AUNT BEL

GUY McCRONE

B&W PUBLISHING

First published 1949
This edition published 1994
by B&W Publishing Ltd
Edinburgh
Reprinted 1998, 2001
ISBN 1 873631 39 1

British Library Cataloguing in Publication Data:
A catalogue record for this book is available
from the British Library.

Cover illustration: Detail from
Mrs St George by Sir William Orpen.
Photograph by kind permission of
Jefferson Smurfit Group plc.

Printed by WS Bookwell

AUNT BEL

GUY MCCRONE was born in 1898 in Birkenhead.
After his parents' return to their native Glasgow, he
was educated at Glasgow Academy, going on to
read modern languages at Pembroke College,
Cambridge, and then studying singing in Vienna.
On his return to Glasgow, he organised the first
British performance of Berlioz's *Les Troyens* at
the Theatre Royal in 1935. He was also one of the
founders of the city's Citizens' Theatre.

Glasgow provided the inspiration for many of
McCrone's novels, including *Antimacassar City*,
The Philistines and *The Puritans*, which were pub-
lished as *Wax Fruit* in 1947. Two sequels followed:
Aunt Bel (1949) and *The Hayburn Family* (1952).
His other novels include *The Striped Umbrella*
(1937), *James and Charlotte* (1955) and *An
Independent Young Man* (1961). Guy McCrone
retired to the Lake District in 1968, where he
died at Windermere in May 1977.

Other B&W Titles by Guy McCrone

WAX FRUIT
THE HAYBURN FAMILY

*Once again I must disappoint Glasgow readers.
I have not yet acquired enough impertinence to
draw for them portraits of their grandparents,
their parents or their friends.*

Chapter One

IT WAS A COLD, clear morning in March, 1892.

The sun was shining as Mrs. Arthur Moorhouse, of Grosvenor Terrace in the West End, and therefore the most fashionable part, of the City of Glasgow, stood before her mirror getting ready to go out.

Mrs. Moorhouse had no cause to be displeased with her reflection. She was a handsome woman of forty-six; still as slim as a life of prosperity and the bearing of three fine children had allowed her to remain; still reasonably slim, still fair-haired, and still possessed of a smile that was not without elegance. An air of distinction, indeed, hung about Bel Moorhouse, wife of a self-made merchant though she might be. If she was over-careful in her dress, too meticulous in her appointments, still fearful, a little, of what her neighbours might think, she could not, at least, be called vulgar, aggressive or loud.

Satisfied with her appearance, Bel took her way downstairs. The hall fire was blazing up pleasantly in the handsome fireplace of black marble, having been replenished just after breakfast. A large pot of hyacinths on a table sent up a wave of perfume to meet her as she descended. A door had been left off its catch, and the sunlight was throwing a beam of silver into the sombre comfort of the hall.

Bel found herself humming. Life was good to her. Secure, prosperous, the possessor of a husband who was, of course, everything to her—when it occurred to her to think about him—a boy of twenty-one, a boy of seventeen, and a daughter of nineteen; all of them handsome, all of them behaving—for the most part at least—as she would have them behave, all of them drawing the eye of approval when they ventured abroad. Add to that a fine terrace house, solidly furnished, three devoted maidservants, who had for years now been part of the family, and a shining carriage in the lane behind, with her husband's monogram discreet and unobtrusive on the panels of the doors, and it was no wonder that Bel Moorhouse was humming.

Besides, just tonight she was taking her daughter Isabel to her first important ball.

But as her parlour-maid, Sarah, appeared in the hall, Bel stopped. The mistresses of Grosvenor Terrace houses did not hum before their servants; even before those who had been with them since marriage and were held in strong affection.

"What a lovely morning it is, Sarah! I have some shopping to do in town. But it really is so nice this morning, I think I'll take a turn round the Botanic Gardens first. Do I need brushing?"

Sarah smiled, took a brush from the hall table, ran it over her mistress's shoulders, helped her to reset the lavish Russian sables about them, gave her back her muff, and, going to the front door, threw it open for Bel to pass out.

The opened door revealed Bel's sister-in-law, Sophia Butter, standing on the mat.

"Bel, dear! Have you heard the news?"

Bel was not particularly pleased to see Sophia. She had wanted, this morning, to be left with the sunshine, her plans for tonight's ball, her consciousness of her own and her family's virtues, and the knowledge that, just for the moment, in the large circle of relatives into which marriage had thrown her, nothing was happening to trouble herself or her good and conscientious husband.

2

"News, Sophia? What news?" Her elegant smile was forced and a little broader than usual, in the hope that it might cloak the annoyance she felt at the appearance of this untidy, chattering relative.

"It's about Wil, Bel dear. He's engaged to be married. How nice and warm it is in here!" Sophia came into the house, drawing off a seedy sealskin jacket, and thus taking it for granted that Bel would not now go out, but would return indoors to hear the great news of her nephew, Wil Butter's, engagement.

Bel followed reluctantly. She felt that the news might very well have kept for a less sunny morning.

"And do you know who he's engaged to, dear? You'll never guess!"

The sun was streaming into Bel's back parlour—which she herself called the library—as she pulled the bell for a cup of tea. The bright light did not flatter Sophia. How shabby and old she was looking! And she had no reason to. She was only fifty-four, and her husband, William Butter, was comfortably off. Her grey hair was straggling from beneath a ridiculous fur bonnet, in a way that only hair that was never properly brushed could straggle.

"Do tell me, Sophia." Bel, exasperated at being required to guess what she had little interest in guessing, hoped her voice did not sound querulous.

Sophia Butter settled herself in an easy-chair by the fire, a pleased smile irradiating her good-natured but, Bel could not help feeling, not particularly clean face, and uttered the single word "Polly!"

"Polly, Sophia? Polly who?"

"Polly, Bel dear. Your niece Polly. My niece Polly! Wee Polly. Mary's Polly."

"Oh."

For a time there was a silence, which at last Sophia felt impelled to break.

"Well, Bel dear? Aren't you pleased?"

"Yes, of course, Sophia."

At this moment Sarah appeared to receive orders.

"A cup of tea for Mrs. Butter, Sarah. And Mrs. Butter has just told me that young Mr. William is engaged to Miss Polly McNairn. Isn't it nice?"

"Yes, Mam. Very nice." Sarah withdrew with a wan smile and just the suggestion of a flounce, conveying thus to Bel that the news had not killed her with pleasure.

Perversely now, Bel found herself resenting Sarah's manner. Sarah, however good and trustworthy she might be, had no right to express anything but interest. What were servants coming to? Besides, now that Bel came to think of it, it *was* nice—very nice.

For little Polly was one of the twin daughters of her husband Arthur's widowed sister, Mary McNairn. The child was only eighteen. But the sooner these two girls found husbands the better. Their mother's income was fixed and none too large.

Bel was not ungenerous. But Arthur had been more than good. And there had been times when Bel had felt that Mary took Arthur's generosity with too much patient resignation. Now there would be young Wil Butter to help.

No. Really, it was splendid! The more she thought about it, the better she could bear with Sophia's enthusiasm. For Sophia's son, Wil, a large young man of twenty-nine, was, she understood, becoming a force in Glasgow's shipping world. He must already be well able to support a wife, and, if necessity arose, stretch out a helping hand to the aunt who would also be his mother-in-law.

Somewhat softened, Bel now found herself pouring out tea.

"And when did this happen, Sophia?" she asked pleasantly enough.

"It was only arranged last night, Bel dear. Wil came home very late, so I didn't see him until this morning. And then, I don't know how it is with breakfast in our house, nobody ever has much time to talk. Everybody grabbing and running for things at the last minute."

Bel could well picture the Butters' noisy, untidy breakfasts. But she turned her inward eye from what it saw and let Sophia go on.

"And it was so like Wil, dear. He just looked up from his porridge and said: 'By the way, I'm getting married.' Just as if it was something quite ordinary. William nearly collapsed."

Sophia's husband, William Butter, was a corpulent bear of a man one year older than herself, who, in the twenty-two years of Bel's connection with the Moorhouse family, had, so far as Bel knew, expressed neither joy nor sorrow, pleasure nor pain. It was seldom, indeed, that she had even heard him speak. The idea of William either collapsing or expanding was something that defeated thought.

"Margy was very quiet about it," Sophia continued, referring to her twenty-seven-year-old daughter. "But I know she's pleased. Poor Margy! I think she feels she should be married too. There was a young man in the church that we thought— Just last autumn it was, dear. And I think it has left her a little nervous. But after breakfast Polly came up to see us, and Margy couldn't have been nicer. She went back with her to visit Mary. And I said I would come up and tell you."

"That was very kind of you, Sophia," Bel said, rising and making some attempt to stop the flow; for really she must go out. "They won't be married for a long time yet, I suppose?" she asked.

"Polly said Wil thinks a six weeks' engagement will be enough."

"Only six weeks, Sophia!"

"Well, you know what Wil is, Bel dear." Sophia's voice had a ring of pride. "If he wants to get a thing over and done with, he does it at once. He's so determined."

II

Sophia's words were still in Bel's mind as, half an hour later, she found herself in a tram-car making her way towards the centre of the city. Yes, she supposed Wil Butter must be determined.

Some twelve years ago, David, the youngest Moorhouse brother, had taken his sister Sophia's adolescent son into Dermott Ships, the firm of which he was the chairman. At the time it had seemed almost a charity on David's part. Now people said Wil Butter was the mainspring of the business. It was very admirable, of course. Especially in this city, where success in business counted for so much. But for Bel life contained other successes, other kinds of sons than those who turned themselves into mainsprings.

Her own son Arthur, for instance. As the tram clattered along in the sunlight, Bel, as mothers will, gave herself up to comparing Arthur with his cousin. And again, as mothers will, she found herself making the comparison in Arthur's favour.

At Belmont Street the horses were halted to let passengers descend, then, once more, they started up and trotted on towards Kelvin Bridge.

Arthur; her son. And the very core and centre of her. He was a Moorhouse, of course, like his father and his uncles. With their good looks, their natural distinction, their self-control. But young Arthur, at twenty-one, was a variation on the Moorhouse theme. His fair hair and skin were Bel's own. And he had both a shyness and an arrogance about him, at times, that seemed, in his mother's eyes at least, only to add to his attraction.

Yes, a fine boy. Far superior to his cousin, William Butter. And in his two years with the merchant firm of Arthur Moorhouse and Company he had shown himself conscientious and persistent. His father was proud of him. When the time came, the second Arthur would be a worthy successor to the first.

The tram-car had brought Bel to St. Vincent Place. As she stepped down and turned towards Buchanan Street, intending to make one or two final purchases in preparation for the Lord Provost's Ball tonight, she met the son she had been thinking of. Her pulses quickened. It is always pleasant and a little exciting to encounter, thus unexpectedly, someone near and well-beloved.

"Hullo, Arthur! What are you doing?"

"Father wasn't sure if he had a white tie, so he sent me out to buy him one. And I want some things for myself."

"I'll come and help you."

Bel was well aware that her husband had several white ties at home. But she wanted to walk about in the cheerfulness of the city side by side with her handsome son.

"All right." Arthur took his mother's arm, and they walked along the pavement in the sunshine.

"I've got some things to buy too for myself and Isabel," Bel said, "but I'll get them later." She was enjoying herself. She was pleasantly aware of her son's masculinity this morning, and her pride in him made her feminine and charming. She stood by while he made his purchases, offering advice only when it was asked of her, allowing him his own decisions. Presently they were on the pavement once more.

7

"Come and have lunch, Mother."

"But isn't it too early, Arthur? And can you spare the time?"

"It's half-past twelve. We can go to Ferguson and Forrester's."

Yes, vastly superior to Wil Butter, Bel decided, contemplating the top of Arthur's head as it bent over the menu card in the restaurant, his fair hair falling over his brow, the round of a clear, flushed cheek, the light growth of boyish side-whiskers.

He ordered for both of them, sat back and looked across at her. "Funny meeting you like this."

Bel's eyes danced like the eyes of a young girl. "Are you sorry?"

"Of course not."

They sat silent, waiting for the meal to be brought. Arthur was basking in his mother's approval. Bel was wishing that sons could remain twenty-one for ever.

"I came down in the tram with Wil Butter this morning," Arthur said after a moment.

"Oh, so you've heard?"

"About his engagement? Yes. Quite a good idea, wouldn't you say? Even if Polly is his cousin."

"Oh yes. Very good. It should be a help to your Aunt Mary."

"He wants me to be his best man."

"Oh."

"Any objections?"

"No, I don't suppose so."

"You don't seem very sure."

Their soup was brought, and Bel supped it, pondering. Yes, she supposed it would be all right. But it would be a style-less affair, this wedding that would join the son of Sophia Butter to the daughter of Mary McNairn.

Still, her husband and she had always been the centre of

the family. Yes, she dared say Wil Butter was right. It was in recognition of this, no doubt, that he had asked their son to be his groomsman. But she liked style, she liked distinction, she liked importance. And the Butter-McNairn wedding would have none of these things.

Their soup plates were taken away. Arthur looked at his mother.

"Well, Mother? Anything wrong?"

"No, nothing."

"Going to enjoy the Ball?"

"I hope so."

And she supposed this handsome boy opposite her would, one of these days, be in want of a wife too. She must get herself used to that. Suddenly, Arthur would present some chit of a girl to her and request her to love her as a daughter. Well, she must try. But she wanted the best for Arthur: the best looks; the best manners; the best position in Glasgow's aristocracy of riches that the ever-increasing Moorhouse name could command for him. Bel looked about her, as though, for a moment, she were seeking some escape.

But, after all, these were fences that could be taken when she came to them. And if Arthur could not remain twenty-one for ever, he was at least twenty-one now.

"How nice this looks!" she said, rallying and smiling approvingly at the food of Arthur's choosing that was now being set before her. "I *am* enjoying myself! Are you?"

III

The age of twenty-one might be just the right age to set the bloom upon a son's charm, but now Bel was not so sure that nineteen did the same for a daughter.

It was shortly after two. Home only ten minutes ago, and standing on the first-floor landing, Bel cast eyes of exasperation, of frustration, of real anxiety about her, as Isabel, coming down from above, passed by glumly, carrying a hot-water can on her way to the kitchen in the basement.

"How is Tom now?" Bel asked, daring the blackness of Isabel's mood.

"If he had to cut his head open, he might at least have cut it open some other time."

"Isabel!"

"Well, what about tonight?"

"How can you even think about tonight now?"

But Isabel merely continued on her way downstairs in quest of yet more hot water. Bel stared at her daughter's descending and indignant back. How callous young girls were becoming! How intent upon their own pleasures!

But this was serious. Her second son, Tom, had had an accident. He was for ever falling about, of course. But this time there might be concussion. Or perhaps blood-poisoning. Or a permanent and disfiguring scar.

Impotently, Bel looked about her. She turned automatically to close the door of her bedroom, from which, some minutes ago, she had hurried so abruptly, preparations for her afternoon rest interrupted. Now the March sun, bursting for a moment through gathering rain-clouds, was flooding the room with cold shafts of light. A carafe of water on her table had caught its beams, and, forming a prism, was making a little dazzle of rainbow colours. In the bedroom fireplace the flames flickered lazily in the sunshine. Over an easy-chair her husband's tail-coat had been spread out, that it should be creaseless for the evening. On a sofa her own dress of fine lace and black satin, costly, elegant, and new-made for tonight's function, was spread out to the same purpose.

The sight of it was too much for Bel. She closed the door quickly, turned, and went upstairs to the bedside of her son.

There was little of the natural nurse about her. She shrank from the sight of blood, even when, as now, it belonged to her own son. It should, she felt, be running tidily in Tom's veins and arteries. But in poor Tom's room it seemed to be everywhere.

He was now in bed. Sarah had stripped him of his dusty clothes, cleaned down his seventeen-year-old body as best she could, and got him into a nightshirt with the same firm purpose and as little embarrassment as when Tom had been a baby of three.

Sarah tyrannised over the household, as devoted servants will. There had been moments in the last years when Bel could almost have wished her away. But this afternoon she was thankful for her. Had there been no Sarah, she would have been forced to do all these unpleasant things herself. Now, Sarah being as she was, merely to offer to help would be to give offence.

Bel stood looking down upon her son. "How do you feel now, darling?" she asked weakly.

"I don't think the cut can be very deep."

"I wish they wid get a haud o' the doctor." In moments of crisis Sarah was inclined to revert to the speech of working Glasgow.

"He's here." Isabel, coming in with additional hot water, was followed by the man they were seeking. She explained how, quite providentially, Cook had recognized his brougham standing outside another house in the terrace.

The doctor was flushed and without breath from climbing two flights of stairs. He gave Mrs. Moorhouse a friendly and deferential hand, speech being impossible for the moment, and shook a chubby and elderly fist with reassuring and

11

professional playfulness at the boy on the bed. Thereafter he crossed over, sat down and took the patient's wrist in one hand, while he stroked his beard with the other.

"Pulse all right," he said presently. Then he bent over Thomas Moorhouse and asked: "And what do you think you've been doing to yourself, young man?"

Bel explained for him. Tom *would* ride his bicycle to school. This was quite unnecessary, with Kelvinside Academy so near. But there it was. Tom was always in a hurry. And Tom had a trick of using only one hand, while the other grasped his schoolbooks and what not. He had set out thus after the midday meal. So far as his mother could gather, he had swerved to avoid a flying hansom, got his wheels stuck in the groove of a tram-rail, and come down, cutting his head on the metal rail itself.

The doctor, who had been examining him, sat back, and said thoughtfully: "Yes. Now I see what's what." Adding: "Good thing the trams are not electrified yet, or you might have been electrocuted into the bargain, Tommy." He stood up. "I'll have to do a bit of sewing. I think I'll take off my coat to it. So perhaps Mrs. Moorhouse— I'll look in and tell you how he is when it's finished. In the drawing-room?"

Only too glad to take the hint, Bel and her daughter withdrew, leaving Tom with the doctor and Sarah.

IV

Bel was not alarmed any more. The doctor had reassured her. She had begun to share her daughter's annoyance at Tom's very inconvenient, irresponsible behaviour. Today of all days! Aimlessly she now followed Isabel into her bedroom. Like her mother's, Isabel's ball dress lay waiting, virgin white and new.

12

On her dressing-table were a mother-of-pearl fan given her for the occasion by her father, one or two trinkets and long white gloves. In tissue paper, white and unsullied, were a pair of satin slippers.

Bel stroked the dress disconsolately. No. It was too bad of Tom. They had looked forward to the Lord Provost's Ball for weeks now. Although there had already been two such balls given in the new Municipal Buildings, this was to be by far the most brilliant; in celebration of the extension of the City of Glasgow's boundaries. Everybody was going. She had read that the Lord Mayor of every English and Irish city of consequence had been invited—beginning with the Lord Mayor of London. And, of course, the Lord Provost of every other Scottish city that was important enough to possess one. And, in addition, many of the real aristocracy were to be present.

Just after Christmas she had asked her husband, Arthur, to make certain that he, she and their elder children should receive cards. They would be nobodies, she had insisted, if their names did not appear in the published lists of those present.

Then, in the middle of January, a blow had fallen. The Prince of Wales' elder son, the Duke of Clarence, had died of the influenza that was then sweeping the country. The Court was in mourning. National and municipal functions throughout the land were cancelled.

But suddenly the ball had been reannounced for the middle of March. Bel and Isabel breathed once more. Now they could order their dresses. Black for Bel. White for Isabel. They must remain on the side of discretion this spring. Besides, what could be more becoming to a fair and comely dowager of forty-six than elegant black? Or virgin white to her nineteen-year-old counterpart?

And now Tom had appeared at the front door in a welter of dust and worse, on this the very afternoon of the great day! Just when his mother and sister had gone to rest themselves, that they might be in the best of looks for the evening.

"I think," Bel said to Isabel, her voice full of exasperation, "you might ask Cook to make a cup of tea."

"It's only half-past two."

"Never mind. I feel we need it. And perhaps the doctor, when he's finished with Tom—"

As Isabel descended the stairs yet again she became aware that her spirits were rising. She knew now, that if her mother could find a loophole, they would still go tonight.

V

In half an hour more the doctor was sitting in the drawing-room, drinking tea and telling Tom's mother and sister just what a nasty gash Tom had given himself, implying modestly that he, the doctor, was not quite unskilled, perhaps, in the sewing up of faces, and reassuring Bel that her younger son's handsomeness would, in the end, be none the worse for having had a difference with the tram-rails of Great Western Road.

"But what about poisoning, Doctor? Or concussion? What if he starts a temperature?"

"Well, Mrs. Moorhouse, you could take his temperature— let me see—in the late afternoon; and again in the evening. My assistant would come round at once if anything was wrong." And in answer to a look from Bel: "You see, I'll be going with my wife to the Municipal Buildings tonight."

"That's what *we* were hoping to do, Doctor!" The words burst from Isabel.

Bel was grateful to her. Now, without seeming unmaternal, she could smile at the child's impulsiveness, exchange knowing looks with the doctor and say: "Isabel is going to be very disappointed. Do you think, Doctor—?"

The doctor put the tips of his fingers together, and sat gazing out into the Botanic Gardens opposite. "Well, Mrs. Moorhouse, I don't know really," he said with maddening slowness. "I wouldn't quite say—"

"Then we'll just give up the idea," Bel said hurriedly, not because she had made up her mind to do any such thing, but because the doctor's pompous slowness had become unendurable. This produced the result she sought.

The doctor became alert. "No, no, no! Go by all means, if your arrangements are made. The lad is fine. That's a grand woman that Sarah of yours. And it would be a pity for my young friend Isabel to miss—"

VI

But all obstruction was not yet at an end.

At the proper tea-hour, Bel's mother, Mrs. Barrowfield, descended from a cab. Mrs. Barrowfield was vigorous, masculine-featured and very old. The Battle of Waterloo had been won when she was ten. She declared that she still remembered the bonfire and other celebrations on Glasgow Green. In so far as her clothes followed any fashions, they were those of the 'sixties. Even Bel was not now sure if the hard, grey side-curls were still her own. As old people will, Mrs. Barrowfield doted on her grandchildren and bullied her daughter.

She found Bel in the drawing-room by herself. "I just came up to see ye gettin' dressed," she said, seizing her and giving her a vigorous kiss.

Bel received these advances coldly. "How will you get home again, Mother?" she asked.

15

"I thought, maybe, you could leave here ten minutes early. That would give you time to drop me at the Row." Mrs. Barrowfield chose a comfortable chair and looked about her, beaming.

Bel was furious. The old lady had a flat in Monteith Row overlooking Glasgow Green—a decaying locality that Bel had wanted her to leave years ago. And now Mrs. Barrowfield was suggesting that she, too, should squeeze into the family carriage on its way to the Municipal Buildings, crushing their finery, forcing Arthur, Senior, who would be cross enough already, to hurry his dressing, and causing them all to make a tiresome detour for nothing.

Besides, she hadn't wanted her mother to be here this evening, taking in every detail of her toilet. Bel had just discovered the virtues of tinted rice-powder. If she locked herself in the bathroom and applied it discreetly, it did wonders, Bel found, to a forty-six-year-old face. Her husband, Arthur, never really looked at her now, and she could count on the children noticing nothing. But it would not escape the old lady. Mrs. Barrowfield's glasses were strong.

"Tom fell off his bicycle today and cut his head very badly," Bel said maliciously, intent upon destroying her mother's smug cheerfulness.

"Tom? Have ye had the doctor?"

Already Bel regretted what she had said. She was beginning to glimpse the trouble she had loosed upon her own head. "Oh yes, Mother. The doctor had to put in several stitches. But he says he'll be all right—that we needn't worry."

"That's all very fine."

"What do you mean, Mother?" Bel resented her tone. It implied that she, Bel, was taking Tom's mishap lightly.

"What happened?"

Dutifully, and at length, Bel told Tom's grandmother all that had occurred.

16

"Puir lamb!" Mrs. Barrowfield took up her cup and stirred it thoughtfully.

"Yes; it's unfortunate," Bel hazarded.

The old lady swallowed down her tea and held out her cup for more. "Well," she said with decision, "that's the finish of your high jinks."

"I don't understand, Mother." But Bel understood perfectly; had, indeed, expected it. Her mother would, of course, now disapprove of her going tonight. But to have this entertainment given by the Lord Provost of Glasgow to the more important of his fellow-citizens, to the Mayors and Provosts of other towns, and to the aristocracy of the West of Scotland, called "high jinks", jarred upon Bel's sense of propriety. Couldn't her mother see that their appearance tonight, and the mention of their names in tomorrow's papers, would add cubits to the family stature?

"You canna go when the boy's had a serious accident."

"But the doctor says it's not serious."

Mrs. Barrowfield merely drew herself up, looked at Bel coldly, and said: "You can never be sure."

"The young doctor's coming in tonight just to make certain he's all right."

"Fancy." Mrs. Barrowfield had brought the baiting of her daughter to a fine art. Now she was implying that Bel was a heartless pleasure-seeker, quite unworthy of two fine sons and a pretty daughter.

"Hullo, Granny!"

As Isabel came into the room, Bel signalled to her with raised eyebrows and a look of desperation. She added the cue: "Your granny says we are all to stay at home tonight and look after Tom."

As Bel had intended, the Grosvenor Terrace ranks closed with a snap.

17

Isabel came forward, kissed her grandmother's glum face and sat kittenishly on the arm of her chair. "You don't really, do you, Granny?"

"It's yer duty."

"Did you never want to go to balls, Granny?"

"Not if anybody's life was in danger."

Isabel's voice took on a note of panic. "Danger? Is Tom's life in danger? Oh, Granny, I didn't know!"

"Well, maybe not in danger, but—"

"Granny! You've no right to frighten me like that! I thought you had heard something I didn't know." She grasped her grandmother's hand as though she sought its comfort.

The old lady's face relaxed. That was better. "You're a silly wee thing," she said, patting Isabel affectionately.

"And Mother and I have our new dresses," Isabel added dejectedly.

Bel watched her daughter with amazement. If she herself had tried any such crude tactics at Isabel's age, Mrs. Barrowfield would have reacted very differently.

"I tell you what I'll do," the old lady said. "If ye give me a bed here, I'll stay and see that the boy's all right. And ye can all go out and enjoy yerselves."

"Oh, Granny! How kind!"

Isabel's mother was not, for the moment, sure that she did not want to smack Isabel for this. But an instant's reflection told her that the child had been right. It would save a stand-up battle and all the fuss about taking her mother home. The old lady would have the satisfaction of seeing them adorned in all their splendour, and the invalid would not now be overlooked. If, in the course of the evening, Mrs. Barrowfield came to blows with an equally domineering Sarah, she, Bel, would not be there to see.

And thus it was that when the two Arthur Moorhouses—

father and son—arrived home rather earlier than usual, they were received by a loving old lady, who kissed them both affectionately, told them that young Tom had had a little accident, but there was nothing whatever to be alarmed about, that it was really little more than a scratch; that she had consented to stay overnight, as anxiety must in no way be allowed to mix with their enjoyment; that Bel and Isabel were already gone to dress, and would look lovely in their new ball dresses. And were the Arthurs quite sure they wouldn't like a hurried cup of tea before they, too, went up to change?

Chapter Two

THEY made a handsome group, the Arthur Moorhouses, as they waited in the long queue that coiled itself up the marble staircase of Glasgow's new Municipal Buildings; moving inch by inch upwards and along the gallery in the direction of the Satinwood Saloon, where the Chief Magistrate and his lady stood giving the many guests a hand of welcome.

A handsome group, but in no way conspicuous. It was firmly fixed in the Moorhouses, as in so many of their kind, that to draw notice upon oneself, however blamelessly, was in the worst of taste. You dressed well, avoiding all exaggeration. Your charity must be as liberal as discretion would allow. But rather none, than a charity that might seem showy. If duty forced you into public office, then you must see to it that others drew the limelight, that you might perform what was required of you in peace. Not a creed perhaps to kindle the imagination, to breed a race of leaders; but one that gave a backbone of complacent dependability to this great commercial city.

Arthur Moorhouse leant his long, spare body against the balustrade of the staircase, and for once took time to look at his wife and elder children. She was a handsome woman still, Bel. Her fine, fair hair was a little faded now, perhaps; but her face was glowing tonight, and her handsome eyes were bright, as they took in the spectacle about her.

And her daughter was Bel all over again—Bel as she had looked when, a green farmer's son from Ayrshire come to make his way as a city merchant, Arthur had learnt that the stately child who troubled his senses of a Sunday morning as he sat in the Ramshorn Church was called Bel Barrowfield. Perhaps Isabel's face didn't quite hold the magic her mother's face had held for him in those days of the 'sixties; but now, of course, he was fifty-five, and Isabel was his daughter. It would have magic enough for some other young fellow, he dared say.

The movement of the waiting people forced Arthur Moorhouse a step or two upwards. When he turned to look about him once more, he found himself looking down into the face of his son, who came behind him.

Young Arthur smiled. "We're moving faster now," he said, looking up at his father.

The elder man nodded. "Aye." His deep-set eyes softened under their black eyebrows, and he knew a moment of sharp pleasure, that this handsome boy should have been part-created by himself. He turned away, fearful that he should show his feelings. Queer, how you took your family for granted day in, day out, then suddenly you found yourself seeing them as though for the first time.

Now they had reached the upper floor, and were passing along more quickly. Palms, ferns, alabaster and multicoloured, over-elaborate civic marble. A noise of welcome provided by the band of a brigade of Scottish Rifles, playing with an ear-shattering brassiness, and—Mrs. Arthur Moorhouse could not help feeling—rather unsuitably, the too-popular "Ta-ra-ra-boom-de-ay". Now they had received their welcome in the Satinwood Saloon; recognised some of the important, who stood around the Lord Provost, guessed at the identity of others; now they were in the main ballroom looking about them and noting who was who. Now the young people, hailing friends, had received programmes and were busy filling them.

For the moment Arthur, seeing a business friend, had quite forgotten about Bel, and stood in deep and amicable talk. Bel,

21

used to this treatment, let him be and, setting a vague and, she hoped, decorative smile upon her face, moved to a point of vantage, took a seat and fanned herself elegantly.

There was much for her to see. The wealth of the city was here made manifest. The mourning at Court had, perhaps, laid its restraints upon military splendour; but many men present wore the kilt, thus adding the vividness of dress tartan and the brilliance of Highland stones and silver to the finery of the women.

Bel, behind her detached smile, had eyes for everything. Many of the daughters of the rich were dressed at great cost. The fashions of this winter were simple. The 'nineties had not yet taken on the exaggerations that were to come presently. But there were many beautiful colours—others had been less restrained than herself and Isabel—and much splendid jewellery.

The dance orchestra, conducted by a certain Herr Iff, had finished its opening overture, and was playing a Viennese waltz. Young people she knew—friends of her children—were beginning to swing past her, smiling down upon her as they danced. Bel, mustering the poise of a dowager, returned gracious greetings. She wished now that her husband would remember her existence and come to sit beside her. Not that she wanted him for himself, particularly. But she felt it would look better.

Her own son and daughter passed her, dancing together, well and with restraint. Her eyes followed them with satisfaction. Everything about them was quite unexceptionable— Isabel's simple white; young Arthur's evening clothes, cut by the best tailor in Glasgow. There was nothing over-dressed about them; nothing showy. Let others entertain her with display. Her own children must not be conspicuous. Bel's fixed smile became a little complacent. The final expression of her own careful good taste had just danced past her.

"Hullo, Auntie Bel!"

"Wil!" Bel looked up in surprise at the large young man whose name was Wil Butter. "And Polly!"

Bel did her best, although she was not sure if she were much pleased at the sight of these young relatives. But her nephew and niece seemed pleased to see her. They bent down and saluted her with kisses that expressed vigorous family affection, rather than the deference she could have wished for. There had been times, indeed, recently when Bel had wondered if Wil's extreme heartiness towards her did not carry overtones of derision.

"How nice to see you, my dears! Your mother told me the great news this morning, Wil. We are all delighted. I had no idea you were coming tonight. This is a surprise!" She schooled her feelings and strove to be as gracious as possible.

"It was a surprise to us, too," Wil Butter grinned broadly. "I didn't know we were coming either until this afternoon. Uncle David came into my room at the office and chucked his tickets at me."

Bel winced a little. She did not like the expression "chucked", nor the implication that the tickets for this important function —tickets Arthur had gone to some trouble to obtain—were things to be taken lightly.

But Wil Butter continued cheerfully: "Uncle David said he didn't feel like coming. And could we use them? He said you would be here to chaperone. I knew Polly would like to come. You see, it's a kind of celebration. Hope you don't mind."

Polly McNairn, a plump little thing with the bloom of eighteen years upon her, grinned in corroboration.

Bel assured them that of course she didn't mind. What else could she say? And really, after all, why should she? But she had hoped to join forces tonight with her husband's youngest brother, David, impeccable socially now, and very rich, being married to the only child of old Robert Dermott, the founder of Dermott Ships. To be in company with David and Grace Dermott-Moorhouse at any public function gave Bel a pleasant sense of having arrived. And in addition, just tonight, she had rather depended upon Grace to present one or two eligible young men to Isabel.

"There's nothing wrong with your Uncle David?" Bel looked up at her nephew, noting that his vigour did not, somehow, go with the indifferent cut of his evening clothes.

"Oh no! Don't think so. Slight cold coming on. Or perhaps he was just feeling petted."

Bel did not care for this last remark either. Wil had no right to talk so familiarly about his uncle. She stiffened. "Your Uncle David never used to be petted, William," she said coldly.

Wil laughed loudly. "Well, he is now, Auntie Bel. Often. In the office, at any rate. Old age, probably."

Nor did this reference to David's age please Bel. David was a year younger than she was. But she allowed her face to relax. It was no use. What could she expect from Sophia Butter's son? Sophia could never teach her children manners. Besides, Wil was a well-meaning creature, and very much in favour with everybody at present, by reason of having engaged himself to take one of his Aunt Mary's daughters off her hands.

The twin who was being thus auspiciously removed looked up adoringly at her remover, appalled and pleased that he should dare to say such things to their important Aunt Bel, said "Oh Wil!", and blushed becomingly.

Wil Butter beamed down at her.

Bel Moorhouse, who was very human beneath the overlay of provincial snobbery, felt suddenly touched by the sight of them. They were deeply in love, she could see, these two imperfect creatures. And, to Bel's sentimentality, young love could not help being as lovely as the blossoms of the cherry and the sloe—even if the vessels that contained it were a vigorous young man with large hands and a strong jaw, and a plump little fledgling in an improvised evening dress.

"I hear you are being married very soon?" she said genially.

"Yes. Six or eight weeks."

"Would you like me to give your reception in Grosvenor Terrace?"

"Oh, Auntie Bel! Would you? Such a lovely house!" Polly gave a hop like a little girl, striking her hands together.

Bel had spoken without giving herself time to think. She did these impetuous things when she was touched. She would hear about this from her mother, who was for ever scolding her for taking upon herself obligations from which she could not withdraw herself gracefully. Already she was regretting a little.

"You're sure your mother wouldn't like to have a quiet reception in your own house?"

"Oh no, Auntie Bel! Our house is so shabby."

"Well, I'll see what your Uncle Arthur says. Now, children, there's the music begun again. It's time you were dancing."

They did as they were told, Polly wondering a little why she had been thus dismissed.

But Bel had seen her husband crossing the floor accompanied by a gentleman.

The gentleman was presented to her. He was new to Glasgow, it seemed. He had been introduced to Arthur only yesterday at Arthur's club.

And presently Mrs. Arthur Moorhouse was to be seen waltzing with just that right amount of unfluid dignity, that regal stiffness that comes with middle age, a touch of rheumatism, and an ever-growing sense of one's own consequence.

Bel's partner was a little surprised to find himself dancing with this strange Scotch lady. His name was Colonel James Ellerdale. He was English, and he was sixty-five. An advanced age to go to balls, perhaps. But he had come in the company of his wife—a lady some twenty years younger than himself—and, just like the Moorhouses, they had with them a son and daughter.

"My wife is dancing with my boy, and my girl is dancing with some young fellow from Maryhill Barracks. Looks as if they were trying to leave me out of it. Would you care to have a turn round the room with me just to show 'em, Mrs. Moorhouse?"

The Colonel had always possessed a figure. Even now it was very good. His hair was quite white, but it was thick, and went well with a face burnt to mahogany by Eastern suns. In his uniform, indeed, he looked striking. Which may have had something to do with Bel's accepting his arm.

The Colonel was a permanent adolescent. He hopped round cheerfully. He had always enjoyed dancing, he told her, and saw no reason why he should stop. It stirred up your blood, kept you fit and helped you to get to know people. As a soldier, stationed here, there and everywhere, you had always to keep getting to know people, hadn't you? Otherwise where would you be?

"I suppose so," Bel said, not quite certain what she should suppose.

"Ever been in the East, Mrs. Moorhouse?"

Realising just in time that the Colonel did not mean places like Aberdeen and Dundee, but places like Egypt and India, Bel hastened to regret that she had not.

"Do you know Scotland well, Colonel Ellerdale?" she asked,

when her breath would allow her, feeling it was now her turn to introduce a subject.

"No, I don't. Not really. Done a bit of shooting up here now and then, of course. But we've just got a house in Ayr. Have to get to know people all over again. But we're used to that."

This was fortunate. Bel had her brother-in-law, Mungo Ruanthorpe-Moorhouse, the Laird of Duntrafford, as a trump card to play against all comers from Ayrshire. But for the instant she could not play it, as the Colonel was still talking.

"My boy has gone into business in Glasgow. Shipping. Elsie, my wife, wanted to be near, for his weekends. He should have been a soldier, but it went against the grain. Don't know why. Have you a boy?"

"Oh yes—two."

"Either of them in the Army?"

For a moment Bel felt embarrassed. The Colonel's question made her feel for a moment that one at least should be. But she could not help herself. "No," she said. "My elder boy is with my husband in business"—she did not say her husband was a cheese-merchant, though a quite special one—"and the other is still at school."

"Oh? Where have you sent him?"

"Kelvinside Academy."

There was a silence at this. The Colonel seemed puzzled. But he was a cheerful soul, and tried to keep the conversation going. "You'll soon have him home for Easter," he said presently.

"But he's always at home."

"Then he's not gone to a public school?"

"Oh no! It's a very good private one."

Again her partner fell silent. Why was her boy at a private school? Was he mentally deficient? Better not probe, perhaps.

According to their kind, neither of them realised that the term public school in Scotland meant quite a different thing from public school in England. Rich middle-class Scotland still, in great part, found education for her sons in day schools.

The Colonel continued to swing Bel manfully. But it was hard work. It was evident that she didn't dance much, or she would keep better time and hang less heavily. To this worshipper at the shrine of eternal youth it was ridiculous for a woman of Mrs. Moorhouse's looks not to be a better dancer.

IV

"Oh, there's Elsie and Jim sitting down! Do let me introduce you, Mrs. Moorhouse." Glad of this excuse to stop, the Colonel led Bel to a rather faded woman of much the same age as herself, seated beside a young man who had some of the Colonel's looks.

Who had James found this time? Mrs. Ellerdale wondered, watching her husband advance across the floor with a handsome fair-haired woman in black. In the course of her married life she had seen him dance with many partners. Feminine novelty had, in other days, been a trouble with James. But now, poor man, he was getting on. There was nothing left of all that but his frosty good looks and his vacant cheerfulness.

"Elsie, my dear, let me introduce Mrs. Moorhouse."

She seemed a pleasant sort of woman, this Mrs. Moorhouse, Elsie Ellerdale thought, as Bel sat down beside her. A little prim, perhaps. A little anxiously regal. Really, there was no knowing whom James would get in tow with next. A wealthy Glasgow burgher's wife, she guessed, and one who had not amused James much, otherwise he would not thus have got rid of her. That Mrs. Moorhouse should bore the Colonel, however, did not in any way count against her with the Colonel's lady. Still, she found Bel puzzling. But, then, there was so much in Scotland that *was* puzzling.

Bel was pleased with this new acquaintance. It was not often that Arthur was so helpful. The Ellerdales were English. And to be English—unless, indeed, you spoke broad Midland or dropped your aitches—counted for much with Bel and her kind. And these ones had children who might make nice friends for her own.

Bel fanned herself, beamed graciously and expanded. Now she might play her trump card safely. "You've just bought a house in Ayr, Mrs. Ellerdale?"

"Rented it. We're much too poor to buy. Did my husband tell you?"

"Yes. *My* husband's brother lives quite near Ayr," Bel said, conversationally offhand.

"Oh yes?"

"Well, about ten miles away. The Ruanthorpe-Moorhouses of Duntrafford. You may have heard their names?"

"We've been in Ayr for such a very short time, Mrs. Moorhouse. We are still very much outside of things, aren't we, James?" But turning to find the Colonel, his wife saw his soldierly back in the distance disappearing through the ballroom entrance. But her son was still standing by respectfully.

"Ruanthorpe?" he asked. "I've heard of an old lady called Lady Ruanthorpe."

"My sister-in-law's mother." Bel waved her fan as a well-fed cat might wave her tail. She wondered if she ought to say she would ask Mungo's wife to call upon Mrs. Ellerdale, but decided the acquaintanceship was much too new. "You're going into business in Glasgow, Mr. Ellerdale?" she said, looking up at the young man. "Your father gave me all the news, you see."

"Yes. I'm in the office of Dermott Ships to learn the ropes. Then after that I hope to launch out on my own."

"My brother-in-law, David Dermott-Moorhouse, is the Chairman, you know," Bel said, smilingly taking to herself this additional importance.

"Yes—I gathered—when I heard your name—that perhaps—"

Bel laughed. "It looks as if we were being forced into knowing each other, Mrs. Ellerdale."

Elsie Ellerdale smiled. Yes, all this made a difference. It was difficult to assess people in this northern city. They were not cut to the English pattern. This Mrs. Moorhouse might be quite influential, with relatives in the county and in the chairs of important concerns. It was a good thing that James had danced with her, after all, perhaps.

And so it came about that these women of widely different backgrounds set about making advances, the one towards the other. When, a little later, Arthur came to claim Bel and lead her to other friends, all the James Ellerdales had met all the Arthur Moorhouses. The Ellerdales' daughter was a nice child, Bel noted. Less expensively dressed than Isabel, perhaps. But simple and quite pretty. Young Arthur's mother was pleased to see that he still had a dance on his programme for her. She expressed suitable, unemphatic hopes that Mrs. Ellerdale might come to see her sometime soon, now that she would often have occasion to be in Glasgow.

As she stood up to leave these newly-found friends, Wil and Polly polkaed past her. They looked delighted with each other.

Bel decided there was no point in introducing them.

Chapter Three

FOR an instant, as he slowly came back to consciousness, Arthur Moorhouse lay drowsy and serenely aware of feeling rested.

The cans of a milk-cart were rattling somewhere in the lane at the back of Grosvenor Terrace. An errand-boy could be heard whistling. City sparrows made a springtime twitter.

Presently he would get up, dress, eat his ham and eggs, read his morning paper, take himself into town—walking part of the way if the morning tempted—and, having arrived there, devote the rest of his day to the far from distasteful routine of earning his living.

These things made no hard outline in Arthur's emerging consciousness, but they had joined themselves to make the background of so many mornings that automatically they did so now. As he became more alert, however, other more troublesome things intervened. Today the routine would be broken by the Butter-McNairn wedding.

Arthur turned in bed and sighed. He could not shake himself free from his sense of responsibility towards his brothers and sisters and their children. He supposed he liked them. Or was it that Bel and himself were born to lift the burden of others, whether they liked them or not?

Arthur sighed and turned about once more. His brother, Mungo, was the only one he had never worried over. Mungo, the eldest Moorhouse, had stayed to succeed their father at the Laigh Farm in central Ayrshire. And Mungo was perhaps the one among his brothers and sisters he liked best. Was it because Mungo had remained simple and given no trouble? Yet later, much to the surprise of everyone, especially the "girls", Sophia and Mary, Mungo had married Margaret Ruanthorpe, the daughter and heiress of the old laird, Sir Charles Ruanthorpe of Duntrafford.

Arthur himself had taken the way most natural to a farmer's son, forced to the city to earn his living. He had become a dealer in the produce of the land. On the second marriage of their father to a Highland maidservant, Sophia and Mary had followed him to Glasgow. Each in her turn had kept his bachelor home for him, before they had found husbands and homes of their own. Thus he had helped them, step by step.

With the "girls" married off, that had left young David, socially adroit, and good-looking. Arthur had worried over David. But in the end David had settled down, turned his natural assets to the best advantage, and, with a shrewdness that ran in his peasant blood, married himself to the daughter of a shipping magnate. David was rich.

As Arthur lay thinking of them, going over them all one by one, he was taken by surprise to find he had forgotten his half-sister, Phœbe, the child of his father's old age.

Phœbe had come to Glasgow when she was only a child. Bel had brought her up. A queer girl, Phœbe. And she had married a queer man. Yet in some ways she was the best of the bunch.

Arthur yawned, rolled on his back and opened his eyes.

"I was just wondering when you were going to wake up, dear." His wife's voice came to him from the other pillow. "I have been lying thinking of everything I have to do today."

"Ye didna need to do it, Bel, if ye didna want."

"Oh, I know, Arthur. I suppose I wanted to do it in a way. Still—"

"Of course ye did!"

"But think of it! The reception, and the church arrangements, and everything!"

"You'll manage. Ye always manage."

"Oh yes, I'll manage."

They fell silent for a time. In the distance the city's voice was becoming more insistent. Inside they could hear the sounds of housework. Their bedroom clock struck seven, and as it was striking Sarah appeared with shining cans of hot water.

When she had gone Arthur became aware that Bel was laughing softly to herself.

"What's wrong with ye?" he asked.

"I was thinking, Arthur, how we'll see the whole menagerie today."

He was not offended that Bel should liken his family to a menagerie, but he said: "What's funny about that?"

"Oh, I don't know. They're so awful when you see them all together. But, then, perhaps most families are."

"Aye, maybe." He did not tell her he had been lying thinking about them. He merely said: "Well, I'm getting up."

"So am I."

Thus Mr. and Mrs. Arthur Moorhouse arose, prepared to face this day of family rejoicing.

II

Sophia Butter could not really say that she had slept last night. Here and there she had dozed, she supposed. She lay, now, beside her solid, snoring husband, listening to the six o'clock horns from the far-off shipyards calling to the workers to begin their day. There was so much on Sophia's mind, so much for her to think about.

From the front bedroom in Rosebery Terrace she could hear

the water, as it roared over the weir down below in the gulf of the Kelvin. Now and then there were the sounds of hooves and footsteps passing over Kelvin Bridge. As the morning advanced these sounds would join themselves together, becoming one continuous roar of traffic.

Sophia was not conceited. And as there was no conceit to blind her to the image of herself, Sophia had few illusions. She saw herself very much as she was: a plain, fussy woman of fifty-four.

She was, she knew, the stupidest of all the Moorhouses. She couldn't even assume an air of saintly resignation like her widowed sister Mary. And certainly she wasn't beautiful, moody and aloof, like her half-sister Phœbe.

Weary and under-slept, Sophia sighed and turned about in bed. It was easier to decide she was the failure of the family and be done with it. An early-morning depression settled upon her. Why wasn't she smart and effective like the others? Even Mary, living on a narrow income, seemed to manage to put a better face on things.

William, her husband, snoring here beside her, was, after all, comfortably off. There was nothing exciting about William. Still, he provided support. For a moment Sophia wondered how he managed to do this. Perhaps it was that customers mistook William's stolid, lifeless behaviour for dependability.

Seeking in her mind for compensating thoughts, Sophia turned to her children. Wil, her boy, who was to be married today. She loved him dearly. And yet, in all the twenty-nine years of Wil's life, what had their relationship amounted to? Seeing that her son was fed, clothed and mended. Futile attempts at endearment on her side. A peremptory, male taking for granted on his. She couldn't say that the boy had ever shown his feelings much, except to be cross when she fussed around him.

34

Sophia resented none of her son's behaviour. Wil was like that towards her. That was all. But if she had courage enough she might tell this clever, forceful young man that if he wanted to keep the love of the little cousin who was to be his wife, he had better show her he remembered her existence now and then. Still, better say nothing. Perhaps he would remember. Perhaps wives were different. Sophia was so long past passion that it did not strike her that Wil's senses might encourage politeness.

But she was proud of Wil. He had the sharpest business head of the next generation, his uncles said. David had been reluctant to take him into Dermott Ships, but now, she was assured, Dermott Ships and David could not do without him.

If only her daughter Margy had been born a boy, too! Margy had all Wil's qualities. But, translated into feminine terms, they did not, somehow, seem effective. Like her brother, she was large, tireless and energetic. And she was good-looking, in a big sort of way. But, as Sophia put it to herself, as she lay now considering, Margy had too little of the "parlour puss" about her. By which she meant that Margy had neither softness nor allure enough to induce an eligible male to set an engagement ring upon her finger.

And yet Margy was a fine girl. Strong, bright-witted and loyal. She could be a splendid wife for some man; could bear him a dozen children; run an establishment of servants and come up smiling at the end of it.

The grandfather clock in the little hall downstairs struck seven. Sophia could hear the servant-girl raking ashes in the kitchen. And Wil was on the move already. She could hear his bedroom door bang. The snoring on the pillow beside her stopped. She saw her husband's eyes open drowsily.

"Good morning, William." Sophia's bright tones came

rather from habit and good nature than from her present feelings. "Wake up, dear! It's your son's wedding morning!"

III

At about the same time as these happenings the sun was breaking through the mist that hung over the lower reaches of the river Clyde. From the windows of Aucheneame, Dumbartonshire, residence of David Dermott-Moorhouse, Esq., youngest of the three Moorhouse brothers, the world, this morning, seemed silvery and unsubstantial. The distant hills, where you could see them, were mere pale outlines. The trees of the drive, fledged with May green, stood up rootless from the denser mist that lay close to the ground. The shrubs standing on the lawn outside the window dripped and gleamed with dew. The river itself could only be discerned here and there, where glittering reflections pierced the haze that veiled it.

David Moorhouse was awakened by the booming of a ship's horn. A familiar awakening this, and a pleasant part of the pattern of his easy life. The tide was in. A great ship must be moving in the river. He wondered if it were one of his own. As the chairman of Dermott Ships, Limited, he should, he supposed, have been alert to the exact position of all his steamships, as they moved about the surface of the globe. But he had never been alert in the business sense. And at the office he had only to ring his bell to have the daily chart laid before him. He didn't even have to expose his ignorance. His dead father-in-law, old Robert Dermott, would have known their whereabouts by instinct. As would, indeed, his younger partner, Wil Butter—the bridegroom of today.

But David was not made of the same stuff. Had he remained unloved and unwed by old Robert Dermott's daughter, life would have been very different for him. And David knew it.

He turned his head and looked at his wife, Grace, as she lay beside him. A thick plait of fair hair straggled on her pillow. Her face was pink with sleep. It was a moment before he realised that her eyes were half open.

"Hullo, dear! Awake?"

Grace turned to smile her soft smile at him. "Hullo! I have just been thinking about the young couple. Especially Wil."

"What about him, dear?"

"I was just thinking how queer it is that he's so important in Dermott Ships, and yet Father never knew him."

"Yes, I saw that Wil would be useful."

"That was very clever of you, David."

David sighed, turned on his back and looked at the ceiling. "Oh, I don't know," was all he said.

But he was forty-five now, and Grace was forty-three. Wil's presence in the firm would allow him to retire early, to buy an estate somewhere, which, in turn, he would leave to his twelve-year-old son, Robert David. With Dermott Ships continuing prosperously in the background, there would be ample fortune for all of them. So far as David's thought could reach on this May morning of the year 1892, only prosperity lay ahead.

He found his fair-haired children in the garden. His six-year-old daughter explained that she had been to see to her white rabbit. Her nurse had told her that she had better do so now, as there would be little time after breakfast. The child, delighted with her importance, explained to David that she must be very carefully dressed, as she had to bear her Cousin Polly's train today.

Young Robert was dreaming about the garden, doing nothing much in particular.

37

If there was any passion in David Moorhouse, it was for this dreamy boy. Father and son understood each other perfectly.

"Well, Robert?"

The boy grinned back at him, saying nothing—only half aware, it would seem, of the things around him.

"That's a big steamer going up," David said.

Robert turned, threw it a glance and nodded, the morning sunshine glinting in his hair. David saw that he looked without interest. The boy was so very like himself, as he had been in boyhood. Sensitive and misty; with no gift, no enthusiasm to give him direction or purpose. Yes, the best thing to do with Robert was to turn him into a gentleman. There would be enough money for it.

Or was this ambition for him shallow? David had an instant of uncertainty as he stood looking about him, at the trees, the river, the sunshine and the mist that was now so quickly dispersing.

He called his son to him. And together they went into breakfast.

IV

Phœbe Hayburn came out into her garden while still it was white with dew. Last night, her husband, Henry, had said that as he must waste a whole afternoon at the wedding of their nephew and niece today he would get up early. And would Phœbe please see to it that breakfast was in time? Disturbed by his rising, Phœbe had got up, too.

Mr. and Mrs. Henry Hayburn occupied one of the smaller villas standing pleasantly in its own garden on the top of Partickhill, a district which, even as late as the 'nineties, had much of the country about it. When the prevailing west wind came blowing up to them from across the river it was little contaminated as yet by the smoke of Partick, and bore the tang of the sea and the Renfrew hills. Gardens up here were still rural and unsullied.

The grass was damp under Phœbe's feet. A mavis was singing somewhere among the white blossom of a cherry-tree.

She went about with her fork and basket, humming softly to herself. It was a small garden, tended by its mistress and an occasional labouring man. The morning was delicious. How pleasant it was to be out here alone! Spasmodic hammering sounds of shipbuilding, distant and muted, were coming from yards down there, veiled in the silver mist. Now and then, too, there came the far-off drone of a tug's horn, as it nosed its way cautiously in the river. Flowering shrubs were in full bloom. The pageant of the year would presently wave farewell to spring and move on into the early summer.

"That's me away, then, Phœbe. I've had breakfast. I'll be back in time."

Phœbe turned to see her husband standing bareheaded in the pale sunshine—a long, bony, snub-nosed man with black, untidy hair and side-whiskers. Yet Henry's thirty-seven years were beginning, somehow, to make him look distinguished. He had improved in his twelve years of marriage. She was glad she had persuaded him to shave his beard.

"All right, dear. Goodbye."

But Henry did not go away at once. He was looking at his wife, seeing her anew, as she stood there in her garden, a rough tweed cloak thrown over her dress. At thirty-two, Phœbe looked slim and young. Her hair was raven black, and this morning her dark, Celtic-blue eyes, with their gipsy slant, had what he had come to call her "wild-cat look".

Henry came up the path, seized Phœbe in his arms, gave

39

her a sudden, hot kiss, and went off down the hill to Hayburn and Company. Neither had uttered another word. And neither was surprised at the quick flame that had flared between them.

Phœbe went back to her gardening, her blood pulsing with awareness of her husband. She had married Henry very young and gone with him to Austria. It had not been easy. Indeed, it had been quite the reverse. And the experiences they had there had left them different from the others of the home-keeping Moorhouses.

Henry, an engineer, was now the head of a small firm of his own founding. Henry had brains and diligence.

Phœbe worked away. She had lost count of time when she became aware that a boy of eleven was standing beside her.

"Hullo, Robin. Good morning. What time is it?"

"Nearly eight o'clock, Mother."

She raised herself on her knees and smiled. The boy, finding her thus at a convenient height, put his arms about her and kissed her.

There was a lot of kissing going on in this dour Scotch family this morning, Phœbe reflected, as she smiled thoughtfully at the child. He was sentimental and demonstrative, this half-Austrian foundling they had brought back from Vienna eleven years ago. Now she found herself looking at the boy's handsome face, seeking and finding the proofs of an old story. Her adopted son. The son of her husband's loneliness.

"Run along, Robin. I'm just coming." She patted his shoulder and got up.

The boy ran off down the path. He could see that his mother was in one of her moods. Not that he was afraid of them, for she was seldom anything but tender with him.

Phœbe followed him slowly.

40

V

The window of the dressing-room occupied by Mungo Ruanthorpe-Moorhouse, of Duntrafford House, Ayrshire, faced east. And thus it was that Mungo was awakened by a dazzle of sunshine this morning. He blinked and thrust up a hand to shade his eyes.

Starlings were chattering outside. Somewhere in the distance a cock was crowing. Sparrows chirped and quarrelled in the shrubbery. A breath of air moved the curtains of his window, and he caught the scents of early morning—of the damp earth; of a flowering shrub; of the sprouting May-time woodlands.

Having shifted his head on the pillow to avoid a shaft of sunlight, Mungo yawned and stretched himself. He would not be at his farm. Today he would have to dress himself in city clothes and go with his wife and son to the wedding of his nephew and niece. What a nuisance! How much better just to be going up to the Laigh Farm as usual!

He heaved a sigh of impatience, stretched himself once again and lay thinking. He would see everybody, of course: all his brothers and sisters; and their husbands and wives and children. The prospect did not enchant him. He liked them individually very well, but the Moorhouses in the mass, with their city ways and their city interests, could be too much of a good thing. He and Margaret, his wife, could never quite grasp what the family were talking about. Perhaps because they were not interested. That, he supposed, was because he and she were of the country.

Mungo put his hands behind his head and stared at the ceiling. The barking of dogs came from the kennels. The keeper must be feeding them. A gardener had begun to rake the gravel of the drive. The voices of the country, of the pleasant life of comfort he and Margaret were leading.

He had not sought it; he had been a plodding, unambitious farmer. Yet he had made a match of it with Margaret Ruanthorpe, the old laird's daughter. The most unlikely match on earth. And it had worked out excellently. And even though neither of them was young, they had succeeded in bringing a son into the world. Margaret would be—what now? Fifty-three. And he was fifty-seven. Young Charlie must be thirteen.

But he had kept the Laigh Farm, the family farm of the Moorhouses, and given his days to it. Mungo lay regretting that he could not go up there today. His work, his interests, everything that gave him a separate personality, lay across at the Laigh.

But what time was it? He put out his hand to pick up his watch from the bedside table. In doing so he knocked it on the floor.

"You're awake, too, are you, Mungo? I was just wondering when you were going to move." Margaret's voice came from the open door of her bedroom.

"What time is it?"

"Just after six. Do I hear you getting up?"

"Aye." In another moment Mungo's sturdy bulk was standing in his nightgown at one of the windows of his wife's large, comfortable bedroom. He stood now, looking down upon the gardener, busy with his rake.

"I must run over to the Dower House to see Mother before we go this morning. She is a bit upset about Miss MacMinn's marriage."

"That's no' very reasonable. The lassie had to get married when she had the chance."

"Oh, of course. Mother knows that. Still, old people don't like changes, I suppose. She's been Mother's companion since Father died. That's quite five years. She's been very good with Mother. And Mother can be very difficult."

42

Mungo was very well aware of this. But, having acquired some of the art of being a husband, he left criticism of Lady Ruanthorpe to Lady Ruanthorpe's daughter. He merely yawned and said: "Oh, yer mother's all right." Adding as he turned: "Hullo! What do *you* want?" as he spied his son, Charles, standing in the doorway of his dressing-room.

The son of the house looked at his parents with the popping eyes that had belonged to his grandfather, the old laird, and said: "Hullo! What's happening? We *are* brisk this morning! Feeling excited about the wedding or something?"

"Why are you up so soon, darling?" Margaret's teeth flashed in her handsome, weather-beaten face.

"Don't know, old lady. Couldn't sleep. The fine morning, I expect. Are you using the bathroom now, Dad?"

Mungo disapproved of Charles calling his mother "old lady", but he couldn't be bothered to take that up now. He merely said: "Aye, I'm goin' to shave, so ye can keep out of it," testily, and went back to his dressing-room.

That boy didn't know he was born. He had everything he wanted in the world. He was served hand and foot just because his mother thought he was delicate. Life was far too easy for Charlie. In fact, Mungo could not quite suppress the thought that life was too easy for all of them. Here he was, going to a morning bath in one of the new, up-to-date bathrooms Margaret had installed less than a year ago. Already it had become a daily habit with him. Mechanically, he put on a dressing-gown, picked up a thick white towel and slid his feet into slippers of lambs' fleece.

No. When he himself was Charlie's age he had tumbled out of bed straight into his working clothes—usually by candle-light—and gone down to the byre to help with the early milking.

Mary McNairn's eyes opened as her little maid-of-all-work turned the handle of her door, kicked it open and brought in her breakfast tray.

Since the death of her husband, twelve years ago, Mary had decided to become an old lady. Not deliberately, perhaps. But Mary's instincts—her complacency, her laziness, her piety, her love of comfort; a shrinking from unpleasant obligation, a conviction that she was very sensitive—all these joined to decide her to present a picture of ageing dignity to the world. Her actual age was fifty-two.

She sat up in bed, thanked the girl for setting the tray in front of her and asked to have a shawl put about her shoulders. The smell of ham and egg was pleasant.

"I think, Jessie, you might take this toast away again and brown it a little more, please. Were you late in lighting the kitchen fire this morning? And bring me some other kind of jam. You know I don't like rhubarb. Wait. I'll keep this slice, so that I can begin. Thank you."

With a sniff and a determination to seek less critical employment, the little maid went to do as she was bid.

Mary buttered the slice of toast, poured out her cup of tea and looked out of the window. From her bed she could see blue sky, white, piled-up clouds and sunshine. She could hear the ships sounding their horns as they moved far away on the river. It was high and pleasant in this Hillhead flat where she passed her widowhood.

Yes, it was going to be a nice day for the wedding. She could hear her twin daughters, Anne and Polly, getting up. They must have heard her tray come in. Why didn't they appear to say good morning? Especially Polly, who would be leaving her for ever today. Mary lay considering the loss of her daughter. Already she had lost two sons, she told herself. Her elder boy, George—or Georgie, as she still called him—was far away in America. And her younger boy, Jackie, was as good as taken from her, too. For Jackie had married very young and very unsuitably. A dreadful girl, Jackie's Rosie!

Adept, as most selfish people are, at excluding the unpleasant, Mary's mind dropped a veil over Rosie.

And now Polly was going. That left only Anne.

A nice, good-natured girl, Anne. Mary lay drinking tea, savouring ham and egg, and considered the daughter who was left. Would Anne marry, too, now? It was nice, of course, to be able to say you had married off your daughters. But, after all—and here Mary's piety reproached her—wasn't that just being a little worldly? Wouldn't it be nicer to keep Anne comfortable by her, so that she could look after her real old age when it came, and drive back the spectre of loneliness from her? Anne was a quiet, docile little creature, and would be very happy. She wasn't energetic and troublesome, like Margy Butter. Wil and Polly would have children, and Anne could find her interest in them. No. It would be much better if Anne did not marry.

The toast, properly browned, and a jam better to her liking were now brought by the little maid, whose face was red with annoyance and bending over the kitchen fire. "Thank you, Jessie. That's better. Ask the young ladies to come and say good morning."

They came together, hand in hand. Even their mother had difficulty in telling which was which. They both bent over Mary and kissed her carefully, taking care to disarrange nothing.

Her little twin girls who were everything to her. She smiled, saint-like, at the two plump young things. "Well, Polly? I hope you're feeling very, very happy."

"Yes, Mamma." Polly's little, round face exploded in a flood of tears. Almost simultaneously Anne's did the same.

"Girls! Girls! What a way to behave on Polly's wedding morning!"

"I don't want to leave Anne," Polly cried.

"But you don't mind leaving me? Is that it?"

"I don't want to leave you either, Mamma."

"I knew that, dear. I was just teasing. Now run away, both of you, and don't be so silly. It's going to be a lovely day. And just think how kind your Auntie Bel is being, arranging such a lovely wedding for you."

With a brave smile, Mary settled back and poured herself another cup of tea. Foolish, dear little things. Yes, Bel was really very kind, doing all this.

Now she lay considering Bel with that unconscious lack of charity with which we tend to think of those who force their benefactions upon us. She couldn't really deny how kind Bel was being. But, then, after all, Bel liked that sort of thing. Entertainment was the breath of Bel's nostrils. Besides, she had a grand house and servants to keep busy. Arthur seemed to let Bel spend just what she liked. Mary set down her teacup and stared before her. Bel. Wait until young Isabel got an eligible admirer or two, and Bel's entertainment would burst all the bounds of reason.

Suddenly self-conscious, Mary chid herself for thinking any such worldly thoughts—for allowing the sting of jealousy to enter her widow's heart. After all, she had so much to be thankful for.

She put aside her empty ham-and-egg plate, buttered a slice of toast, spread it with jam, refilled her teacup and settled herself among her pillows, harshly bidding herself count her blessings.

Chapter Four

BEL could be snobbish and ambitious. But her affections were real. Family responsibility came to her as naturally as it came to her husband. She was ever ready to stretch out the helping hand.

Now, on this bright morning, the helping hand was setting late spring flowers, half-sprouted, green branches and pots of conservatory plants about her pleasant house in Grosvenor Terrace; all this in preparation for the wedding reception of her niece, Polly McNairn.

It had ended up, of course, in herself taking all the responsibility for Polly's wedding-day. While Arthur did the paying.

"Mary hasn't got very much of a margin, dear," she had said to her husband. "I think perhaps—well, what I mean is, if these two are determined to be married in Kelvinside in a nice church"—nice, with Bel, was a word that supported a pyramid of overtones—"we had better see that everything is done properly."

Bel felt a twinge of envy that Mary, now living modestly in a small flat in Hillhead, should worship in a fashionable West End church, while she and her family must continue to worship in a church in the centre of the city. But her husband had begun his Glasgow days in the Ramshorn Church, he had long been an elder and had no intention of changing.

Arthur was no great reader of hearts. Thus, fixed in his admiration for his handsome wife, he did not bother to question her motives. Too much care for appearances; self-importance; family pride? Kindliness; sentimentality; affection? A real desire to help? He merely said: "Aye, we had better." And that had decided the matter.

Bel turned, a spray of almond blossom in her hand, to find Mary McNairn in the drawing-room doorway.

"Oh, good morning, Mary! I'm glad to see you."

The bride's mother advanced to kiss her sister-in-law. Mary was a good-looking woman in her way, Bel thought, seeing her afresh. Black suited her.

"And how is the little bride this morning, Mary?" Bel bent to kiss her.

"Very happy, Bel. Very, very happy." Mary spoke solemnly.

Bel thought of the bouncing, virile young man who was to be Polly's husband. "I'm glad, Mary," she said brightly. "That's just as it should be." Mary's widowed resignation annoyed her.

"What beautiful flowers, dear!" Mary said, looking round. "How kind you all are to us!"

"David and Grace sent up a load from Aucheneame this morning. And Mungo and Margaret sent up an under-gardener with white lilies and roses. And Phœbe and Henry sent this almond blossom." Bel smiled briskly. Mary was in one of her thanking moods. And Bel detested them. Rather illogically, perhaps. And yet somehow there were tones in Mary's voice suggesting that, of course, she knew Bel liked doing this sort of thing. It was easy for Mary to stand there, all emotional thankfulness, taking little or nothing to do with her own daughter's wedding. "The young people have gone round to the church," Bel added. "I sent most of the flowers round there. Isabel says the church looks lovely. Are you going to have a look at it?"

Mary wondered if this were a hint. But as it was a bright morning, and as the house was in too much of a turmoil to yield cups of tea, she bade Bel good morning and took herself to have a look at the decorations.

48

Bel looked at the gilt clock in its glass dome on the drawing-room mantelpiece. The morning was getting on. But the house was ready, and Isabel had reported there was little left to do in church. Bel was happy. This organising was just what she liked, and she did it easily and well.

The young people—the bridegroom, her son Arthur, Isabel and the other bridesmaid—were to have some kind of rehearsal in church at eleven. The organist would be there, and they would make sure of their places. That must be all over now. They would be dispersing to dress.

Bel could relax, but did not feel that she wanted to do so. The ceremony was not until two, and, after all, only the family would be present. She need neither be nervous nor fussed. She would put on her things and follow Mary across to the church to see how it looked.

A moment later Bel was coming downstairs, pulling on her gloves. It was a sunny morning. The front door was open. The stairway, the hall, the stone steps outside and the pavement to the carriage-stone had been covered with red baize. Already there was rice in Indian brass bowls to be thrown at her newly-married nephew and niece as they left for their honeymoon. The sight of them made Bel feel pleasantly sentimental.

"Arthur! What is it?"

Her son had suddenly appeared on the pavement outside, hatless and out of breath.

"Wil and the others came for the church rehearsal at eleven. We waited, but the organist, Mr. Netherton, didn't appear. Then at ten past they sent someone to say he had fallen and broken his wrist this morning."

"What a nuisance! Who have they got to take his place?"

"They haven't got anyone."

"But, Arthur, they must get someone! What are they going to do?"

Arthur looked vague. "We thought I had better come round to you first."

This made Arthur's mother angry. "And am I the only person in the family who can arrange anything? Wasn't Wil there? Hadn't your Aunt Mary come? Why should you all come to me?" It did not strike her that this was just what she had spent her life teaching the family to do. If there was one person who drew obligation upon herself, it was Bel.

But here was a challenge to her generalship! She stood thinking for a moment, then rang her own front-door bell. "Sarah, go and tell McCrimmon to put the horses into the carriage at once, please. Say I'm sorry. I know he wanted everything shining to take Miss Polly to church. But something has happened. Tell him to bring it round to the church. I'm walking there now. Come along, Arthur."

The sight of the bridegroom, her son Tom, her daughter Isabel, Margy Butter and the other McNairn twin, Anne, standing in the decorated church, merely waiting, without any appearance of anxiety, increased Bel's exasperation. What was the younger generation coming to? Had they no sense of responsibility? No idea of doing things for themselves? Had the thought of marriage paralysed Wil Butter's ability to think? Why didn't *he* do something? He was the director of a company. Was it beyond his powers to find another musician? And there was Mary, sitting like a Madonna Dolorosa behind a pot of white lilies!

But this was not the moment to lose control. "Well, children?" Bel's voice was very crisp. "What are we going to do?"

Their faces displayed a maddening blankness.

"Oh, get the church officer, someone!"

The church officer was old, slow, white-haired and tremulous. All these attributes suited him well as, dignified by his black coat, his cuffs and his dickey, he held the door of the little pulpit staircase open on Sundays for the minister to pass upwards and begin the morning service. The members of this prosperous and pleasant place of worship felt that here was a frail and reverent spirit, a simple creature purged of all grossness, ready likewise (but this time in a spiritual sense) to pass onwards and upwards.

But now the church officer was cross. He had been seeing to his coal cellar. He wore no collar, his sleeves were rolled up, a pair of frayed braces supported his working trousers, and coal dust marred the whiteness of his beard and hair. Soap, hot water and a comb would be needed before the light once more shone through.

Bel advanced upon him. "Good morning. I'm sorry to trouble you. But have you heard that the organist has broken his wrist and can't play?"

Like most half-deaf people, the church officer had long since discovered that, nine times out of ten, there is little profit in giving oneself the trouble of grasping what is said. Utterances can be so trivial. He merely allowed a look of sharp resentment to dart from beneath his bushy eyebrows, and said: "Eh?"

Bel summoned Wil Butter. After all, this was Wil's affair. "Wil dear, will you please ask him for the organist's name and address? He must have it. If nobody has bothered to do anything, I must go to the organist's house myself. I am sorry about his wrist, but he'll have to tell me where to find someone else to play. It's twelve o'clock now. We have only two hours. I think I hear the carriage. I told McCrimmon to find me here. Arthur, you had better come with me."

Wil Butter had a strong voice, and the church officer had to listen, however much it pained him.

And so it came about that the children in a street of tenement flats in the nearby suburb of Partick stopped their games
of hopscotch to stare at a handsome carriage with its pair of
dark, sleek horses standing before an entrance.

Who was the grand lady? Who was the young man? And
what could they be wanting here?

III

The staircase was untidy and none too clean. Boys had been
chalking their own kind of decoration on its walls. But on the
second landing Bel found a letter-box and a brass bell-pull
with a little nameplate beneath it, shining with polish. The
name-plate bore the name Netherton. She pulled the bell.

The door was opened by a little, twittering lady. In spite of
her troubles, Bel's practised eye took in her appearance at a
glance, and straightway labelled it "artistic".

Though she must be about Bel's own age, and might still
have a figure if she tried, everything about the little lady was
loose: a loose dark dress; a loose housejacket of mauve linen,
with wide, loose sleeves embroidered with square roses; several
gun-metal chains dangling loosely round her neck, and sus-
pending "artistic" ornaments of metal and enamel. Her dark
hair was parted in the middle, looped loosely over her ears
and caught loosely at the back.

The little lady looked up at Bel and Arthur somewhat
timidly. Perhaps they would tell her what she could do for
them?

A strange little person, Bel decided, but neither a slattern
nor ill-bred.

When she spoke, the little lady's pleasant voice confirmed
this. Yes, this was the house of Mr. Netherton, the organist.

Yes, she was Mrs. Netherton. Yes, it was all most unfortunate; and would they come in?

The little sitting-room was full, but tidy. It contained an upright piano, and, not surprisingly perhaps, its decoration waved a hand to the newer art. Stencilled water-lilies coiled their sinuous stems up the wallpaper in the corners, bursting into conventional leaves and blooms on the cornice. There were one or two long-backed chairs with hearts cut out of them. Two armchairs by the fireside were protected by rough linen antimacassars adorned with square mauve roses.

Bel's sense of order applauded the room's cleanliness, although she hated these new ideas of decoration. "Well, as I say, I've come about your husband, Mrs. Netherton," she said, taking the chair that was offered her.

"Yes. The doctor says his wrist is broken. It's unfortunate for us. He'll be able to teach, of course, but it will be some time before he can play. He tripped going downstairs this morning. He put out his hand to save himself."

Yes, a strange little lady. Bel could not, even now, help wondering what this woman's story was. But time was short.

"I'm very sorry, Mrs. Netherton. I do hope your husband will be better soon." But artistic people could be so irresponsible. "I hope you won't think me heartless, but, you see, my nephew is to be married in less than two hours. And there's no other arrangement about the music. I felt I had to come and ask your help."

"My daughter has gone to get someone else. Surely the boy we sent told them at the church? The organist of"—she mentioned a place of worship in the city. "He's a friend of John's. They always help each other when they can."

Again Bel was angry. Not with this woman, but with the young people she had left behind. Were they so irresponsible that they hadn't even taken the message properly?

"Arthur, why didn't you tell me?"

The little lady hastened to reassure her. "I don't think you need worry, Mrs.—"

"Mrs. Moorhouse—Mrs. Arthur Moorhouse of Grosvenor Terrace."

"It should be all right, Mrs. Moorhouse. Elizabeth will be sure to find him. She promised to come back at once and tell me."

Mrs. Netherton's words had only a part effect in reassuring Bel. "Is there nothing more I can do, then?" she asked doubtfully.

"It should really be all right, Mrs. Moorhouse. You see—" But there was the rattle of a key in the lock. The little lady brightened. "That must be Elizabeth."

The door was burst open with the words: "Oh, Mother! What are we to do? He wasn't there!" A young girl stood before them, panting and dishevelled. Her cheeks were flushed, strands of dark hair were out of place, and her eyes were big with distress. The sight of Bel and Arthur halted her. "Oh, I'm sorry; I didn't know."

There was silence for a moment. Bel's heart sank within her. Even Mrs. Netherton could twitter no suggestion. She stood fumbling with her chains and looking impotently at her daughter.

It was the girl who pulled herself together first. "You're here about the music for the wedding, I suppose?" she addressed them without introduction or ceremony.

"Yes. My nephew's wedding."

Elizabeth Netherton considered once again for a time, then said: "I must ask Father to try to come in. You'll just have to excuse what he looks like."

She went, leaving her mother to make timid, reassuring conversation to the handsome young man and his fashionable mother.

Bel turned to Arthur. He was looking out of the window! "Arthur!" Had he taken leave of his senses? Were all the young people mad today? "Arthur!"

He turned. "Yes, Mother?"

"Well? This is very upsetting, isn't it?" What was wrong? She felt for a moment as though she were calling to him from a distance, trying to attract his attention.

"This?" Why was he suddenly so vague?

"Oh! The music, Arthur!"

John Netherton came back with his daughter. He was a gaunt man with a face that was pale, even at normal times. A thin red-grey beard and sparse, overlong hair gave him something of the look of a faded Messiah. He wore a worn dressing-gown, and his right arm was splinted, bandaged and held in a sling. He nodded morosely to Bel. She guessed that he was suffering.

"What are we to do, John?" His wife ran to him. There was little time; and pain, she could see, had not improved his patience.

The man looked around him and sighed. They were fussy, these West-Enders, with their functions and their importance. But they were his bread and butter. He had better help, pain or no pain. He sought for a moment in his mind, then looked at his daughter. "Could *you* manage it?"

"Father!"

"I think ye could get through. I'll put on my things and come up and sit beside ye."

"I'm frightened." Elizabeth Netherton stood in the room looking at them.

"Oh, Miss Netherton! Could you? I didn't know you played. And if Mr. Netherton could! We couldn't thank you enough."

"But I'm not an organist. I play the piano a little. And Father lets me try the organ sometimes when he's working alone in church."

55

Bel turned to the clock. "It's a quarter to one. Who else can we find now?"

The girl looked about her. This fashionable woman. Her father dishevelled and suffering. The slim young man. Her mother. "But there must be hundreds of people who can do it."

John Netherton leant himself wearily against the mantel-piece. "We havena time to find them."

She turned again to her mother.

"Do it, Lizzie."

Her mother was appealing to her. It was a family responsibility.

"All right." But her voice wavered.

Bel, overcome with relief, promised to send a cab for them.

The door closed behind the visitors. Elizabeth Netherton went to dress. John Netherton turned to his wife. "That lot'll not know the difference."

Cynicism comes easily to those in pain.

IV

And it all went splendidly. The sun shone. The church was full of spring flowers, reverence and red baize. The church officer had got the coal dust out of his hair, and, once again, the spirit shone transparent through the frailness of the flesh. And the organ seemed to be pealing out very much as organs should. At all events, no one bothered to listen. Why should they? Unless it were the bride's Aunt Bel, who had her own very real reasons to congratulate herself that things were, after all, going so smoothly. If there was a wrong note here, a neglected harmony there, the happy ears of the guests did not catch at such trifles.

For this wedding within the family was a cheerful affair. There was no need for the relatives of the bride and the bridegroom to examine each other across the central aisle, as enemy tribes examine each other across a river. They need not wonder how the relationship now being formed would, in the end, result. How this one could possibly get on with that. Everybody knew everybody else already; knew their qualities, good and bad; knew where to lean and where to go lightly.

People whispered that the little, pink, round-faced bride was beautiful. And if happiness could make her, then Polly was so. And that the bridegroom was handsome. Which came nearer to the truth. For young Wil Butter, although he was a large young man with loosely knit bones, had some of the Moorhouse distinction, fine eyes, black hair and a pale skin. In his grand new wedding clothes, even Bel could not but admit that Wil had some kind of an air.

But not so much, Bel thought, as his Uncle Mungo Moorhouse, Laird of Duntrafford, who gave the little bride away. And certainly not so much as her own son, Arthur, who stood up, slim and young beside the bridegroom.

Now the service proper was over. The bridal party had gone into the vestry to sign the register. The others could for the moment sit back and relax, smile, and wonder at the astonishing taste of each other's hats.

David Moorhouse of Aucheneame was sitting behind Bel with his pleasant wife Grace, his son, and his wife's mother, Mrs. Robert Dermott. This good, but formidable lady tapped Bel on the shoulder.

"A very pretty wedding, my dear. Don't you think so?"

Bel thought so.

Mrs. Dermott went on: "Beautiful flowers! I wonder which David sent from Aucheneame?"

As Bel could not answer this difficult question, but merely

said that, yes, the flowers were beautiful, Mrs. Dermott raised her lorgnette, looked about her and went on: "Now why is that odd-looking man sitting beside the girl at the organ? Is his arm in a sling?"

Bel stopped for a moment to listen to Elizabeth Netherton as she meandered through the simplest church music her father could find for her. Then she turned back to Mrs. Dermott, told her of the morning's excitement and how plucky the girl up there was being.

Mrs. Dermott was an old woman of spirit, and it pleased her to find it in others. "What a capital child! I like people with pluck. Especially young ones. Young people can be so flabby."

Bel remembered that her young people had certainly been flabby this morning. But she merely said: "The music is perhaps a little—" and hesitated for a word.

"Never mind. It's putting the thing through. The great thing is to put things through. I would like to meet her. You're asking her to the reception, of course?"

Bel had not thought of this. There had, indeed, been so little time to do anything but dress herself, give final orders in the house, and come with the family to church. But somewhere in Bel's mind there had been thoughts of a present, a gracious note of thanks, and a parcel of delicacies, perhaps, to help knit together Mr. Netherton's bones. Now Mrs. Dermott's admiration, however, had given his daughter added importance.

"It has all been so hurried," she said. "The poor man will want to go home. I've arranged a cab. But it would be nice to have the girl. I'll tell Arthur."

And now the bridal procession was coming down the aisle, while a very sketchy wedding march sounded above and around them. The newly-married Mr. and Mrs. William Butter smiled

58

bravely. Little Meg Dermott-Moorhouse bore the bride's train. Mrs. Dermott waved her lorgnette at her granddaughter. Then the grown-up bridesmaids; Anne McNairn, Polly's twin sister. Anne was a replica of the bride. So much so that people wondered why Wil had chosen Polly and not Anne, and how, when he had done so, he could know which was which. Anne was supported on the groomsman's arm. Margy Butter on Jack McNairn's. Margy was looking nipped and spinsterish, Bel felt, making a mental note to do as much entertaining as possible for Isabel now. And then came Mary, smiling bravely and tearfully on the arm of the hairy and unresponsive William Butter. While Sophia, excited, anxious to greet everybody as she passed, and inclined to stumble in a home-made dress that was a little too long in front, brought up the rear with a resolute Mungo who was giving his mind to keeping his sister's progress steady.

Now all the guests were outside the church. Some were still chatting in the portico. Children were being kissed by uncles and aunts, and were being told how they had grown. Some had already driven away. Some were preparing to walk the easy distance to Grosvenor Terrace in the spring sunshine.

Now the music could stop. Elizabeth Netherton laid her hands in her lap and turned to look at her father. "Is your wrist hurting you?"

"Aye." He did not think of praising her. But his stretched nerves had played every note with her. And now, with that, and the shock of his fall in the morning, he was utterly exhausted. He moved towards the vestry door.

Elizabeth followed him. Her little mother came towards them, offering anxious support. Now they would drive home together, and her father could rest. She had got through somehow. It had been like a dream, dreamt in a fever when one is pushed upon a stage to act a part one does not know. When she got home she would probably shut herself up in her room and cry away the tension.

But in the vestry the fair young man she had seen this morning was waiting. He had come to beg her to go with him.

Chapter Five

MRS. ROBERT DERMOTT, the mother-in-law of David Moorhouse, was an old lady possessed of admirable qualities. There was nothing small about her: her body, her mind or her outlook. Mrs. Dermott filled every room she entered, no matter how full that room might already be. She had a personality that must make itself felt. And if at any time Mrs. Dermott became aware that her personality was not doing so, at once she became unhappy.

She was unhappy now, as she stood by herself in the window of Bel's large drawing-room, while the Moorhouse tribe—always delighted, whatever they might say, to come together in family reunion, whether it be a wedding, a Christmas dinner or a funeral—having saluted and forgotten the little bride, hastened to rush one at the other in greeting—brothers to clap brothers on the shoulders; uncles to kiss pretty nieces and compliment them on their looks; sisters to tell sisters-in-law how well their spring clothes became them and how each wished she had the other's figure.

All this was very well. But it did not include Mrs. Dermott. She tried to attract the attention of her grandson, Robert David. But the dreamy Robert David was being stirred up, for once, by his cousin, Charles Ruanthorpe-Moorhouse, who was using him to demonstrate different methods of boxing. Much to the inconvenience of uncles and aunts. And much to the delight of the third boy of the family, Robin Hayburn, who stood, offering encouragement and applause, but taking care to keep out of range.

Robert David was no use, then, to his grandmother. It was impossible to catch him; even to give him a scolding for being so noisy. Her little granddaughter, Meg, taking her train-bearing seriously, had refused to quit the bride and bridegroom. She had found, to her gratification, that in this position, standing near them, everyone was forced to take notice of herself.

No, neither grandchild was of use to Mrs. Dermott. But now there was young Arthur Moorhouse arriving with a pretty girl in a plain straw hat and a white summer dress. That must be the organist.

Mrs. Dermott was delighted. Was it not on her own suggestion that Bel had asked the girl here? She would know no one. Herself, Mrs. Dermott, had better take her in hand.

As a Dermott liner made nothing of Atlantic billows, so Mrs. Robert Dermott, slipping her moorings by the window, cut her way through the mob of Moorhouses, bearing down upon Elizabeth Netherton.

Elizabeth was bewildered. She was not, indeed, sure why she had come. In the vestry she had been excited—in tears almost. Then Mr. Moorhouse had come with his mother's invitation. Hardly knowing what she did, she had said it was very kind, received a nod of encouragement from her mother, and forthwith set out in the company of this solemn, polite young man, walking by his side in the sunshine.

But what was she to do now, here in this noisy room, full of people she did not know?

Mrs. Arthur Moorhouse was coming to welcome Elizabeth. She was explaining her to the bride, who seemed friendly and flustered and gave Elizabeth her thanks. Now, for a moment, her busy hostess was looking about, wondering perhaps how to dispose of her, while the young man who had brought Elizabeth stood by looking as though he were shyly ready to resume his guardianship.

"My dear Bel! You must introduce me to this wonderful young lady at once! Miss Netherton, isn't it? My name is Dermott—Mrs. Robert Dermott. Now, my dear Bel, you're busy. I'll look after Miss Netherton. Come along with me, Miss Netherton. I think it was splendid of you to be so plucky today. There's nothing I admire more than pluck. And you must tell me about your poor father. Dreadful about his hand! Or was it his wrist?"

Elizabeth's bewilderment did not diminish. This must, of course, be *the* Mrs. Robert Dermott. But why had she descended upon herself with this exaggerated friendliness? And did she always talk so loud?

Established with Elizabeth beside her on a sofa pushed against the wall, Mrs. Dermott set up a sort of court. One after the other people were called upon to shake hands with this clever young lady who had played so beautifully; to have her helpfulness explained to them; to be told about her father's accident. These people seemed to hold Mrs. Dermott in awe. The stamp of her approval seemed to mean much.

Elizabeth blushed at being taken so seriously. People hurried to shake her hand. Several said they would be pleased if she would come to see them. Yet what could they really want of her? She decided they were all making a fuss for fussing's sake.

II

On the whole, Mary McNairn was enjoying her daughter's wedding day.

It was nice to find oneself at the centre of things without being put to any trouble. She had never wholeheartedly liked Bel since her brother Arthur had brought her into the family some twenty-two years ago. Bel was too effective. Too handsome. Too capable. Too generous. To put the matter shortly, Mary had always been a little jealous of Bel.

But now, sitting in Bel's drawing-room, Mary could not but feel that Bel's prosperity, Bel's ability to organise, Bel's amiable self-importance had their uses. Today Bel had given little Polly a wedding day to remember.

Mary took a sip from the glass that she had, unwittingly perhaps, allowed to be replenished, savoured the champagne upon her tongue and marked its pleasant descent to lower regions. She looked about her. Bel's handsome room. The well-dressed people who thronged it, nearly all of them her relatives. The scent of flowers. Familiar voices. Familiar talk and laughter. As the widowed sister of this prosperous clan, it gave her a sense of support.

Her thoughts went back to her husband, George, a dull, self-important baillie of the city, now some twelve years dead. For a moment Mary felt a primitive stab of loneliness. They had been very happy. They had been smug together. Complacent together. Slow-witted together. It had been a perfect union. Yes, she missed George. For a moment the room trembled before her.

"Let me fill up your glass, Aunt Mary." It was young Tom Moorhouse.

"Oh—just very little, Tom." Mary smiled bravely. "How are you? Is your head all right again?"

"Yes. All right, thanks. I've forgotten about it. Aren't you having any, Rosie?"

"No, thanks, Tom. Tea's what I want. You can keep your champagnes for me. Tea's the thing. Are you sure that won't do you any harm, Mother?" Rosie McNairn was standing over Mary.

She had never got used to her son Jack's wife calling her

"Mother". In very few respects indeed had she got used to her son Jack's wife. It had been a ridiculously early marriage when the boy was only twenty-two. Rosie had been a sales-girl in the warehouse where Jack had found himself employment.

Mary had done everything to stop it. She had wept to Jack. She had reminded him that his father was dead; that he was the son of a widow; that his only brother was in America. She had even prevailed upon his Uncle David to lecture Jack. But it had all been of no use. Jack, paying his mother back in her own sentimental coin, had taken his stand, declaring that his life would be broken if he could not marry the girl he loved.

Rosie was hopelessly ordinary—an over-dressed, shoppy little thing, with a crude, jocular heartiness, that seemed to proof her against all the influences of refinement. Rosie was irrepressible. The only way to repress her, indeed, was to keep her out of sight. All that you could say of her was that she had pluck. She lived frugally in a cheap two-roomed flat with her husband, made her own preposterous clothes, and asked charity from no one.

When Jack and she had settled down at first, Anne and Polly had shown signs of accepting too many invitations to Rosie's. Rosie, they reported, was just a caution, did killing imitations of music-hall ladies, and cooked the most wonderful fish teas. But Mary had determined that this was no kind of entertainment for growing schoolgirls. She had not forbidden them to go. But she had pointed out that poor Jack had very little money; that they must not be so selfish as to go eating poor Rosie out of her house; and that they were perhaps too young to realise that newly-married people who love each other like to be left to themselves a great deal.

And now, after a year, there was to be a child. Looking at her, Mary could take no pleasure in this prospect. She could only wish that Rosie wouldn't wear that conspicuous pink dress in her present condition.

The girl sat down beside her uninvited. "Get tired standing on your feet, don't you, Mother?"

"Look. Take this." A cup was thrust in front of Rosie.

"Sure you don't want it?"

"I'm offering it to you."

"Oh, well, thanks." Rosie giggled. "I needed this." She looked up at the dark elegance of the young woman standing before her. She had seen her before, but she had to think for a moment. "Now—you're Jackie's Aunt Phœbe! That's right, isn't it?"

"Yes."

"You look younger than he does!"

"I'm exactly eight years older."

"Funny to think you two are sisters!" the girl said, with unintentional impertinence, looking from Phœbe to Mary.

"Half-sisters," Phœbe said.

She seemed a queer, sharp kind of young woman, Jackie's Aunt Phœbe. She had hardly even bothered to smile. Still, there was something about her. Style. That's what it was, Rosie McNairn reflected. But it was impossible, now, to tell what she was thinking. Jackie hadn't told her much about the Hayburns.

"You've never come to see me, Rosie," Phœbe was saying.

Again Rosie giggled. "I've never been asked."

"Well, I'm asking you now. Come across and see me to-morrow morning. You live near George's Cross, don't you? I'm in Partickhill. I've got some things of Robin's you could use when your child comes."

Rosie thanked her.

"Any time in the morning." Phœbe turned away to talk to Mrs. Barrowfield.

Mary felt puzzled and rebuked. Why had her strange, off-hand half-sister shown this sudden friendliness towards Rosie? But you could never tell anything with Phœbe.

III

Elizabeth had not been sitting long beside Mrs. Dermott on the sofa before she was confirmed in what she had begun thinking. A fuss, it seemed, was what Mrs. Dermott wanted.

"Sophia, how are you? I think your daughter makes a charming little bride. So pretty, too."

"But Polly is Mary's daughter, Mrs. Dermott. I'm the mother of Wil, the bridegroom. You remember, Mary's twins, Anne and Polly. Some people thought—"

"Of course, Mrs. Butter. I'm a silly old woman." (Mrs. Dermott had a way of addressing the women of her son-in-law's family sometimes as Mrs., sometimes by their Christian names. They were long used to it.) "Yes, very silly. But there are so many of you. Still, it's time I had you all properly sorted out. I can remember faces, but not names. Don't you find that, Miss Netherton? When I was younger and had all my committees I used to find taking notes of people's names was the only thing. Especially when—"

"No. I was just going to say that some people thought it was a bad thing for first cousins to marry. You see, Miss Netherton, the bridegroom is my son and the bride is my niece—my sister Mary's girl. Muddling, isn't it? And so, as I say, some people think—but I could never see any real reason why not. Can you? I suppose there's an idea that cousins' children are sometimes—but dear me, there's time enough to think about all that later. And as William, my husband, was saying this morning, we all come from a splendid healthy

67

stock. And as far as daughters-in-law go, I couldn't have wished—"

"Margaret dear! Margaret! Miss Netherton, I want to introduce you to another Mrs. Moorhouse. Mrs. Ruanthorpe-Moorhouse of Duntrafford."

Thus Elizabeth found that very little was required of her in the way of conversation. Everyone around her was so busy trying to say things.

The large, handsome, middle-aged woman who now held out a hand was, she gathered, the wife of a Moorhouse who lived in Ayrshire. As she stood over Mrs. Dermott, the voice of Mrs. Mungo Moorhouse boomed loud, friendly and aristocratic. It was difficult to connect her with this Mrs. Butter in dowdy silk, her untidy hair surmounted by a bonnet of battered velvet flowers, who was still in full flow over the eugenics or otherwise of a marriage between first cousins.

"And how is my dear friend, Lady Ruanthorpe?" Mrs. Dermott was asking.

"Mother is very well. She is very old now, of course—eighty-eight—and missing Father. And the young woman who is with her is being married. Isn't it tiresome? It's so difficult to find anyone. Mother is so fond of her. Perhaps if you hear of anyone— Charles! Charles dear! Come and say how-do-you-do to your Aunt Grace's mother."

Sophia, having proved to her satisfaction that the mating of first cousins was the healthiest thing possible, provided that their blood was Moorhouse and pure, tried to fight her way back into the general conversation by way of her nephew Charles. "Charlie! Charlie dear! Are you not going to say how-do-you-do to your Aunt Sophie? And this is Miss Netherton, who—"

But she was swept under once more by the louder conversation of Charles's mother and Mrs. Dermott.

"I must try to get down to see Lady Ruanthorpe, Margaret. I'm very fond of her, you know. She's a very old friend of mine. And you see, my dear," Mrs. Dermott added playfully, "we old people must stick together."

Margaret was well aware that Mrs. Dermott and Lady Ruanthorpe had only come together some three or four times in their lives. But she assured her mother's very old friend that her mother would be more than pleased to see her.

"And I'll try to find someone really nice for Lady Ruanthorpe, Margaret. I'm in the way of hearing about people, you know. Well, Charles? I hear you're going to Eton in the autumn."

Charles received Mrs. Dermott's last remark with no great enthusiasm. The prospect of school, after a somewhat autocratic boyhood, filled him with little rapture. You had to fag for people and do unpleasant things, instead of having everything done for you by manservant, maidservant, tutor and stable-boy. He merely said: "Yes, I am, I'm sorry to say," and turned once again to his Aunt Sophia and the pleasant young lady.

"I say, it was wonderful of you to play the organ like that, when you couldn't really play it at all," he said, making what he considered a suitable opening.

His mother descended. "Charles, don't be impertinent. Miss Netherton plays beautifully."

"Of course she does. Haven't I just said so? Marvellous! I don't know how she does it. I couldn't." And now Charles, who took in most things, having taken in his mother's words concerning a companion for his grandmother, was struck by an idea. "Miss Netherton, you wouldn't like to go and look after my grandmother, I suppose? She's a fearful handful. But I believe you're clever enough to manage her. Mother's at her wit's end."

Margaret burst out laughing. "Oh, run away, Charles!

You're quite impossible. I'm sorry, Miss Netherton. You see how badly he needs to go to school. He should have gone before now, but he's been ill. He thinks he can arrange the universe."

Charles's mother, with her commanding ways, gave Elizabeth the impression that she too, perhaps, might not be averse to arranging the universe. But Elizabeth could not quite dislike Mrs. Ruanthorpe-Moorhouse.

"Ladies and gentlemen."

The room was hushing down. Elizabeth turned. Young Arthur Moorhouse, pink and bothered, was beginning his first public speech.

Mrs. Dermott turned to Elizabeth, as the girl's bright eyes took in the stammering young man in the middle of the floor. Yes, a pleasant, attractive young woman. And plucky. Young Charles, in his impertinence, hadn't perhaps been so far wrong. Elizabeth might be just the person for her old friend Lady Ruanthorpe. She must talk to Bel about it.

"It is my great privilege this afternoon to propose—" For a moment Arthur's bashful, wandering eyes met Elizabeth's across the space that had cleared itself.

She dropped her own eyes quickly and fumbled with her gloves.

Chapter Six

BEL MOORHOUSE was much attached to her mother. But there were times when Mrs. Barrowfield could be so inflexible, so wilfully stubborn, that she drove her daughter to the frontiers of exasperation. She was doing so now.

It was a week since the wedding. And during that week Mrs. Barrowfield had been ill. On the day after it, over-tired, perhaps, she had collapsed in a sudden faint on the floor of her sitting-room in Monteith Row. Her maids had picked her up, put her to bed, and sent for Bel and the doctor. By the time these had arrived the old lady was sitting up in bed drinking tea, asserting that she had stupidly tripped on the hearthrug and demanding of those around her what all the fuss was about?

The doctor, with a doctor's diplomacy, had agreed that, yes, it must have been the hearthrug, had winked across her mother's bed at a tired and anxious Bel, and told the old lady to stay where she was until such time as he gave her permission to get up. Mrs. Barrowfield, always pleased to have a man paying her attention, promised to do so.

That evening Bel laid her troubles before her husband. It was ridiculous that her mother, a woman of eighty-seven, should remain down there in that old-fashioned terrace over-looking Glasgow Green. Until now, Mrs. Barrowfield had known no illness worse than gout. But she was very old, and this collapse must be taken as a warning.

"It's hard on the old body to ask her to move at her time o' life," Arthur said.

71

"Oh, I know, dear. But she's so difficult to get to. It's half an hour in the carriage. And her maids are old, too, now. And think if anything happened in the night. They would have to send word to us here somehow, then we would have to go down."

"Could she not come and stay here?"

"Do you mean permanently, Arthur?"

"Aye."

Bel, who had been standing in front of the fire, bent down and kissed her husband. It was nice of him to suggest that. She had always been grateful that so much goodwill existed between her husband and her mother. But no. That would never do! The old lady was much too strong-minded. She, Bel, would no longer be mistress in her own house. Her forty-six years were as nothing to her mother. To Mrs. Barrowfield she was still a green girl, a flighty, silly creature, who would, of course, be expected to give way to mature experience. And the maids! The children! Oh, no! Never! Rather the prospect of numberless midnight excursions through wind, rain and darkness, than have her strong-willed parent installed in Grosvenor Terrace. Besides, her mother's habits tended to be homely. Quite unsuitable, really, for the children and their friends.

Bel did not say these things to Arthur. You couldn't expect a man to grasp the finer points. He would only think her hard and unfilial. She merely said: "Oh no, dear. I could never think of allowing Mother to be a burden on you."

"I tell you what, then," Arthur said presently. "Yer mother had better get in a telephone, and we can get one here. And you can talk to her whenever you want."

"Arthur! But wouldn't that be very expensive? And would it be quite easy for Mother to use?"

Arthur explained that the telephone he had just installed in his warehouse was the easiest thing in the world. All you had to do was to look up the little book of subscribers' numbers that the National Telephone Company supplied with each instrument, turn the handle to ring a place called the exchange, and repeat the number when a voice answered you. Thereafter, and in no time at all, you were speaking to the person you wanted.

Bel was delighted. That solved everything. She had taken the opportunity of looking through just such a little book as Arthur had mentioned, and noted that, for the great part, it was only those who were important and fashionable who were going the length of having private telephones in their homes. Already she heard herself saying to that nameless duchess who was a permanent shadow at the back of her mind: "Yes. My husband has just had a private telephone put in. Perhaps you would care to ring me up sometime?"

"We'll need to ask yer mother if she'll use it," Arthur said, bringing her back to earth. "Some old folks are frightened to touch them."

"Mother? What nonsense, Arthur! Mother's frightened of nothing. And her hearing is as good as ever."

II

Now, a week later, Mrs. Barrowfield, bored with bed, got out of it, hired a cab and came all the way out to the West End to call upon her daughter.

Bel greeted her tartly. "Mother, what are you doing?"

"What do you think I'm doing? Come to see you."

"But you've been ill. Has the doctor allowed you?"

"I wasna ill. I tripped on the rug."

"Well—yes. But to fall down at your age!"

Mrs. Barrowfield did not reply to this.

73

"Did the doctor allow you to come here?" Bel repeated her question.

Still Mrs. Barrowfield did not answer. She merely marched past Bel into her parlour, untying her bonnet-strings as she went and shaking out her side-curls.

Bel sighed and sat down on the other side of the fireplace. "Well, anyway, rug or no rug, you gave us all a fright," she said crossly.

Mrs. Barrowfield smiled and looked at Bel with affection. "It's nice to be out here seeing ye again, my dear," she said, adding: "You'll not be having a wee cup of tea?"

"Sarah will bring it without being told, Mother."

"Ye better make sure."

Bel rose with resignation, pulled the bell-rope and sat down again. "I was talking to Arthur, Mother," she went on. "And we've decided to have a telephone put in here and one put into your house, so that we can hear how you are whenever we want to."

Mrs. Barrowfield was sitting in front of her chair, still taking off her outdoor things. She did not bother to listen properly. She put her sealskin jacket aside, then turned to say: "Telephone? Who's getting a telephone?"

"We are, Mother. And you. So that we can talk to you if you're ill."

Mrs. Barrowfield sat back, looked sulkily across at Bel and said: "Who said I was ill?"

"Oh, nobody! But if you are. Arthur thought you ought to be able to get through to us at once."

"There's no telephone coming into any house of mine!"

"But Mother, why?" Bel had not expected this. Arthur's opinion usually decided things for her mother.

The old woman continued to look sulky. "Dangerous, new-fangled things," she said bleakly.

74

"There's nothing dangerous about them, Mother."

"How do *you* know?"

"Arthur uses one every day at the office now."

"It's different for men."

"I can't see how."

"Have ye seen this morning's paper? There's a bit about a man touching an electric wire and getting killed."

"But was it a telephone wire, Mother?"

"It was electric, anyway."

Bel sighed with desperation. Her chances of conversation with her visionary duchess were showing signs of fading. And she knew her husband. If her mother refused, he would start making a fuss about respecting an old body's wishes. And if there was to be no telephone at Monteith Row, then there would be no telephone at Grosvenor Terrace. Her only chance might be to persuade him of its extreme urgency and take her mother for a holiday while their respective telephones were installed. Thereafter, even if her mother still refused to use hers, the Grosvenor Terrace instrument would at least be there for the duchess.

But now, for the time being, Bel thought it best to drop the matter. She smiled with resignation. "We'll have a talk with Arthur some time, Mother," she said, pleasantly evasive.

"Ye can talk yer heads off. It'll make no odds to me."

Bel was pleased to hear the handle of the parlour door turning. She continued determinedly and diplomatically pleasant. "Well, at any rate, dear, here's Sarah with tea."

But it wasn't Sarah with tea. It was Sarah with Mrs. Robert Dermott.

"My dear Bel! I'm so glad to catch you at home!" Mrs. Dermott's largeness, her white gloves, her dangling gold chains, her feather boa, advanced into the parlour. "And Mrs. Barrowfield! How do you do, Mrs. Barrowfield. You know, you and I should know each other much better than we do. After all, we both belong to the honourable company of Moorhouse grandmothers."

Mrs. Dermott was far from being without social instinct. For long she had sensed that Bel's homely parent had no great love for her; that Mrs. Barrowfield kept out of her way. These facts did not, however, trouble Mrs. Dermott much. It pleased her to think that people liked her, but if they did not choose to, then it was easy for her to forget about them. But now she had come to consult Bel about Elizabeth Netherton, and she did not want to do so in an atmosphere of chill dislike.

Mrs. Barrowfield gave Mrs. Dermott her hand without enthusiasm.

Bel had managed to catch Sarah's eye before she closed the door. A lift of an eyebrow conveyed that Mrs. Dermott's arrival meant heavier silver, finer china, more careful appointments. A tea-party of these strong-minded old women was not what she would have chosen, but now she was so out of temper with her mother that she did not much care.

She was well aware that Mrs. Barrowfield hated Mrs. Dermott. She had, indeed, once asked her why. But all her mother would say was: "That upsettin' old body! I could never abide her!"

Perhaps it was that Mrs. Dermott, used to being of importance, gave those who wanted to dislike her a feeling that she was ready to ride roughshod over them; though this, in fact, she never did. She was a large, generous, noisy woman, with the confidence of a heavy purse, but with sensibilities that seventy-nine years had not yet blunted.

On Bel's invitation, Mrs. Dermott sat down by the fire, pulling off her kid gloves, jangling thick gold bangles, and radiating goodwill with a determination that amounted to fierceness. "Do you know what I have been doing today, Mrs. Barrowfield? I've been talking to my daughter Grace on my new telephone! And I can talk to David at the office! They insisted on putting it in for me. I think it's the most wonderful of all modern wonders. Don't you?"

Mrs. Barrowfield's gloom seemed, unaccountably, to deepen. She merely said: "That's so." And offered no further comment.

Bel felt she must cover up her mother's unresponsiveness. "Arthur has one at the office. Would you advise us to get one in here, Mrs. Dermott?"

"Of course, Mrs. Moorhouse. And you should have one, too, Mrs. Barrowfield. Especially when you live all alone, like me. Think how nice for us both to be able to plague our daughters whenever we wanted to."

Mrs. Barrowfield did not respond. She merely murmured something about having heard that electric wires were dangerous, which caused Bel to say: "Mother manages to plague her own daughter quite enough as it is. Don't you, Mother?" And immediately thereafter to realise that this sounded ungracious. She hastened to go on: "Funnily enough, I have just been telling Mother that Arthur wants to arrange a telephone for her. She was ill last week. It gave us all rather a fright."

"I wasna ill. I fell over the rug."

"Well, at any rate, Mother, you had a little mishap." Bel's became more elegant as Mrs. Barrowfield's speech broadened.

"Oh, Mrs. Barrowfield, I should certainly have the telephone! It's such fun turning the little handle!"

Mrs. Barrowfield looked at Mrs. Dermott with distaste.

What right had this woman, who must only be her junior by a few years, to talk to her thus, as though she were already in her second childhood? "There's no telephone going into my house," she said bluntly, and with finality, refusing to be bludgeoned into good humour.

Bel was genuinely vexed now. Her mother had many fine qualities. Why should she so perversely display the worst of herself to David's mother-in-law? Was it jealousy? A sense of her lack of education? Shyness? At all events, she was doing herself less than justice, and her daughter did not like it.

"Oh, there you are, Sarah!"

Sarah had never seen her mistress more delighted by the arrival of tea.

IV

Reluctantly, Mrs. Dermott gave Mrs. Barrowfield up. She had tried and failed. Well, that was that. She really must get on. She addressed herself to Bel.

"Bel, my dear, I want to ask your advice about something. You see, Mrs. Moorhouse, I had a visit yesterday from Miss Netherton—you remember the girl who played the organ at the wedding?—of course, you arranged all that. Didn't you? Such a nice child! Well, I liked her more than ever. And now just this morning I have a letter from Margaret Moorhouse reminding me of my promise to find someone for her mother. Miss Netherton at once came into my mind. Have you any idea if she would consider taking the situation? I imagine a girl like that might be glad to. What do you think?"

"Ye've put too much cream in this," Mrs. Barrowfield said, tasting her tea with disapproval.

It was difficult for Bel to concentrate. Her mother clung to habits that were not quite genteel, such as pouring her tea, if it were too hot, into her saucer and drinking it from that. Bel had deliberately given her more than the usual amount of cream to cool it down and to avoid this catastrophe.

Bel sat, wreathed in false smiles, doing her best. "I'm sorry, Mother. Give me your cup, and I'll pour some of it away. As she took it from her, she avoided her mother's eye. "I'm sorry, Mrs. Dermott. You were talking about Miss Netherton?"

"Yes. About Miss Netherton going to Lady Ruanthorpe. I just wondered if she would think of it."

Bel gave the cup back to her mother, handed her a plate of the softest things she could find, lest she should take to dipping them, and wrenched her mind round to the topic of Miss Netherton. "The only thing to do is to ask her, isn't it? Yes, it would be splendid for her." She did not, just for the present, really mind what Miss Netherton did. But the awkwardness of the moment drove her to a show of enthusiasm she did not feel.

Mrs. Dermott smiled. Planning for other people was meat and drink to her. "I'm so glad you think so, Bel; I do, too."

For a moment Bel's concentration had slipped. Her mother was feeling her teacup to judge if it were too hot. But after a moment that hung in eternity the cup descended safely to its saucer, and Bel breathed once more. "I wonder what we can do about it?" she said, catching at lost threads.

"Well, that's just what I was going to ask you, my dear. Your daughter Bel is such a clever person, Mrs. Barrowfield," Mrs. Dermott added, her sense of politeness forcing her once more to include Bel's mother in the conversation.

Mrs. Barrowfield merely said: "Sometimes," took a drink of tea and looked bleakly into the fire.

Bel snatched at the first idea that came into her mind. "Wouldn't it be a good thing for you to write a letter to her here after tea? Arthur knows where she lives. He could run down this evening and give it to Miss Netherton."

"Could ye not post it and save the boy the trouble?" Mrs. Barrowfield asked suddenly.

Glad of even this show of interest from Mrs. Barrowfield, Mrs. Dermott exclaimed: "Yes, indeed! Why not? I'll write tonight and post it. But now, let me see, what about her address? How foolish of me! I don't think I have it. But perhaps you—?"

"Not at all, Mrs. Dermott. Arthur can run down with it easily. He knows just where to go."

"Well, it's very kind of you." Mrs. Dermott put down her cup. "If you would allow me to write it now? You see, I have to go on somewhere else in a moment." She looked towards Arthur Senior's writing-desk in the corner.

"There's paper in the drawing-room. It would be much better for you to write there," Bel said, with a firmness that was born of the chance of getting Mrs. Dermott from the room.

"All right, my dear. Lead the way. I must make it quite plain to Miss Netherton what a charming woman Lady Ruanthorpe is!"

Mrs. Barrowfield looked with contempt at the door which had just closed behind Mrs. Dermott. She got up and helped herself to another cup of tea. By the time she had done so, the door had opened once again to admit her granddaughter Isabel.

"Hullo, Granny!" Isabel bent down and kissed her. "Who's in the drawing-room with Mother?"

"That Mrs. Dermott. She's writin' a letter."

"Did you see her?"

"Oh, aye."

Isabel picked up a piece of cake and munched it, standing in front of her grandmother. "Granny," she said at length.

"What is it?"

"I believe you've been rude to Mrs. Dermott."

"What way should I—?"

Isabel turned to her mother, who, having arranged Mrs. Dermott's materials for her, had come back into the room. "Mother, was Granny being rude to Mrs. Dermott?"

Bel, who was highly displeased with her mother, found much relief in snapping: "Yes. Very."

"I thought so. I knew just from the look of her."

In face of this double attack, the old woman twisted herself in her chair with the petted gesture of a bad child. "Me? I never—"

"You've no right to be rude to people who come to this house, Mother. Even if you don't like them." Bel stood over her like an avenging fury.

"Granny, how could you?" Isabel sat on the edge of the old woman's chair and laid a cheek against her own.

"And I don't like Arthur going to see that lassie again."

"Who do you mean, Granny?"

"Oh, Miss Netherton, Isabel! Mrs. Dermott wants Arthur to take a letter to her, that's all. I suggested it. Besides, Miss Netherton has nothing to do with it. Your grandmother was being rude long before Miss Netherton was mentioned." Bel's voice was hoarse with exasperation.

Mrs. Barrowfield looked still more glumly at her daughter. "Maybe you'll be sorry ye suggested it."

"Don't talk nonsense, Mother! Anyway, what on earth do you mean? Arthur's a young man in quite a different station from Miss Netherton."

"Just so. That's what I'm trying to tell ye."

Bel merely said: "Rubbish!" poured herself some tea and stood drinking it angrily, drumming with one foot and listening for Mrs. Dermott to come downstairs.

She was amazed as she turned back to Mrs. Barrowfield to see that there were tears running down the wrinkles of her cheeks. The sight of them stabbed her sharply, bringing home to her that her strong-minded, vigorous mother had become a very old woman. "Mother? Whatever—? Oh, there's Mrs. Dermott. I won't bring her back. I'll make an excuse for you."

Isabel watched the door bang behind Bel, then she bent once more over her grandmother.

"Yer mother's awful nippy," Mrs. Barrowfield said plaintively.

"Well, dearest, perhaps you deserved it."

The old lady wept a little more, then wiped her eyes and said: "No, I didna deserve it." She sniffed dejectedly yet again, and added—much to her granddaughter's mystification: "And, what's more, I'm not going to let yer father put in a telephone!"

Chapter Seven

THERE WAS LITTLE that was remarkable about the Netherton family, if one knew their type.

John Netherton, a farmer's son from Perthshire with a turn for music, had, at the age of twenty, won a small scholarship and taken himself to Dresden. There, for the best part of a year, he had studied; practising, necessarily, a rigid economy. It had been hard for him, in this city where musicians were two a penny, to find hack-work to expand his slim resources. But now and then there had been an unmusical singer seeking, at a low fee, to be stuffed with an operatic rôle. And his landlady had let him have his room cheap in exchange for his giving her son English lessons.

John Netherton's life in Dresden had been narrow. Too narrow, perhaps, to allow him fully to expand the talent he possessed. He had come home, competent to make a modest living—nothing more. And yet the lonely young Scot studying unnoticed had worked with passion, had heard the great ones of the day, and dreamt his dreams. For John the year in Dresden had softened and become a golden happening: a memory to lean upon in despondency; a flash of arrogance, if his musician's knowledge came to be questioned.

On coming home he had obtained a post in one of the many new churches of a quickly expanding Glasgow. At twenty he had hopes of really doing something. And he had gone about the town seeking, as young men will, to look as though he had already done so. He affected a velvet jacket. And the hair that was now thin had been a bushy, red crop, worn recklessly long. At thirty his ambitions had faded somewhat, though his competence assured him of steady work. And still, when one of his fellow-students, now become a public figure, came to perform in the city, John would call round at his hotel, take him by the hand and talk of old times.

A year later the light of another hope was bright within him— the hope that a young woman who sang a piping soprano in church of a Sunday might be induced to consider him as a husband. She was a well-bred little thing, the orphan of a country manse, living with relatives in Glasgow, and now teaching "artistic" sewing to such young ladies as cared to learn it. Ellen's manner was young for her twenty-four years. But her birdlike admiration, innocent and obvious, had flattered, somehow, this sombre young man who took himself so seriously.

At forty he had a wife and child, and the knowledge that he would never be other than he was. Now, at fifty-three, it was not often that John Netherton remembered he had ever had a dream. If a fellow-student, turned virtuoso, came to the city, his wife, still bright and a little irresponsible, might say: "Surely that's someone you knew when you were in Germany, John."

"Oh aye, I knew him fine. He wasna such a big man in those days."

For a moment Ellen Netherton might wonder dimly why luck had been against her husband. But she would ask: "Don't you feel like going to see him?"

"Oh, he wouldna have mind of me now. It's a long time." And then, to lay the wraiths of old hopes that refused, in spite of everything, quite to cease from haunting, John might let himself appear, for a little, more than usually cheerful. But at these times he, too, would wonder how it had come about that he had stopped short, while this other had gone on.

But on the whole the Nethertons were contented. The husband and wife, taking each other comfortably for granted, joined together to find pleasure in the daughter they had brought into the world.

An unremarkable, demurely bohemian family. But one that did very well. Mrs. Netherton was pleased to take each day as it came, uncritically cheerful, making allowance for the darker moods of her husband, and taking pride in her daughter. If all hope of being more than a local organist and teacher had long since left John Netherton, his love for the music he served did not leave him, but continued his interest and delight.

And as for Elizabeth, at twenty the world was opening before her, and that was interest and delight enough. She was quick, comely and not without spirit. As the daughter of a simple-minded mother, she had learnt responsibility early. That, and the fact that she must earn her own living when and as she could, had given her pluck, independence and a will of her own.

II

Bel Moorhouse was the sun of her own universe. And the planets that circled nearest to herself were her sons, Arthur and Tom. Her husband and daughter, belonging, too, of course, to Bel's solar system, made wider circles about her, catching the light from a rather colder distance.

Until now young Arthur Moorhouse had swallowed Bel whole. He was not a stupid young man, but, as happens with the newly grown-up sons of most charming, self-confident mothers, to criticise Bel did not enter young Arthur's mind. What Bel thought, what Bel said, her son was used to thinking and saying after her.

And Bel was thinking and saying many things these days. For a week or two after the Lord Provost's ball the Ellerdales had occupied her mind. How pleasant Mrs. Ellerdale was! How handsome the Colonel! She had wondered how the young man liked Glasgow, what David thought of him at the office, and if it would be kind to ask him to visit them at Grosvenor Terrace. He would, she had said often and brightly, be a nice friend for the boys. And even more brightly, and especially when young Arthur was by her, she had praised little Miss Ellerdale, exclaiming—perhaps because the girl was not particularly beautiful—how very fresh and young she looked; how simple and unspoilt her manners.

Once, alone with young Arthur and losing her head a little, Bel had told him that she would be more than delighted if, when the time came, he found a wife half as nice as Winifred Ellerdale. But Arthur's fair colour rose hotly, so she had hastened to say that, of course, she did not expect this to happen for a long time; and that she had no wish to lose him, even to the nicest girl in the world. And thereafter she had not risked coming out thus into the open. Bel saw that even adoring sons cannot be pushed into love with suitable young women merely by the enthusiasm of their mothers.

But now, with the wedding and its alarms, there was another young woman to talk about. Caught unawares, and quite unheedful of the harvest she might reap, Bel had taken to extolling Elizabeth Netherton. Her pluck, her bravery and all the rest of it.

It is difficult to disentangle the motives that forced Bel to talk about Elizabeth. A sense of gratitude? Because other members of the family were making a fuss; especially Mrs. Dermott? In order that she might not appear to be for ever extolling Winifred Ellerdale?

At all events, Arthur's mother praised Miss Netherton without stopping to consider the dangers. She did not see that, to Arthur's innocent thinking, he had been given permission by her faultless self to take a hesitant step along a new and tremulously interesting path, that somehow held Elizabeth Netherton at its shining end.

And now, tonight, his mother was asking him to take her a letter.

"It's from Mrs. Dermott, dear. Miss Netherton came to see her, but she didn't leave her address. I said you would remember where she lived."

Arthur showed no alacrity. His voice could not have been more casual as he said: "Why is Mrs. Dermott writing to Miss Netherton?"

Like most mothers who protest they can read their children like books, Bel was completely deceived. "You *will* go, won't you, dear? It's quite a nice evening for a walk. I promised Mrs. Dermott you would. And it's really important. Mrs. Dermott thought Miss Netherton might care to go as companion to Lady Ruanthorpe."

"Where? At Duntrafford?"

"Of course. Why not? Please, Arthur. If you're not too tired. Tom, dear, would you like to walk down with Arthur? Just to keep him company?"

But ten minutes later, Arthur, bearing the letter in his pocket, had succeeded in eluding Tom, and was taking his way to Partick.

III

Ellen Netherton answered the doorbell. She greeted Arthur with simple enthusiasm. "Oh! Mr. Moorhouse. Come in! It's funny, I was just thinking about you."

Arthur allowed himself to be led into the little sitting-room. John Netherton was sitting by the fire, tired, lean-faced and more like a prophet than ever. The piano was strewn with music.

Mrs. Netherton's talk continued, high-pitched and friendly. "John has just finished his teaching, Mr. Moorhouse, so we were just going to have a cup of tea. Sit down and I'll bring one for you, too. I'm sorry my daughter's not in. She'll be sorry to miss you. But she may be back."

Arthur's conventionality flinched a little. Was he not, after all, a plant reared in a forcing-house of social consciousness? He was here in the Nethertons for the second time in his life, and already his friendship had been taken for granted. It was difficult for him to understand that this fluttering, talkative little woman saw him quite simply as a friend. Should he excuse himself, leave the letter and go? Or should he submit to having the too easy hospitality thus thrust upon him? Elizabeth was not here. What was the use of waiting?

Yet Arthur's instinct told him that if he ever wanted to come back to this house he had better stay now. He knew nothing of John Netherton. But he saw at once that he must make an effort to put himself into the good graces of Elizabeth's father. He therefore accepted Mrs. Netherton's offer, if, indeed, acceptance was necessary, for already she had returned and was pouring tea for him.

Arthur thanked her. "I came down for two things, Mrs. Netherton," he said. "First, Mother wanted to know how Mr. Netherton's wrist was, and second to give Miss Netherton a letter."

"Oh, his wrist is getting better. Isn't it, John?" Ellen Netherton said, answering for her husband, innocently officious. "It was a little painful after it was set, but it's not so bad now. You see, Mr. Moorhouse, I can tell what John's feeling, just about as well as he can himself. Isn't that right, John?"

"You seem to know." Netherton looked up half whimsically, half defensively. It was so easy for him to resent youth and prosperity.

Arthur blushed, confused and unsure of himself. He could have done nothing better.

So this young man was not necessarily a puppy? He did not behave as though he owned the world. John Netherton relaxed a little. "Oh, yes. It's better. But I'll have to give it time." He was siding with Arthur now, and a little ashamed that his wife should be chattering vacantly.

John Netherton's sensibilities were much more quick on his own account than they were on anybody else's. He had known for twenty years that his wife talked too much. But still her chatter could make him feel uncomfortable. He did not see that the present good-natured flow had the effect of covering the young man's awkwardness.

And she was talking hard. What a beautiful wedding it had been! What flowers! What nice clothes! What a handsome mother Arthur had! And was the fair young lady who had been a bridesmaid his sister? What was the relationship of this one to that? Dear me! What a large family they seemed! How kind it had been of Arthur's mother to ask Elizabeth to the reception! Elizabeth had enjoyed seeing everyone. And she had been to visit Mrs. Robert Dermott only yesterday. Now, to whom was Mrs. Robert Dermott related?

Here Arthur took the chance to say once more that he had a letter from Mrs. Dermott. He brought it from his pocket.

A letter? What could she be writing about?

Arthur knew very well. But he did not think it right that he should appear to do so. He shook his head and smiled, as Elizabeth's mother took it into her hand, silent for a moment, and turned it this way and that, as though she would open it.

The man in the armchair said nothing. A little clock of

beaten brass ticked away the seconds on the white-enamelled mantelpiece. The slanting rays of the late May sunset had caught the windows of the tenement opposite, setting the panes of glass on fire.

"No, I don't know what she can be wanting." Mrs. Netherton put down the letter reluctantly.

Arthur could hear the bang of a door, then a voice singing as young people sing, casually cheerful, as they move about the house. Elizabeth's mother called her. She came into the room briskly. "Oh, Mr. Moorhouse!"

He rose and gave her his hand. He knew that he was excited. He knew, now, that this young woman had scarcely left his thoughts since the day of the wedding.

Yes, she was a remarkable young woman. His mother had, as usual, been right. Right, in singing Elizabeth's praises to the skies.

IV

But first he must, if he could, find out what Elizabeth thought of the letter. This was important. If she went to Lady Ruanthorpe, then it would be easy for him to see her. He watched her break it open, and saw her colour change a little as she read. Again the room was silent. Her father bent over the fire. Her mother waited, grasping the chains about her neck and dangling the enamels that hung on them, curious to know what Mrs. Robert Dermott could have to write about.

Presently Elizabeth put down the letter and said: "Is there any tea left? I'll get myself a cup." She rose and went to fetch it.

"Can I see the letter?" Mrs. Netherton called after her.

"Yes."

90

More communicative than her daughter, Mrs. Netherton exclaimed as she read: "Lady Ruanthorpe? Who is she? Well, I don't know. Of course Lizzie was with an old lady in Helensburgh for a month or two, but I couldn't say whether she would—"

The girl had come back.

"What do you think about this, Lizzie?" And in answer to a question in the eyes of John Netherton as he looked up from the fire: "Mrs. Dermott wants to know if Lizzie will go to Ayrshire as companion friend. What do you think, dear?"

"What does *she* think?" John Netherton asked, almost, as Arthur thought, resentfully.

He did not know that artists, contrary to tradition, can be very conventional creatures; that Elizabeth's father was blaming himself because he could not keep his daughter at home, prim and unoccupied, like richer young ladies.

Elizabeth did not seem to notice her father's dry tone. She poured herself out a cup of tea, saying: "How do I know? I haven't had time to think about it."

This self-confidence was new to Arthur. His sister—any of his women relatives—would have been upset at the idea of having to leave their homes to earn money. This girl took it calmly.

"What kind of woman is this Lady Ruanthorpe, Mr. Moorhouse?" Mrs. Netherton asked.

Arthur flinched a little at being forced to explain a relative so august as Lady Ruanthorpe. "She's the mother of my Uncle Mungo Moorhouse's wife," he said.

Elizabeth smiled. "Mother! You can't ask Mr. Moorhouse about his own relatives!"

"Oh, I'm sure she's very nice! But why shouldn't I ask him? If she's asking you to go and stay with her, we had better know something about her. What do you think, John?"

But Netherton said nothing. His eyes were again upon the fire.

Until this moment Arthur had thought little about Lady Ruanthorpe. He took her for granted. She was merely a rather grand old lady to whom he must, on occasion, be polite. Now, surprisingly, he found himself extolling Lady Ruanthorpe. She was kind. She was generous. She had great personality.

The girl watched him with curiosity. His face was flushed and vivid as he talked of Duntrafford, of his uncle, of this old woman. What could it matter to him whether she, Elizabeth, went or not? He seemed absurdly in earnest about it. She would tease him.

"Did you know what was in this letter, Mr. Moorhouse?"

Arthur's caution was driven to bay. He could not be untruthful. "Well—I had an idea."

"Did they tell you to persuade me?"

"Oh, no!"

"I see. Just doing a little on your own?"

He murmured something about liking the people at Duntrafford, then stopped.

Mrs. Netherton's easy talk came to his rescue. "Of course," she said; "why shouldn't he like his uncle's people?"

Elizabeth now remembered the Ruanthorpe-Moorhouse boy at the wedding. She wanted to tease Arthur further, telling him that his cousin Charles had already offered her the situation; that Charles had warned her, however, that his granny was a bit of a handful. But something in Arthur's expression stopped her.

She crossed to the window and looked out of it for a moment.

For some reason she was thinking of her walk with this young man on the wedding day, back from the church to Grosvenor Terrace.

"Do you mind walking, Miss Netherton? It's not far."

"Oh no! Of course not."

She saw now the phaeton that flew by them, making for the open country; the bright harness, the polished carriage. Leaves were bursting on the trees—pale green and not yet made grimy by the city. She saw the children spinning hoops. In the Botanic Gardens the hawthorn was flowering. It had been pleasant.

She turned. "I'll think about it," she said presently. "I'll write and let them know. If you see Mrs. Dermott you can thank her for giving me the chance. I told her I had to work for my living."

Arthur took this as a dismissal. He stood up, disappointed, saying he must go. But he did not know that his shyness, his well-bred lack of confidence, his movements, youthful and male, might be doing something to influence Elizabeth's decision, however little this might yet be known to herself.

The street lamps were lit. Papers and dust blew before a soft evening wind. Even down here, with the sounds of the river traffic within earshot, the clatter of late-working shipyards, it was impossible to forget that the month was May.

He could still see every corner of the little room he had just left: its cheap, modern decoration; the strange, worn man by the fire; the bright little lady, with her chains and enamels. These he could see clearly.

But already the girl's face eluded him. It had become a radiance in his mind; a will-o'-the-wisp, that would not let him be.

Chapter Eight

ONE SHOULD NEVER, Bel Moorhouse would often say, let slip an opportunity of getting to know nice people—nice in this particular sense, meaning people whose social foundations were deeper dug and fixed more firmly than one's own. And to this she would add that you never knew what might come of it.

Now, the wedding of her nephew and niece over, Bel's thoughts returned to just such a nice family—the family of Colonel James Ellerdale. She had thought them particularly nice. And she had no intention whatever of letting them drop.

This time Bel did not bother to deceive herself with false reasons for seeking the friendship. Her son Arthur was newly twenty-one, and the more she could ring him about with suitable young women the better. She did not count upon Arthur's marrying for four or five years at least. She knew him through and through, she felt, and he was not susceptible. But she knew, too, that some very young men *did* catch the divine fever; whereupon, like the prince in the fairy tale, they were apt to attach their affections to the first young woman who then presented herself before them. Bel had given this eventuality much thought. If the girl were really nice, then little harm would be done. Rash young marriages, after all, turned, if you gave them time, into reasonable old ones. But if the girl were not nice—if she were like poor Rosie McNairn, for instance—then all would be disaster.

Now, on the morning after Arthur's errand to the Nethertons', his mother, as she arranged the flowers in the drawing-room, was thinking of all these things. Rosie. If Arthur— No! Bel dropped her task and, going to one of the long windows, gazed unseeing across the road at the green and blossoming Botanic Gardens.

The thought of Rosie always gave her an odd, hollow feeling. The girl was so noisily cheerful, so irrepressible, so undefeatably common. And she wouldn't be hid away: she had to obtrude. There was no doing with her. Others said she was good-natured; that she didn't take umbrage; that she was ready to laugh at her own shortcomings. But Bel detested Rosie's laugh, whether it was directed against its owner's shortcomings or not. It was harsh and insistent. It was the least attractive thing about Rosie. No! no! Please heaven, not a Rosie! And Jackie McNairn's marriage to Rosie had been a young marriage! Yes, it must be the thought of Rosie that made her so nervous for Arthur.

Bel tore at the stem of a flower, her eye following mechanically the progress of a landau as it passed up the hill going farther west. But her mind could not take in the horses, the flunkeys and the ladies with their furs still about them against the coolness of the northern May.

Rosie. Poor Mary! She must really forgive Mary everything when she thought of Rosie. Mary had behaved a little casually, Bel felt, over Polly's wedding. Mary's thanks to herself and Arthur might have been more effusive; her gratitude more humble. There had been a taking for granted that Bel didn't quite care about. But in the blaze of Rosie's vulgarity all these shadows must vanish. If only Jackie, instead of Georgie, had been the McNairn nephew to cross the Atlantic—and, of course, taken Rosie with him! The Wild West was just the place for Rosie, Bel felt. Oh no! Not a Rosie!

Bel returned to her task with decision. She must set herself to open up this friendship with the Ellerdales. She blamed

95

herself for having wasted so much time. Sweet young girls like Winifred Ellerdale did not grow on every bush. And perhaps, being English and strangers, they would be glad to make friends. Then, of course, there was always the young man in David's office. She must invite him to come to see them. After all, it would only be kind. Grace, David's wife, had written that she hoped to drop in to tea this afternoon, as she would be in town shopping. Perhaps she knew something of him. Jim was the young man's name, wasn't it? Jim Ellerdale.

Then Bel wondered if the Mungo Moorhouses would mind her running down for a day or two to Duntrafford. She could say she was overtired and would like a few days' rest. Her sister-in-law, Margaret, was for ever insisting that she should. And having got herself there, she might persuade Margaret to drive her into Ayr. Just for a reviving sniff of the sea, she could say; and while they were there she could leave her own and her husband's cards upon Mrs. Ellerdale and the Colonel. And perhaps, if Isabel were with them—yes, she had better take Isabel, too—Isabel could invite Winifred Ellerdale—no. That would be too forward, too thrusting; not on a first visit. Still, young girls became great friends almost at once. But perhaps on the second visit or the third—

II

"Hullo, Mother! Nice flowers." Isabel had come in. And was sounding, Bel was happy to find, amenable.

"They are pretty, aren't they, dear? I'm trying to make the room nice. Your Aunt Grace is coming to tea."

Isabel wondered why her mother's tone had dropped some of its usual crispness. Why there was a note of coaxing.

"I've been thinking, dear," Bel went on, "that it might be nice if you and I took a run down to Duntrafford for a few days."

A little unexpectedly, Isabel merely said: "Why?"

"Well, why not, dear? I'm feeling a little tired, with Wil and Polly's wedding. And your Aunt Margaret is always at me to go. And think how wonderful the Duntrafford rhododendrons must be looking!"

Bel's honeyed tones automatically increased her daughter's resistance. Isabel thought about the Duntrafford rhododendrons for a moment, wondered idly what her mother was up to, and said: "I don't see how you can go just now."

"But why, Isabel?"

"Granny's been ill."

"Yes. But she's all right again. And she would hate to think—" Bel stopped. Her invention had given out. She could not, for the moment, imagine what Mrs. Barrowfield would or would not hate to think.

"Hate to think what?" Isabel asked provokingly.

"My dear, I don't know!" But even now Bel kept exasperation out of her tone. "Well, hate to think she was tying me down, dear."

"I don't suppose she would mind."

For a moment Bel was silent. Isabel's last retort was only too true.

"Besides," Isabel went on, "I want to invite someone to stay."

"Stay?" Bel was astonished. This was new. What friend could Isabel possibly have that she might want to invite to stay? The Moorhouses were Glasgow people. They had few friends, other than relatives, outside of it. And, like her kind, Isabel had been educated at an establishment for young ladies in the city. All her former school friends could drop in to see her.

"Yes. I want to ask Winifred Ellerdale to stay. I don't think she's got much in her head. But I think she's lonely. She said she would be glad to come."

Bel was so surprised that she could only repeat the words: "Winifred Ellerdale?"

"Yes. You remember the family we met at the Provost's Ball in March?"

"Of course I remember!" This was truly amazing. She must give herself time. "Isabel, we can't ask her just like that. They might think us very impertinent."

"Oh, I saw her again the other day. I met her, with her mother, in Buchanan Street last week. They invited me to tea in Stuart Cranston's."

"But, dear, why didn't you tell me?"

"I forgot. Besides, there was all the fuss of the wedding. You seem very surprised. I don't see why."

"And were they as nice as they seemed at the ball?" was all Bel could think of to say.

"D'you think I would invite Winifred Ellerdale if I thought she was nasty?"

"No, dear, of course not!"

"Well, then, what's the objection?"

"Isabel, I'm not *making* any objection."

"You seem very queer about it."

At another time Bel would have reproved Isabel's impertinence, but in the face of this accomplished and gratifying fact, she returned to her honeyed tones and said: "No, dear. A little surprised, that's all. Of course she must come if you want her. I've always been determined that my children's friends should have a welcome in this house."

As her mother still seemed strange, and in serious danger now of becoming noble, Isabel decided to leave her. She would discuss her guest in a calmer atmosphere later.

Bel tried to stop her. "But, Isabel, tell me about the Eller-dales. Did you only meet Mrs. Ellerdale and Miss Ellerdale?"

"No. Winifred Ellerdale's brother was there, too."

"And did you like him?"

"He seemed quite nice." And Isabel disappeared.

But that was only the beginning of it. As the day went on it looked as though Ellerdales were to be piled upon Ellerdales.

In the afternoon the post brought her a letter from Dun-trafford. Margaret Ruanthorpe-Moorhouse wrote to persuade Bel to come down into the country. It had just occurred to Margaret that Bel must be tired. Bel was always so good, and wore herself out for everybody. And, by the way, a charming family had come to live in Ayr—English, and called Ellerdale. They had met Arthur and Bel at a reception or something, and had liked them so much. Perhaps if Bel came she might care to call with Margaret. And the Ellerdale boy was in Dermott Ships with David. Wasn't it extraordinary how small the world was? Margaret *did* hope Bel would come.

Ellerdales piled upon Ellerdales.

Then at four o'clock Grace Dermott-Moorhouse arrived for tea with her small daughter Meg. The child had been with her grandmother, Mrs. Dermott, most of the day, and was, in consequence, out of hand. She met her Aunt Bel's offer of a nursery tea with Sarah upstairs by threatening to go into hys-terics, so she had to remain on the drawing-room hearthrug eating cake, defacing her cousins' discarded but still sentimen-tally beloved picture-books with crayons, and joining loudly and insistently in the conversation. Her gentle mother, fore-seeing a pitched battle, decided to postpone it until she got Meg home.

Yet even through Meg's many interruptions the Ellerdales managed to obtrude themselves. Silencing her daughter mo-mentarily with a piece of marzipan cake—there would be

99

castor oil tonight, anyway—Grace told Bel how David had brought such a nice young man to Aucheneame last weekend. He had met Bel and Arthur at that Ball Grace and David hadn't been able to go to. Which was it? And he had liked Isabel and young Arthur so much. Grace wondered if her nephew would care to spend a weekend at Aucheneame and renew the acquaintance. There was a Miss Ellerdale, too, Grace understood. About Isabel's age.

"Oh, a sweet girl!" Bel hastened to say, noting that the last bite of marzipan cake was going into Meg's mouth, and wondering if weakness and folly would prompt Meg's mother to give the child another piece. Oh yes. Indeed, she was a friend of Isabel's already. And wasn't it funny? Only today Bel had got a letter from Margaret to say she had got to know Colonel and Mrs. Ellerdale in Ayr. And Margaret had said in her letter that she wanted—

But the cake was now swallowed. The noise from the hearthrug redoubled itself. There was nothing left for Grace but to take Meg home.

Bel stood on the doorstep waving the Aucheneame carriage out of sight. When it was gone she remained for a moment, watching the late afternoon traffic on Great Western Road. Now she felt almost cheated. She felt she had been given the key, along with the puzzle. It was all too easy.

III

But that, of course, was nonsense. Before the day was out Bel had written to Margaret Ruanthorpe-Moorhouse accepting her invitation, and saying she would come with her husband, Arthur, who would spend the weekend, leaving herself for a few days thereafter. On second thoughts, Bel had decided she would have a freer hand if she left Isabel at home. And thus at the end of the week the Arthur Moorhouses arrived at Duntrafford.

On many counts now it gave Arthur Moorhouse pleasure to find himself back among the rolling uplands of central Ayrshire. The family had their roots there; and as Arthur grew older the place of his childhood was taking on a glamour. As a youth, it had been the city that challenged him. Glasgow was the nut he must crack open. But the nut was cracked, and for long now the kernel had been his for the eating. Glasgow had yielded to Arthur's diligence and wit the fortune that he sought, the established way of life he had once dreamed of. But in the realisation his dream had turned into a proud commonplace, and it was the things of his boyhood, becoming ever more remote, that began to hold magic.

It was really very gratifying that Mungo had married the old laird's daughter. He had set the Moorhouse family on a pedestal. And it was no bad thing that he had kept on the Laigh Farm of their childhood as a profitable hobby. It was pleasant for Arthur to go from the padded luxury of the Big House to sentimentalise over the scrubbed and spartan rooms of his boyhood; to be treated with deference by the resident grieve; to show his children—when they could be persuaded to come with him—how simple the beginnings of his life had been; to point out what his industry and hard work had done for them; and to feel, perhaps, some quite genuine pangs when he remembered the hopes and fears, the daring and the shrinking back, of the boy who had once been himself.

It was never difficult, then, to persuade Arthur to spend Saturday and Sunday at Duntrafford, Bel found. He could be counted upon to go off with Mungo, visiting the old haunts, seeking out such friends of his boyhood as still remained among the country people, and holding long conversations with them—a little ungenteelly, Bel couldn't help feeling—in broad Scotch. But at any rate he was off her hands, leaving herself to move on higher levels with her hostess.

This morning Margaret took Bel to visit her mother, Lady Ruanthorpe, at the Dower House. Young Charles, who must be everywhere, came with them. Lady Ruanthorpe was one year older than Bel's own mother, and, like Mrs. Barrowfield, she had a mind of her own.

It was not yet eleven o'clock, but already the old woman was settled before the fire in the little Dower House parlour. Two very old house spaniels that had belonged to Sir Charles, her husband, were sleeping at her feet. The sweet, somewhat limp woman of thirty, who had been Lady Ruanthorpe's companion since his death, rose to greet the visitors.

Bel held out her hand. "Lady Ruanthorpe! And how are you?"

Charles pecked his grandmother's cheek and sat down at her feet among the spaniels.

Lady Ruanthorpe pulled out her glasses from a spring on her bosom, placed them on her nose, looked at Bel through them, and returned her handshake. She did not bother to reply to Bel's question. She merely said: "Good morning, Bel. Charles, don't tease those dogs! It's very kind of you, my dear, to come to see an old derelict."

Seeing Lady Ruanthorpe's wrinkles shape themselves into something that might be construed as a smile, Bel did her best to wave this last word aside with an elegant gesture, and again asked Lady Ruanthorpe how she did.

Yet again the old lady seemed to think this question beneath her notice. She said: "Sit down near me, my dear. I want to talk to you." And to her companion: "Miss McMinn, ring for the cake and sherry. And Master Charles's lemonade." While the young woman was doing this Lady Ruanthorpe continued.

102

"Your friend Mrs. Dermott has been writing me about a Miss Netherton, who might be willing to come here. Says she is a wonderful young woman."

"She's quite right, Granny. Miss Netherton is marvellous. I've met her," Charles interjected.

Lady Ruanthorpe merely rapped her grandson on the head with her fingernails, said: "Hold your tongue, sir," and went on: "Do you know anything about her? Mrs. Dermott seems to think she's splendid."

Bel cast a questioning glance at Margaret and the companion whose place Miss Netherton might fill.

Through her gun-metal glasses the old lady's eyes were quick. They caught Bel's meaning. "Oh, don't bother about Miss McMinn. She's leaving me. I'm not sending her away. Am I, Miss McMinn?"

The limp young woman said: "No," and Bel was surprised to see tears in her eyes.

Lady Ruanthorpe was looking at the girl severely. "Don't be a baby, Miss McMinn. What is there to be sorry about? You're leaving a dull old woman for a home and husband of your own." And as Miss McMinn murmured something about Lady Ruanthorpe's being very kind, Lady Ruanthorpe continued: "Kind? Why? Just because I'm not a monster? Go and see about the cake and wine, my dear."

"And my lemonade, please, Miss McMinn," Charles added.

Lady Ruanthorpe turned to Bel when Miss McMinn had gone "A good girl, my dear. But it's time she was married."

Charles asked: "Why, Granny?" But nobody paid attention.

"She seems very fond of you, Lady Ruanthorpe," Bel said, seeking to please her.

The old woman merely looked at the fire severely and grunted.

Margaret answered for her: "Yes. I think she is fond of Mother. She may well be. Mother has been very good to her

103

people. She paid for everything when Miss McMinn's father died."

"Old Mr. McMinn was the beadle in church, wasn't he, Mother?"

His mother answered reprovingly: "Hush, Charles! Yes, dear. The beadle."

Lady Ruanthorpe fixed her daughter through her eyeglasses. "Well, as I've said this morning already, I'm not a monster. What else was there to do but help? Now tell me if you know anything about this young woman that Mrs. Dermott has found for me."

At another time Bel might have reflected, with some annoyance, that Elizabeth Netherton was her find, not Mrs. Dermott's. But her mind was filled with what had just passed. She had had a demonstration that Lady Ruanthorpe's sharp ways were skin-deep, and that she would not be recommending the girl to a harsh mistress. She set herself, therefore, to tell the old lady all that was good about Elizabeth.

IV

The following Monday afternoon found Mrs. Ruanthorpe-Moorhouse of Duntrafford and Mrs. Arthur Moorhouse of Glasgow calling upon their new acquaintance Mrs. Ellerdale. As Duntrafford was some ten miles from the market town of Ayr, it was no great matter to drive there.

The Ellerdales had rented a large Victorian-Gothic villa overlooking the sea. It was built of sandstone, and most of its woodwork was of white pine stained to look like something better. When it was windy, which was nearly all the time, everything rattled and admitted draughts. From the front windows of the upper rooms and from its crenellated battlements there was a superb view westwards, of the Firth of Clyde, of the Island of Arran, of the stretch of pleasant greensward behind the promenade, and of the yellow sand ringing the edge of Ayr Bay.

Bel and Margaret, who had been conducted to the drawing-room on the first floor and told that Miss Ellerdale would be with them presently, stood at the great plate-glass windows admiring this remarkable view. It was a day of sunshine and squalls. Over yonder the mountains of Arran made grey shapes on the horizon, the cone of Goatfell standing up from the rest. The sea between was slate-blue flecked with white. Near the beach it was milky-green, where the sand was churned up by incoming breakers. Promenaders held their hats and leant against the wind, as they walked along in the sunshine. On the sands, trainers were exercising racehorses.

"I'm so sorry to keep you! Mother's out with the dogs. But I think I see her coming in."

They turned, as Winifred Ellerdale came across the large room to greet them and bring them to a seat by the fire. She was charming, this English girl, Bel could not help thinking. She could not be much older than Isabel, but already she was crisp and poised. She seemed neither confident nor impertinent. Bel could not feel that Winifred's manner was particularly warm. It was, indeed, a little impersonal. Yet she seemed quite unembarrassed at having to entertain two matrons who were, each of them, more than twice her age. Winifred Ellerdale was a foreigner to Bel's West of Scotland provinciality, but Bel had come very prepared to admire her.

Margaret and Winifred had much to say to each other. Already, it seemed, the Ellerdales had picked up county gossip. Their family, it would appear, had been accepted. Bel sat smiling elegantly, looking about her, and wondering how they had managed it.

It was not because of their wealth. One look round the room told her that. There was nothing the Moorhouse ideas of substantiality would have given twopence for. A worn Persian rug or two on the newly varnished floor. The skin of a tiger the Colonel had shot in Bengal. The skin of a leopard over the worn plush of a sofa. Brass Benares tray-tables. An oriental curtain with little mirrors sewn into it, draping a tired grand piano. Another such curtain draping the door. And everywhere photographs in frames of velvet, brass and fretwork—photographs of soldiers; photographs of ladies in presentation feathers; photographs of children; a photograph of the Queen. The wallpaper was of faded blue—less faded, here and there, where someone else's pictures had hung. It had not been renewed, obviously, at the Ellerdales' incoming. This soldier's drawing-room had, to Bel, a temporary air. It seemed as though they had arranged things thus merely for the time being.

"Oh, hullo! There's Mother now. I hear her talking to the dogs."

Two immense creatures followed by Mrs. Ellerdale burst into the room. To Bel, for a moment, it seemed as though two lions had come in with their trainer. The great beasts lumbered amiably about, wagging huge tails, much to the danger of the ivory images, spice-boxes and the other knick-knacks on the Benares trays, and snuffling at everybody, including Bel, who found these attentions terrifying. But everybody else in the room seemed to be utterly enchanted by them. Margaret scarcely gave herself time to shake hands with Mrs. Ellerdale before she was exclaiming: "You beautiful darlings!"

Mrs. Ellerdale gave Bel her hand. "I'm so glad to see you, Mrs. Moorhouse. I've just been taking the dogs for a blow along the sands. That's the great thing about dogs, don't you find? They make you take exercise." As the dogs were now importuning Bel alarmingly, Mrs. Ellerdale turned to them with smiling severity. "Gladstone! Disraeli! Go over there and lie down!"

Much to Bel's relief, the dogs did as they were told.

"That's good doggies," Mrs. Ellerdale said, rather unnecessarily using the diminutive, Bel felt. Her hostess pulled off her gloves, pushed a strand of windblown hair beneath her hat and sat down beside Bel. "Ah! Here's tea!" she cried as yet another brass tray was borne in and set before her.

The great dogs had got up once more and were thrashing their tails perilously near the teacups. Bel was relieved to see that these were not of eggshell fineness.

"They're expecting their sandwiches," Winifred said gaily. "Better let them have them, then we'll have peace." Her mother took a sandwich in each hand. At once there was a sharp and simultaneous snap. Bel was afraid to look. Mrs. Ellerdale must surely be left with stumps! But Winifred and Margaret were looking at the animals as tenderly as ever, as they went back to lie down; and agreeing they were adorable. Bel managed to force a smile and murmur the word "darlings" from a dry throat. With a little practice, she felt, confidence might come.

V

Like others of their kind, the Ellerdales carried their world with them. No matter in what part of the Queen's Empire they found themselves, their manners, their behaviour, their interests remained the same: a life out of doors, as little varied as climate would allow; much easy entertaining of people who followed the same pattern as themselves—refusal, indeed, to recognise any other pattern—some arrogance, or the outward appearance of it; a high sense of public service; and a faith that was real, if simple, upheld by strict orthodoxy. Not a type that was negligible, but one that was puzzling to a Scotswoman such as Bel.

And yet, if their ways were foreign to her, Bel decided she liked them. Now that the dogs lay silent, with their heads on their paws, things went much better. Mrs. Ellerdale, pouring out tea, seemed kind and rational. Her daughter, Winifred, made the rounds with bread and butter. She was a bright little thing with a singularly clear and pleasant "English" voice. To Bel this was particularly engaging. There was something unusually elegant about anyone who could make noises like that.

"We call them Gladstone and Disraeli, Mrs. Moorhouse," Winifred said, looking at the creatures in the corner, "because ever since they were puppies they would squabble and wrangle with each other." Winifred went into a little peal of laughter.

Bel did not see this particularly funny, but the girl's laughter was insistent, so Bel felt constrained to say: "Good idea! Darlings!" And laughed, too.

But, on the whole, a nice, unalarming child. Yes, she would like her son to get to know Winifred. "You met my daughter, Isabel, in Glasgow the other day?" she said, following this train of thinking.

"We were so glad to see her again. She came to tea with us. Winifred and I thought she was a darling." Mrs. Ellerdale helped herself to bread and butter as she said this, and settled back.

The adjective darling could, apparently, be applied either to dogs or daughters. "Isabel was very pleased to see you. It was kind of you to give her tea," Bel answered, smiling.

"Winifred has quite fallen in love with her, haven't you, Winifred? She must come for a weekend some time."

"And Isabel was hoping that perhaps Miss Ellerdale would

come to us." Then, wondering if she were being vulgarly genial, Bel added: "But perhaps you don't like towns in summer."

As the wind had begun to batter the windowpanes with raindrops, that sounded like pebbles, Winifred laughed, blushed a little and repeated the word, "Summer!" Adding: "Oh, Mrs. Moorhouse, I should like to come very much!"

Bel was delighted. She could not see that Winifred was, in her way, quite simple; that she was artlessly pleased to receive the invitation. Had Winifred remembered Arthur, then? And might not something come of it?

The animals in the corner had lifted their heads and were flogging the varnished boards of the floor with their tails. The little mirrors on the curtain over the doorway trembled, and the Colonel had come in. He advanced genially.

"Disturbing a ladies' tea-party? What?" He gave his hand to Margaret.

"You remember Mrs. Arthur Moorhouse, James?" his wife said.

"Of course!"

He was handsomer than ever, Bel thought, as he turned to her.

"I always remember my dancing partners."

His wife said: "Not always, I hope, James," smiling wanly as she handed him tea.

Handsome, very aristocratic, and dressed at greater expense than his women, Bel noted, as he sat chatting with Margaret over county matters and the people he was coming to know so quickly. It seemed to Bel that Elsie Ellerdale and her daughter had somehow gone a little dim in his presence. Bel wondered why. Did he make existence difficult for them, somehow? Was he extravagant? Selfish? Mean? Unfaithful? Bel thought of her own excellent husband, and took comfort.

109

But she did not like the Ellerdale women any the less for this glimpse of worry and disillusion. Indeed, it made them real, somehow, despite their unfamiliar ways.

When Margaret rose to take her away, therefore, Bel repeated her invitation to Winifred with greater confidence. The family came downstairs to bid the ladies goodbye and rejoice that the shower was over.

The Colonel was the mirror of gallantry as he handed them into their carriage.

Chapter Nine

BEL came home from Duntrafford pleased and full of decision. Things were going as she wanted. She had come to know the Ellerdales, making the opening she had sought. If she found their English ways a little strange, their mode of behaviour different from the behaviour demanded by local West of Scotland gentility, still she felt no doubt that the Ellerdales stood above reproach; that circles were thrown open to them that would certainly be closed to herself.

And, when her preoccupation with these things allowed her to think of them as human beings, she really quite liked them. Particularly the mother and daughter. Even the signs of comparative poverty encouraged Bel. It made the Ellerdales less intimidating. If, as she hoped, it came to a friendship between the two families, the Moorhouses would be able, at least, to set prosperity against the Ellerdales' distinction.

Very few days were allowed to pass, therefore, before young Arthur was calling at Dermott Ships with a note that was warm and friendly—even in her moments of high diplomacy Bel could not avoid warmth—inviting Jim Ellerdale to come to a simple pot-luck dinner, begging him to take the family just as he found them, and saying that the young people, particularly the bearer of this note, were anxious to renew his acquaintance. Arthur brought the desired acceptance.

And now, on the day of Jim's visit, Bel found a letter from Margaret Ruanthorpe-Moorhouse awaiting her on the breakfast table. Bel opened it.

Margaret wrote to say that her mother had been considering

Miss Netherton's suitability as a companion, that circumstances had arisen that would take Miss McMinn from her almost immediately. Lady Ruanthorpe was prepared to give Miss Netherton a month's trial entirely on the recommendations of such excellent judges of character as Mrs. Dermott and Bel herself; and would Bel, perhaps, if it were not too much, call upon Miss Netherton at once, explain Lady Ruanthorpe's terms of employment (these were given in the letter) and find out just how quickly Miss Netherton could come.

Bel looked up. "This is from Lady Ruanthorpe. She wants me to see Miss Netherton at once. Can you remember the street number, Arthur?"

Arthur could remember the number.

"I'll run down this morning."

Arthur was grateful to Isabel for saying: "Does Lady Ruanthorpe want her to go to Duntrafford?" It did not oblige him to show undue interest.

"Yes, she does."

"Do you think Miss Netherton will go?" Isabel asked.

"I'll certainly do my best to persuade her."

Arthur's heart sang as he found his hat and stick and set off to walk down Great Western Road towards the office.

It was no wonder the June sun was shining. That everyone was smiling. That trees were green and horses were prancing. That the cool breath of the early day was fragrant, even here in the city. That the world around him seemed as though it were reborn.

Elizabeth would, of course, go to Duntrafford. His mother would see that she did so. Who could withstand his mother? And there, as often as possible, Arthur would take himself and follow the path of this true love of his, that would belie the foolish proverb and run smooth and shining to its misty but, of course, dazzling end.

112

No such dreams were filling the head of the mother who stood so high in her son's regard. Yet Bel's thoughts were not unpleasant. She was glad Lady Ruanthorpe had asked her to do this. Elizabeth Netherton, after all, was her find. There was no reason whatever why Mrs. Dermott should take all the credit for finding her.

Bel rang for the carriage. She would see Cook—she had asked young Mr. Ellerdale to pot-luck dinner, but she must make sure that tonight's pot should be a special pot—then she would drive down to Partick in the hope of finding the Netherton girl at home.

While Cook stood, receiving instructions for the kitchen, Sophia Butter flooded into the parlour.

"Bel dear! I couldn't wait! Oh, I'm sorry. I didn't know you had Bessie with you. Good morning, Bessie. I haven't seen you for a long time. How are you?"

"Verra weel, Mam. And yerself? How's Maister Butter? An' is Maister William back frae his honeymoon?" Cook was round and genial, and her position below stairs denied her contact with the family, in whom, nevertheless, she took a passionate interest. When a rare opportunity presented itself, as it was now doing, she did her best to make the most of it.

Bel stiffened a little. She must deal with this. She was annoyed that Sophia, of whom she had not heard since Wil's wedding, should suddenly appear thus ridiculously early. She preferred, too, to have Cook called Cook, not Bessie, in this familiar way. And she disliked Cook's melting into an easy familiarity. Bel smiled augustly. She must offend neither her husband's sister nor the excellent woman who had cooked the Arthur Moorhouse meals ever since she, Bel, had been Mrs. Arthur Moorhouse.

"Good morning, Sophia," she said a little impersonally, conveying to Cook by her manner that no further conversation with Mrs. Butter was expected of her. "We were just wondering where you had disappeared to." And to Bessie: "Well, that's not quite everything, Cook. But I'll come down to the kitchen to see you before I go out. I'll come in a moment, for I have to go out very soon," she added, hoping that Sophia would take this hint.

Bessie's crestfallen face touched Sophia a little. She waved a friendly hand to her as she went, calling: "Mr. Butter is very well, thank you, Bessie. And Mr. William is home and looking splendid. Thank you for asking about them." But as the door closed behind Bessie, Sophia sat down like a conspirator at the parlour table, where Bel already sat with paper and pencil before her.

Sophia's voice dropped. "I'm glad she didn't ask about Margy, Bel dear. I would have felt so self-conscious. And I'm so bad at hiding things. I shouldn't even be telling you. But, then, I know you won't say anything to anybody. . . . Bel dear! I never knew you had taken to spectacles!"

Bel had not listened to a word Sophia was saying. She was going through Cook's grocery list. But now Sophia's exclamation at her spectacles brought her back. She looked at her sister-in-law through them. They gave her an expression of elegant severity. "My eyes have been tired a little, Sophia," she said. "The oculist thought it would relieve the strain if I could make up my mind to wear these. Oh, just for a month or two, while I'm reading and writing. Of course, I can see perfectly without them." As though to prove this, she took the spectacles off and smiled at Sophia.

Sophia's reply to this was to lay her hands on the table in front of her, displaying as she did so an unmended rent in one of her gloves, to drop her voice still lower, look about her furtively and say: "Well, dear, about Margy—" and stare at Bel with a knowing look that was nothing but exasperating to a busy woman who had things to do.

"Well, Sophia? What about Margy?" Bel hoped that impatience did not colour her tone.

"We think—mind you, Bel dear, only *think*—that Margy has a young man! Only don't breathe, dear—"

Bel collected her papers, stifled a sigh and prepared to go through the appearance of asking interested questions. It was the second visit of the kind she had had from Sophia this year. Twice was really too much. And this time she must be on her guard against rash and exhausting generosity. She smiled artificially. "Do tell me about it, Sophia," she said, mimicking for a moment—and rather to her own satisfaction— the bright, impersonal manner Mrs. Ellerdale had adopted towards herself and Margaret.

III

Sophia was much too preoccupied to notice. To Bel's exasperation, she lowered her voice yet more and said: "You know, of course, Bel dear, where we've been."

Bel did not know.

Sophia explained. She and Margy had been to a well-known hydropathic establishment, a "Temple of Hygiene" as its brochure put it, in Perthshire. "You see, dear, after the rush of the wedding Margy got so impatient and nervous that William and I were at our wits' end."

Irrelevantly, Bel found herself thinking she had never seen any sign of wits in William to have an end. And not many in Sophia, either.

Sophia went on: "Well, dear, suddenly William had the

idea of the hydro. Little did we think! Anyway, that's how we went there. And the doctor recommended the cold needle-spray for Margy's spine. For the first day or two she was a little bad-tempered about having it. I had to speak to her and remind her that her father was paying out good money for her nerves. But Bel dear! In a day or two! You've no idea! If the weather had been warmer I would have tried the needle-spray too! But, then, my nerves didn't need— And, of course, by that time Mr. Findowie had turned into a nice friend for Margy."

Sophia stopped. Her sallow colour deepened, as though she had been caught red-handed in crime, then she went on: "Oh, Bel dear! I didn't mean to tell you his name. I feel I'm being so— They got to know each other holding the same hymn-book at prayers in the drawing-room. Margy had come in late: after the hymn was announced and the organ playing and everything. She couldn't reach a hymn-book without making a fuss, so Mr. Findowie signed to her to look on with him." Sophia leant back in her chair, triumphant.

Bel, after all, was human. Her interest was trapped. Margy Butter's affair might be quite undistinguished, but here, at least, was life. "And what happened next, Sophia?"

Sophia bent forward again and went on: "Well, of course, Bel dear, the young people couldn't help going on meeting. Could they? At croquet, and military whist, and drinking hot water before bedtime and everything."

"Was there dancing?" Bel asked, thinking perhaps that dancing was more helpful to romance.

"Oh no, Bel dear! And I don't think Mr. Findowie would have danced if there had been. It wouldn't have been right in his position. Besides, the poor boy has been ill."

"Ill, Sophia?"

"Just let me tell you, dear. Anyway, Margy turned into a

different girl. So bright and lively. Just as if she was twenty again. You remember what she was like then, don't you?"

"But how do you know she has any feeling for this young man?"

"Oh, I'm certain! He took prayers one night, dear. And he was so eloquent, and his voice was so beautiful, we were both quite carried away."

"Then he's a minister, Sophia?"

"Oh, yes, dear. And in Glasgow!" Mr. Findowie, Sophia explained, was assistant minister in one of the largest and most mixed of the city's churches. "Well, anyway, that night in our bedroom I felt so—well—uplifted, dear, with Mr. Findowie's prayer and everything, that I said: 'You know, Margy, I felt I could almost see a halo round that young man's head'! Oh, quite without thinking, Bel, dear. Just because I was so pleased. And what did Margy do but burst out crying as if her heart would break. I didn't say anything. I just left her to cry." Here Sophia paused for a moment, then added: "But after that I knew."

"But what about the young man, Sophia?"

"Oh, I hope it will be all right. I don't think Alec Findowie would ever be so friendly if— So I was determined Margy must stay on a little longer. I had to come home. But there was a very nice lady from Motherwell at our table. She was staying on, too. So I asked her to— And I was quite frank with William. I said: 'Now, William, men may not understand about these things, and you can take it off the housekeeping money, but Margy is twenty-seven, and she's had too much disappointment already. And he's a fine young man, even if he is a little delicate. You'll be delighted with him when you see him.' "

Here Bel interrupted Sophia to say: "You were perfectly right, Sophia."

117

Thus encouraged, Sophia smiled. "I told Wil," she added. "And he offered me a five-pound note. The bad boy said it was worth five pounds to get Margy off. But that's just his way. Of course, I couldn't take it from him, with all his own expenses just now. Still, it was nice of him to think of it."

"Then has the young man been ill?" Bel asked.

"Yes, dear. Doing far too much. He's full of social work, and slums and all sorts of terrible things. He says people in our position have no idea."

"And is he likely to stay up there for some time?"

"Yes. He's been ordered a complete rest. I'm sure he's very highly-strung."

Bel was a better woman than she gave herself credit for. Her sympathy was too quick to remain indifferent to the picture that had built itself out of Sophia's chatter.

An overworked, intense young pastor, broken for the moment in his unequal fight with Glasgow's underworld. A clever, unmated young woman with a boundless vitality running uselessly to the sands. It would, surely, be a good thing if these two could make a match of it.

She got up and paced the room thoughtfully. "There's nothing I can do to help, I suppose, Sophia?"

"No, dear. We can only hope." Sophia rose, pulled her untidy things about her, and prepared to leave. "I just can't think what I'll do with Margy if it doesn't happen."

There were tears in her eyes. Bel did her best to reassure her. "I'm sure it will be all right, Sophia. Young men are always susceptible when they're run down. Did you say he seemed to like Margy?"

"Oh, yes, I think so. But, then, you can never be sure."

At the front door Bel bent and kissed Sophia. "It was nice of you to come and tell me," she said. "And whenever anything happens don't forget to let me know."

When Mrs. Arthur Moorhouse rang his doorbell later in the morning, John Netherton was teaching a pupil—a lazy, but gifted young woman, who was hoping to earn her living in music, and must therefore be taken seriously.

John was unaware that he was alone with her in the house, that his wife and daughter had gone out without disturbing him. He let the bell go on jangling.

But Mrs. Moorhouse heard the sound of a piano. She knew there must be someone inside who would eventually hear her, so she went on ringing.

At last John Netherton could stand the jangling no longer. He opened the door of his sitting-room and called the names of his wife and daughter.

There was no reply.

Angrily, he went to the door and flung it open, presenting Bel with the picture of a wild man in a patched jacket and carpet slippers, with ruffled hair and a look of extreme displeasure. He was anything but glad to see her.

But he merely threw the word "Yes?" bad-temperedly at her, and stood waiting.

Bel was taken aback. But she kept her poise. "Mr. Netherton! How are you? I see the wrist is still bound up. I do hope it's mending all right?"

"Aye, all right." He stood, his hand on the doorknob, still waiting.

"Your daughter isn't here, is she? Or Mrs. Netherton?"

"No. They're out."

"Oh, what a pity! I'm in rather a hurry to get a message to Miss Netherton."

"Well, she's not here."

It was difficult to make headway against the chill wind of

this ungraciousness, but Bel forced herself to go on. "Then perhaps you could take a message for me."

"Well?"

"Ask Miss Netherton to call on me at once, will you? Tell her my friend Lady Ruanthorpe is anxious"—and here, nerves pushed Bel into tactlessness—"to give her a month's trial as companion at Duntrafford, and that she would like her to go immediately. But I can tell her all about that when she comes up to see me." Bel stopped, smiling uncertainly.

John Netherton did not answer at once. He looked Mrs. Arthur Moorhouse up and down—her stylish summer dress; her trinkets; her prosperity; her fixed, artificial smile—then he said: "There's no girl o' mine going to yer Lady This That or the Next Thing, as if she was furniture on approval!"

"Oh, but, Mr. Netherton! I didn't mean—"

But John Netherton had shut the door.

Bel went down the stairs trembling. This kind of incivility was something she had not yet met with.

V

Elizabeth Netherton came upstairs as her father was seeing his pupil out. From the look on the young woman's face, Elizabeth saw that John's forceful teaching had brought tears. She was used to the sight. His work was thorough, and thus his harshness did not chase pupils away.

"Father," she called, struggling to regain her breath, "was that Mrs. Moorhouse's carriage and pair I saw?"

Her father, preoccupied and surly, nodded.

"Was Mrs. Moorhouse up here? Did you see her?"

"Aye."

"What did she want?"

Sulkily, he turned back into his room and shut the door without replying.

Elizabeth stood in the little lobby considering. She had seen her father in such moods many times. Something or someone— the pupil, most likely—had upset him. And when he was upset he was indiscriminately uncivil to those who crossed his path. Usually herself or her mother. But they were used to that, too—knew his way and humoured him. But what if he had been uncivil to Mrs. Moorhouse?

Elizabeth, as she stood there, felt herself go hot with embarrassment. Yet why, after all, should it matter? But now her sudden excitement and shame showed her it did matter. Now, for the first time, she knew that she meant to go to this place in Ayrshire; that Duntrafford Dower House lay across her path.

What had her father been saying to Mrs. Moorhouse? It was important. Elizabeth opened the door and went in.

He was sitting in his fireside chair, filling his pipe, awkwardly because of his bandaged wrist. He did not look at her.

"I'll fill that for you." She took it from him. When she had done so, she put it in his mouth and lit it.

Still his eyes did not meet her own.

"Father, tell me. What happened when Mrs. Moorhouse was here?"

He took a puff or two, then said: "No' much."

"But, Father, she can't have come for nothing." Elizabeth sat on the edge of his chair.

"No."

"Well, for what, then? Was it something to do with me going to Duntrafford?"

He nodded.

"And what did you say to her?"

Netherton took the pipe out of his mouth, looked up in

Elizabeth's direction for a moment, then looked away again and said: "I told her ye werena going."

Elizabeth jumped up. "But, Father! It wasn't decided!"

"Well, I decided."

"But what did you say to her, Father?"

"It doesna matter what I said."

"Oh yes, it does!"

Some minutes later Elizabeth was on her way to Grosvenor Terrace.

VI

Bel was thus given little time to think of what had happened. She had driven home, shaken and upset. She, Mrs. Arthur Moorhouse of Grosvenor Terrace, was unused to having doors slammed in her face. It was a new experience, and her pride as well as her good-nature had received a shock. She would leave Elizabeth alone. With a father so impossible there was nothing else to do.

But now the doorbell was ringing, and here was Sarah to say that Miss Netherton was waiting in the hall, asking if Mrs. Moorhouse had come home, and would Mrs. Moorhouse see her?

Bel would see her. Would tell her that, as her father did not want her to go to Duntrafford, Lady Ruanthorpe's offer was, naturally, withdrawn. That she, Bel, had recommended her, knowing nothing of opposition in Elizabeth's family.

Bel rose, preparing to receive her stiffly.

But Elizabeth's entrance was disarming. She ran into the room exclaiming: "Oh, Mrs. Moorhouse! You must forgive my father. He didn't mean it."

Bel took her hand and led her to a chair. "My dear girl!

You've been running. Come and sit down and get your breath."

Elizabeth did as she was told. "Father's not really rude, Mrs. Moorhouse. But his arm is still hurting. And he's queer when he's interrupted at work," she said, panting and dabbing her distressed face with her handkerchief.

Bel felt she must keep her dignity. But there was no reason to be unkind. "Take off your hat, child. You've made yourself hot with hurrying. And there's really no reason for you to be upset. If your family don't want you to go to Ayrshire, then of course there's nothing more to be said."

"But I want to go!" Elizabeth was surprised to hear these words come out of her own mouth. She had come up to apologise for her father; that was all. Further than that she had not yet had time to think.

Bel sat for a moment, puzzled what to reply. This young girl was attractive. She had her odd little mother's refinement. On every count she was a lady. If she had been a daughter of consequence, Bel would have been glad to accept her as a friend for Isabel. It was a demonstration of the child's fine feelings that she had come, thus at once, to apologise. But what was Bel to do? She had thought she was doing the girl a service. But if Elizabeth's family opposed it?

"I really don't know what to say to you, Miss Netherton. You see, your father was—very definite. I can't take you away against his wishes."

"But, Mrs. Moorhouse, my father has no real wishes. It's difficult for me to explain. He's always been moody and like a child; always been inclined to—to burst out, without thinking quite what he's saying. You have to understand him." Elizabeth stopped for a moment, hoping that Bel might say something to make it easier, but as she said nothing, the girl braced herself, changed her tone and went on: "I saw your

123

carriage drive away. I ran upstairs and found out from Father you had been to see me. I know him. I saw at once he hadn't been—polite." Elizabeth's distressed voice sank to a whisper.

Bel was sorry for her. "Not very. But please don't—"

"Tell me what he said to you, Mrs. Moorhouse."

Bel hesitated. Then she said: "I'm afraid he just shut the door."

"What! In your face?" Elizabeth half rose, made a little gesture towards Bel and sat down again.

No! Her father had been cruel! Cruel to herself! To be uncivil like that to Mrs. Moorhouse! It was like a blow to Elizabeth. And a revelation. She sat for a time twisting her handkerchief, lost in distress. Her father was often uncivil. Uncivil, for instance, to pupils who had, no doubt, just as fine feelings as Mrs. Moorhouse. But these pupils were not the mothers of slim, young men.

Bel saw that tears had come into Elizabeth's eyes. She was amazed that the daughter of such a man should show herself thus sensitive. She had never liked Elizabeth more. "My dear Miss Netherton! I quite understand."

Elizabeth stood up. Now she was in open rebellion against her father. "How can you understand, Mrs. Moorhouse? What is there to understand? Rudeness is rudeness. If you want me to go to Lady Ruanthorpe, I'll go. My father isn't sensible enough to decide these things for me."

Bel stood up, too. "I could never send you against his wishes. And he was very—emphatic."

For a moment Elizabeth stood flinching, seeing her father being emphatic; then she said: "My mother would be glad if I went."

"Still, Miss Netherton, I don't—" Bel wondered how to finish her sentence. She had no intention of going back to Partick, to engage once again with John Netherton. She was

124

spared the trouble, however, for the door was thrown open and Sarah announced:

"Mrs. Dermott."

"My dear Bel! And Miss Netherton! What luck! You see, Mrs. Moorhouse, I had a letter from Lady Ruanthorpe this morning, and she asked me to get into touch with Miss Netherton because her present young lady has to leave her almost at once. And now I've caught you here, Miss Netherton. I had just looked in to ask for your address. It would be simply splendid if you could arrange— Do you think your mother—?"

"I got a letter, too." Bel was, for once, a little cool with Mrs. Dermott's augustness. Really, if these two old women liked making a fuss about each other's doings that was their affair. But why should she have her time wasted? And have doors slammed in her face for her trouble!

"If you could come with me now, my dear," Mrs. Dermott was saying to Elizabeth, "the carriage is at the door. We could see your parents and arrange everything at once."

Elizabeth was beginning to say something about Mrs. Moorhouse having seen her father already, but Mrs. Dermott did not trouble herself to listen. "You see, Miss Netherton, I'm going down to Duntrafford myself tomorrow afternoon, and it would be splendid if you went down with me. Come along. I've got to be somewhere for lunch in half an hour. If you came now I could just fit this in. Bel, my dear. So nice to see you! You and your kind husband must come round to dinner soon. Any night that suits you to dine with a dull old woman. By the way, I was told young Mr. Ellerdale was coming here tonight. I saw him at Aucheneame. Attractive boy. English. You'll like him. Well, come along, Miss Netherton."

Bel gave Mrs. Dermott's carriage a bleak, goodbye wave from her doorstep. Not any the less bleak, perhaps, from the half-jealous knowledge that Mrs. Dermott would very likely succeed where she herself had failed. David's mother-in-law was like that. She swept people and things before her. As Bel turned to go in she wondered what qualities Mrs. Dermott had that let her do this. Was it good-tempered obtuseness? Or sheer animal force? Something of both, perhaps.

Sarah came to tell her that Miss Isabel was out, and that a solitary lunch awaited her. Bel sighed, measured her forty-six years against Mrs. Dermott's seventy-nine, and envied the old lady her vitality.

Chapter Ten

TO ANYBODY who would oblige him by listening, Colonel Ellerdale was given to expressing regret that his only son, Jim, had not, like himself, become a professional soldier. He could not, he would say, understand Jim's reasons.

This was strange. They had often enough been pointed out to the Colonel by his family. Soldiering cost money. But, then, reasons were not, perhaps, things the Colonel took much account of. It was, after all, so much pleasanter to float, disembodied, in the upper air of one's own self-esteem.

And this, having inherited a considerable private income and having married an undemanding, anxious wife, who had rescued some of it before it was quite squandered, the Colonel had been able to do. If, in his progress through the blue, he had, here and there, stuck on a mountain-top of reality, he had always managed to push safely off again.

But if the Colonel had illusions and was able successfully to float among them, his son Jim had none. He must earn his living. And he had come to Glasgow to do so in January of this year.

A family friend in London, whose firm sent its products overseas in the holds of Dermott Ships, had offered to write to the chairman, Mr. David Moorhouse, on Jim's behalf.

Mr. Moorhouse could not easily flout the wishes of one who might, only too readily, transfer his merchandise to rival holds; so young Ellerdale received an invitation to come to Glasgow.

And thus, having presented himself before Mr. Moorhouse,

Jim found his services accepted. He was offered a salary which, if it could not be called princely, was enough to clothe him and pay for comfortable rooms—a salary which resulted not so much from Jim's accomplishment, as from the Chairman's fear lest if the young man went elsewhere some thousands of pounds of yearly business might go with him.

But Jim Ellerdale was his mother's son. He had mettle. He meant to deserve this good start. He had come north to succeed. He set to with a will, leading a life of work, study and evening classes. Dermott Ships was pleased with him. The Chairman signified his distinguished approval. And the younger partner, William Butter, who was the whirlwind of the concern and, as Jim quickly found out, the one who counted, was coming more and more to value Jim's diligence.

The young Englishman was glad to follow a life of industry for reasons that were different from Moorhouse ones. The Moorhouses, working farmers only a generation back, had sought and won wealth, dignity and position. Now they were consciously proud of having them. Jim Ellerdale, after his kind, looked upon these things as his birthright, and was very ready to exert himself for them.

His life, so far, had done nothing to turn him from this purpose. A childhood spent at an inexpensive preparatory school, and later at one of the lesser boarding-schools. Advantages for which his mother had striven and pinched; for which she had, in part, sacrificed the education of his sister—as happened so often in this type of family. Holidays spent with such relatives as would put up with a lonely, tongue-tied schoolboy, while the others were with his father, stationed abroad. Brief spells of happiness when his mother was in England. Farewells that cast their heartbreak before them, and were followed by a stupefying gloom. And, when school was over, career-hunting in London. A young man educated to a life about town, but without the money to live it. A country-house visitor who had to worry over his tips to the servants.

Jim's good sense had had enough of it. It was balm to sit on an office stool in Dermott Ships, Limited, earning his living and obliged to keep up no appearances; balm to work at his books of an evening, and spend his weekends with his mother and sister.

II

How fussy Scotch people were! Jim Ellerdale could not help thinking as he sat at Bel's dinner-table. Fussy, but on the whole very kind. Such people of the Ayrshire county as his parents had come to know were rather different; they were much more like their opposite numbers in England. But here, in the town, the difference in manner was marked.

In the circle to which Jim belonged there was none of this seemingly intense interest in what he was eating, how much he ate, and whether it would please his taste. It appeared, indeed, a crime to refuse anything. It was, he supposed, the Scots idea of hospitality. In time this insistence would become tiresome. Jim wondered how Mrs. Moorhouse could keep it up. And yet Mrs. Moorhouse was not vulgar.

"I hope you like simple things, Mr. Ellerdale. Everything we're having tonight is very simple."

"Thank you. It's very good indeed." What was a man to say? It was a much better meal than was usually to be found at home. No. Mrs. Moorhouse's insistence and apology puzzled him. Her manners were as foreign as though she had been French. But they were warm. Jim did not dislike her.

"And who else of the family do you know, Mr. Ellerdale?" Bel was asking.

"My Chairman, Mr. David Moorhouse, of course. He very kindly invited me to Aucheneame last Saturday. He's your brother, isn't he, sir?"

Arthur was not accustomed to find himself addressed as sir by a young man with English manners. On the strength of it he decided that Jim Ellerdale was a splendid chap and would do well. "Yes, David's my youngest brother."

"Beautiful place he's got down there at Aucheneame, sir. He has promised me some shooting in the autumn."

As Arthur did not seem to be able to find anything to reply to this, and as she, herself, did not feel qualified to discuss the pros and cons of shooting, Bel asked: "And who else in the family have you got to know?"

"The Ayrshire Moorhouses, of course. That's another brother's family, isn't it, sir? And then, of course, Mr. William. I have been to his flat several times. He's been advising me about my work."

"Mr. William?" Bel was bewildered.

"Yes, Mrs. Moorhouse. Who's in Dermott Ships. Who has just been married."

"Oh! Wil Butter? Our nephew? The boy who has just married our niece, Polly McNairn."

"Yes. Mr. Butter. He's known at the office as Mr. William. I like him awfully. Marvellous business man. Brilliant. Charming wife, too." Jim's colour rose a little and his voice became hushed with respect.

While Jim continued in conversation with the young people, Bel sat back to consider this. It was indeed a fresh light upon Wil Butter. Was it possible that any child of Sophia's could be thought marvellous or brilliant by anyone so grand as this young man? Wil, up to now, had just been a large, gauche creature—someone for whom Bel had the vague, but normal feelings of any aunt with sons of her own for any nephew. If, by chance, she called his image to her mind, it was to compare it unfavourably with the image of one of her own boys. And little Polly! Polly was Mary's daughter. That was all. To her Aunt Bel, Polly hardly existed as a separate being. Now Wil was marvellous, while Polly was charming! These were indeed new facets!

For an instant Bel's eye caught her daughter's. Surprise and amusement flashed between them. So Isabel felt as she did? No. It was quite absurd that two young people so negligible in the eyes of the family should be given this importance.

But Isabel had not quite come to Bel's conclusions. In the company of her mother, she had been to pay a ceremonial and somewhat patronising call on Polly, on her first "day at home". But she had not yet been to see her newly married cousin on her own account. Isabel had always liked Anne and Polly. They had been a pleasant, if dim, part of the family pattern. But now, perhaps, she might cultivate Polly a little. Drop up of an evening and help her to entertain such pleasant young men as Wil might care to bring home.

"We had Wil and Polly's wedding reception in this house, Mr. Ellerdale, only last month," Isabel said.

"Oh, did you?"

Had Bel held Jim Ellerdale of less consequence, the tone of his voice would have annoyed her. It seemed to imply that in doing this they had done something quite remarkable; that the Arthur Moorhouses had gained in stature; that Wil and Polly had done herself and Arthur an honour. This was quite preposterous. Wil must indeed have made himself of importance in Dermott Ships!

But she only said, "Oh yes, we had the reception here. I'm surprised they didn't tell you. Perhaps I shouldn't say so, but you see, Mr. Ellerdale, my husband has always been very much the centre of his own family. They all, somehow, lean on him."

131

It was difficult for Jim to understand Bel's sudden sweetness. He could not believe that anyone so brilliant and forceful as William Butter needed to lean on anybody. But he felt he had better not say so. He merely directed a look of respectful approval at Arthur, followed by a smile of polite interest for Bel, and said to Isabel: "Then Mr. William and his wife are your cousins?"

"Oh, yes," Isabel said.

She was a pleasing little thing, this girl sitting opposite him, with her shining eyes and her fairness. If he had been on the lookout for a wife, then perhaps— But he had no money. He would be mad to think of marriage for another ten years, perhaps. He must first establish himself. That would take time. Winifred might, of course, marry well, which would help. If only the Colonel had made things easier for them! If only— Jim wrenched his thoughts back to the somewhat pedestrian conversation of Bel's dinner-table.

III

"Why are you making such a fuss, Mother?"

"Fuss, Isabel?"

"Yes."

Bel drew on her gloves, making ready to go out. "I don't know what you mean, dear. I'm only seeing to things."

Isabel wondered a little at this mildness. As daughters will, she was goading her mother a little. "You've been fussing all morning."

"All morning, dear? It's only half-past nine. I want to get to the shops early, that's all. Now what can I have done with my purse?" Bel went out of the room, smiling a misty, benignant smile, that was intended to convey to Isabel that she was a dear, silly child, who really must not worry her kind, busy mother.

Isabel caught Bel's meaning perfectly and resented it. Bel could not really be angry with her children these days. Everything was going so well. They were making such nice friends. Ten days ago they had Jim Ellerdale to dinner. Then last weekend Arthur and Isabel had met Jim and his sister at Aucheneame; and Isabel had invited Winifred to spend this weekend at Grosvenor Terrace.

Now it was Friday morning, and Miss Ellerdale would be here this afternoon.

Isabel was quite right, of course. She, Bel, *had* been making a fuss. Still, Isabel needn't have said so. Bel found herself wondering, as she sought about her room for the purse she had mislaid, from which side of the family the child had inherited this strand of downrightness. Forgetting her own mother, Bel decided it must come from the farmer blood of the Moorhouses.

But she really must try to be a little less fussy. Yes; there was the purse on her dressing-table. She supposed it must be this strange English girl coming to stay. Would Winifred Ellerdale think the Moorhouse family queer and provincial?

Bel took herself to task. This was ridiculous. If the children were going to have the sort of friends she wanted for them, then she must learn to take the entertainment of these friends as a matter of course. She turned once again to her mirror. Her reflection reassured her. Her appearance was right for Great Western Road on a June morning.

As she came downstairs she was surprised to hear animated talk coming from the back parlour. The voice of Isabel and— no, it mustn't be—yes—Sophia! In panic, Bel retreated a step or two upstairs again. Then, taking courage, she continued downwards cautiously. With luck she could pass the parlour

133

door, escape by the basement stairs, think of yet another order to give Cook by way of excuse, and escape by the back door into the lane.

But luck was against her. She was passing the parlour door as a thief might pass it on his way to the silver in the pantry when Isabel came out.

"Mother! Oh, there you are! I didn't hear you. Aunt Sophia's here."

There was no hope now; for Sophia had followed on Isabel's heels.

"Bel dear! It has happened!"

"Happened, Sophia?" Feelings of guilt and intense annoyance had scattered Bel's wits.

"Well, Bel dear! What *could* happen? Think! What were we talking about the last time I was here?"

Trapped, Bel followed the others back into the parlour. She could not, for her life, remember. She was, indeed, so preoccupied and cross that she had little wish to.

For once Isabel was helpful. "Margy is engaged to someone called the Reverend Alexander Findowie."

Bel rallied. She managed to say: "Oh Sophia, I *am* glad!" with some show of interest.

Sophia was sitting now, crying with excitement.

"Did you know about this, Mother?" Isabel asked, filling an awkwardness.

"Your Aunt Sophia told me it might happen. He seems a very nice young man. Just right for Margy." Bel's tone was businesslike. Her wits had come back to her. She must be firm, and disentangle herself. She took Sophia's hand. "My dear! What is there to cry about? Isabel, ring for Sarah to bring your aunt a cup of tea. Sophia, stop it! Why should you cry at anything so splendid?"

Now she could hear Sarah's footsteps coming up the basement stairs. But why wasn't she coming in? Had she gone to the front door? No. Here she was now. Bel called: "Sarah, bring—"

But it was not Sarah; it was Mary McNairn.

"Good morning, Bel." Mary's voice was as flat as ever. But her face was a little flushed. She paid no attention to the others. "I thought you ought to know that Jackie's wife, Rosie, had a son this morning."

Bel could only repeat the words, "A son?"

"Yes, dear," Mary said evenly. She cast a matron's eye at Isabel's nineteen-year-old innocence, but decided the news could not wait. "Rosie has had a terrible time, Bel. Death's door. But the doctor says he hopes her strong constitution may pull her through. Phœbe has been a brick. She's been with her all the time."

Isabel exclaimed: "Oh, Aunt Mary! I didn't know!"

"Of course not, dear. It wouldn't have been right if you had. Sophia, why are you crying?"

Sarah was standing at the door.

Bel called to her: "Tea, Sarah, please." And then, with a flash of inspiration: "Oh, and there's something I forgot to tell Cook. No, don't ask her to come up. I'll come down and see her myself."

Bel ran down the basement stairs. In a second she had escaped by the back door into the lane behind. It was the only thing to do. She would think of an explanation later.

In some minutes more she was walking down towards the shops, wishing devoutly she were walking on the shores of a desert island.

Bel did not reappear at Grosvenor Terrace until lunchtime. She was determined that Mary and Sophia should be gone. She had, she felt, lost face, and she did not like it. She came back with much the same feelings as a truant scholar who hopes to slink into school unnoticed. What could her daughter, what could the maids—above all, what could her sisters-in-law think of her?

Arrived at her own front door, she was seeking her latchkey when it was thrown open by Isabel, who had recognised her through the patterned glass.

"Hullo, Mother. Have you dared to come back?"

Bel flinched, and her colour rose a little. "I don't know what you mean, Isabel," she said.

"Yes, you do."

Isabel's grandmother could look just like that, Bel reflected. But there was Sarah appearing with a soup tureen.

"Oh, there you are, Sarah! Lunch already? Come, Isabel, dear." These words, intended to be normal, sounded hollow even to Bel's ears as she followed Sarah into the dining-room, pulling off her gloves. And was it possible that, as the tureen was placed on the table and its steaming lid raised, Isabel was grinning into Sarah's face, and Sarah was grinning back? Bel stiffened.

But Isabel attacked gleefully. "Mother, don't go on looking like a criminal. We know you ran away."

Bel found nothing to say, but her face went red as she supped her soup.

"But you were quite right! They would have kept you all morning!"

"What did you tell them?" Bel asked, shamefacedly.

"When I came up with the ladies' tea, Mam, I telt them

that ye had run out to see Mrs. McCrimmon at the coach-house," Sarah said smugly.

"But what did they say when I didn't come back?"

Isabel laughed. "I don't think they noticed. Aunt Sophia was so busy telling Aunt Mary about Margy. And Aunt Mary was so busy eating cake and talking about Rosie's baby, that they both forgot about you."

At this, Bel, knowing her sisters-in-law, and recognising the truth of Isabel's picture, was annoyed. If Mary and Sophia could do nothing better than talk about themselves, why must they do so in her house? But there was nothing to do but relax, and be thankful that deep offence had not been given. She laughed. "It's all very silly," she said, smiling and deciding comfortably that the incident could be dismissed.

But this was just what Isabel would not allow to happen. Her brothers heard of it with pleasure. The story of their mother's escape through the basement became at once a family joke in which even Winifred Ellerdale must be allowed to share. To begin with, Bel was ashamed that Isabel should mention such a thing before their guest.

But the result was excellent. Indeed, Winifred laughed so gaily that Bel began to feel herself quite a wag.

Thus, on Saturday morning Bel set out to make amends. She drove first to Sophia's to express the right amount of enthusiasm for the life of energy and devotion that now lay in front of Margy; and thereafter to Mary's, to express the right amount of concern for Rosie and her son; she received Mary's placid, unworried assurances that, thanks to the strong constitution of her daughter-in-law, and to Phœbe's being a brick, the young mother looked like pulling through.

"And what excuse did you make for running away, Mother?" her son Arthur asked.

"Never mind what I said."

"Did you tell the truth?"

"Of course."

"I don't believe it."

Bel laughed and turned to their visitor. "You're not as impertinent as that to *your* mother, are you, Winifred?"

"Quite, I'm afraid, Mrs. Moorhouse."

Winifred Ellerdale was enjoying herself. She found Scotch people different, but kind. She liked them. Her friend Isabel was charming. The boy, Tom, was a great dear. And Arthur was far from unattractive.

All, indeed, was friendliness. As Bel said to her husband: the Ellerdale children had quite become a part of the family now.

Whatever Arthur Senior's thoughts of this remark were, he kept them behind a smile that gave neither denial nor assent.

Chapter Eleven

"YOU KNOW, it was my idea, Miss Netherton, that you should come to be with Granny at the Dower House. I don't know if you realise that."

Elizabeth remained solemn. "Well, I had a kind of idea. I remember you suggested it at your cousins' wedding."

Charles beamed complacently. "Yes, I did, didn't I?" He had attached himself to Elizabeth, as a boy will to a young woman who is lively and sympathetic. At the moment they were walking back from the stables, where he had taken her to see his pony.

Elizabeth was not displeased to have this self-important child look upon her as his property. She was quite well aware that her novelty would presently wear off. But she guessed, too, that Charles might, in his way, be lonely; that he might be glad to find someone whose own childhood was not too far behind.

Charles's approval meant, of course, the approval of his mother and his grandmother. Elizabeth was aware of this, too, and she did not like him the less for it. The boy was making her settling-down at Duntrafford easy, and she was grateful to him.

They took their way through the shrubbery in the direction of the Dower House. The blaze of rhododendrons was passing, for it was late June. Snow from a wild cherry lay on the path and upon the velvet-green by the wayside. Wild pigeons were squabbling and beating their wings in the high trees. The woods were full of the sound and scent of the opening summer.

"And do you find I come up to your expectations?" she asked.

But he was not such a child as that. "That's asking," he said, turning to look at her with eyes popping mischievously. For a moment they walked on in silence; then, seeming to reconsider, he said with an air that was absurdly casual: "If it's of any interest to you to know, I like you awfully, Miss Netherton."

Elizabeth actually blushed. She laid her hand on his shoulder. "Of course it's of interest. I'm glad, Charles." Yes, she liked this queer, outspoken, affectionate boy.

Indeed, on the whole, she liked all of them. Her life at the Dower House would be tolerable. Lady Ruanthorpe, her charge, had seemed at first sharp and demanding. But before many days the old woman had spoken intimately of the loss of her husband, Sir Charles, and sent the girl to find an old daguerreotype of the other Charles, her son, who had been killed as a young man in the hunting-field. No. Lady Ruanthorpe might be old, gruff, and, as her grandson would have said, a handful. But it would have taken someone less quick than Elizabeth to miss her qualities.

Elizabeth had been able to write to her parents to say that her duties here suited her very well, and that she was being treated as an equal. She wrote this last, knowing her father and his pride.

For John Netherton had not been able to stand against the combined forces of herself and Mrs. Robert Dermott.

But now, as she walked, Elizabeth went cold at the thought of that door, banged in the face of Arthur's mother. When next she saw him—as now, at Duntrafford, she soon must—she would speak of it and once more apologise.

"What on earth are you thinking about, Miss Netherton?"

Elizabeth realised that the boy beside her was speaking.

"I've asked you twice already."

"I'm sorry, Charles."

"You looked worried. What *were* you thinking of?"

"I don't remember. My thoughts were in the clouds."

He seemed to consider this, but did not reply.

In the distance she could hear the river Ayr as, swollen with June rains, it rushed among the stones at the bottom of the sandstone gullies. There was a smell of wild garlic, of sprouting larch, of the pregnant, soaked earth.

They could see the little Dower House before them now. Old Lady Ruanthorpe, leaning on her ebony stick, was standing at the door talking to her daughter.

"There's your grandmother looking for me. It must be teatime."

But to this remark also Charles did not reply at once. He raised one hand in a casual, distant greeting, then, at his leisure, he turned to Elizabeth. "My thoughts are never in the clouds," he said a little coldly.

II

"Are you coming down to Brodick next weekend, Arthur?"

"Uncle Mungo has asked me to Duntrafford."

"Well, you're a man now, dear. You must decide for yourself." Bel smiled at her son across the table.

"Does it matter? Do you want help or anything?"

"Help? No, dear. Tom is going to be my right-hand man. Aren't you, Tommy? And Isabel is going to look after Granny on the journey down. It's really Granny's holiday, you see."

All this was happening at the breakfast table. Arthur Moorhouse, Senior, lowered his morning paper to drink a mouthful of tea, pulled the reading spectacles that he must now wear down towards the point of his nose, and looked over their rims at his wife. He said nothing. Still silent, he shifted his gaze to his daughter. The merest ghost of a smile flickered round Isabel's lips. Without speaking, scarcely by moving a muscle, indeed, father and daughter agreed that "Mother was at it again". Arthur Senior put down his cup, pushed back his glasses and was lost once more behind his newspaper.

But if they thought they knew all that was in "Mother's" mind they were mistaken. There was the telephone, of course. Yet that was only part of it.

Bel had agreed to go back to Brodick for the single month of July. In times gone by, the Moorhouse family, following the custom of all well-to-do Glasgow, had taken a house in some rural village in the Firth of Clyde for the months of July and August. Brodick, in the island of Arran, had been their favourite holiday place. But some years ago Bel had decided that its unconventionality was not good for the children; that the effect of Brodick, where you could behave anyhow, wear anything and come to meals at all kinds of irregular times, was demoralising. So they had taken to going up "north"—as it was called in Glasgow: to places like Aviemore and Grantown, where you could meet all the best people from Kelvinside all over again; or to Oban, where you could at least look at real lords and ladies, who had been rowed ashore from their yachts.

These holidays had not included Mrs. Barrowfield. But the old lady was not aggrieved. It was becoming, indeed, continually harder to induce her to leave her home in the centre of the city even for one night.

But now Isabel, Tom and their grandmother had suddenly been caught up in a sentimental wave of longing to go back to Brodick just for a month to see what it looked like. At once Bel saw her advantage. A month was ample time to instal telephones at Grosvenor Terrace and Monteith Row.

But having her way about the telephone was not the only reason for Bel's blandness this morning—however much her husband and daughter cared to exchange glances. It pleased her that young Arthur had decided to break free and take himself to Duntrafford. Jim Ellerdale, she had heard, was to be on holiday; and as Arthur had, to her gratification, struck up a real friendship with him—the young men met quite often for a standing lunch at Lang's lunch counter in Queen Street and thereafter went to Cranston's smokeroom in Buchanan Street—it was thus very likely that Arthur would see something of Jim's sister.

III

Charles Ruanthorpe-Moorhouse showed a certain imperiousness towards those to whom he was attached. And his cousin Arthur was one of these. He insisted upon going in the pony-trap with his father to meet him.

They were early, and as they waited at the village station Charles, excited and pleased, kept pouring out a flood of talk at his placid, unresponsive father. Carriages, traps and dogcarts were coming to a standstill in the evening sunshine, settling down to await the arrival of the Friday evening train. Charles made comment on each and all of them.

"Whose trap is that, Dad?"

"I couldna say."

"Yes, you could. Look. It's one of our own farmers."

Mungo did not care for his son's expression: "our own farmers". But in justice he had to admit that his son's mother would have used it as a matter of course. "Aye, I believe you're right. It's old Tom Rennie of Greenhead." He raised a hand and shouted: "Fine night, Tom."

The old man raised a hand in greeting to Mungo Moorhouse, who had for so long been merely a neighbouring tenant
farmer at the Laigh Farm, but was now to all intents his laird.
"Fine night, Munga."

Charles snapped his eyelids, friendly too, but dignified.
"Good evening, Mr. Rennie," he shouted.

"Fine night, Mr. Charles."

Charles gave Mr. Rennie just such a smile as his mother
would have given him. It was natural to him to copy her
manner with the tenants rather than his father's. "I expect
he's come to meet his daughter. She'll have been shopping in
Kilmarnock," he said to Mungo in an undertone.

"How do ye know?"

"Well, he's only got one daughter who lives with him, hasn't
he? And people *do* shop in Kilmarnock, don't they? People
like that never dream of going so far as Glasgow." Mungo
flicked straight a rein that had become twisted over the pony's
back. He did not bother to reply. It would merely draw forth
further pertness.

But Charles did not seem to expect it. He was still looking
about him eagerly. "Dear me! The train *is* late," he said
importantly. "I expect it's the heavy weekend traffic."

To this also his father did not reply.

"Dad."

"What is it now?"

"Shall I go out on the platform to meet Arthur?"

"Ye'll stay where ye are."

"Well, I could hold Alexandra's head while you went." This,
Charles suddenly felt, would give him importance in the eyes
of his cousin.

"We'll both stay where we are."

"But the platform's going to be awfully busy, Dad."

"Well, never heed."

144

A roar in the distance had taken up Charles's attention. "Oh, there it is now!"

Arthur emerged from the little station to find his Uncle Mungo sitting holding the reins of the pony and giving him a placid smile of welcome, while his cousin, Charles, his black eyes jumping in his head with pleasure, was opening the door, shouting greeting and giving orders to the local porter. "Hullo, Arthur! Here you are at last. Was the train awfully busy? Just one moment, Macmillan. Let Mr. Moorhouse in first, then his bag can go on the floor."

Mungo, seeing that the porter had other luggage to attend to, stretched out a strong arm, said: "Give it to me, John," hoisted Arthur's weekend baggage over the side of the trap and gave the man a shilling.

In a waking dream young Arthur Moorhouse looked about him. The little thoroughbred mare flew downhill towards Duntrafford. The freshness of the country after the dust of the town. The dark green trees that overhung the road; their branches weighted by early July foliage. The birds already sounding notes of evening, although the sun would still be shining many hours from now. The steady trot of the pony's hooves. The constant talk of the boy beside him. It was easy for him to answer his cousin's questions, for they scarcely needed answering. To answer his Uncle Mungo. Yes. The family had already gone to Brodick.

Now they were in the long drive leading to Duntrafford House. Now, in a moment, they would pass the end of the little drive that branched off to the Dower House.

"Oh! There's Granny out having a walk. I wonder where Miss Netherton is? Did you know there was someone called Miss Netherton with Granny now?"

Yes, Arthur knew. Tonight, indeed, he was aware of nothing else. Had he not come to see her? Yet now Charles's mention of her pierced his excitement like a knife. Was she there, too, then? Beside the bent old lady? Merely concealed for a moment by the bushes?

"Hey, Dad! Granny's waving us to stop. She wants to say hullo to Arthur."

Yes, she was there. Standing beside Lady Ruanthorpe, looking at him, and smiling up into his face.

"Shall we come out, Granny?"

"Oh no, don't bother. Arthur must be hungry. How are you, Arthur? You must come across and tell me all about everything."

He gave the old woman his hand.

"Do you know Miss Netherton? I forget."

"Yes. We met in Glasgow."

Elizabeth had stretched up a hand, too. "Yes, I know Mr. Moorhouse." She looked yet again, up into his face, but almost at once she turned away and her colour rose.

"I won't expect you tonight, Arthur. But, Charles, you must bring Arthur to see us tomorrow."

"All right, Granny."

The trap was on the move again, and Charles was waving a casual goodbye to the ladies in the roadway. They were out of sight before it came to Arthur that, for the first time in many days, his senses were at rest. He would see Elizabeth tomorrow. That was enough. The knowledge of her nearness seemed to calm him—why, he could not say.

IV

John Netherton threw open the little gate of the front garden. "Are ye there, Ellen?"

A voice came from inside. "Just coming, John."

146

Ellen Netherton came out, walking-stick in hand, ready for their evening walk.

They were here in Brodick on their annual fortnight's holiday.

"Where? To the shore?"

"No. Up the hill."

"All right." Ellen did not argue. But it was warm this evening, and very still. By the sea, she felt, there might have been a breeze. At least there would have been a refreshing smell of damp sand and sea-wrack.

They rounded the corner of the little white cottage where they had found rooms, and turned into the farm road leading uphill. Her husband seemed cheerful and on good terms with himself. That was all that mattered. Sunday—tomorrow—would be a day of peace for him. Not a day of church-organ playing and hurry.

John, using the hand that was uninjured, seized his wife's and towed her up the steep farm road. Yes, it was warm. He wished now that he had followed Ellen's wish and gone to the sea. But flexibility was not in John Netherton's make-up. Having taken his decision, he felt that he must keep to it.

The cart-tracks in the road were deep and sandy. In between them were loose stones. The going was not easy. Overhead the evening midges danced. Moths fluttered among the grass and harebells. The air he had now begun to breathe so heavily was aromatic with the scent of bracken, larch and birches.

He felt very warm now. But yet he did not give in. Presently they would be through the cutting and up at the top among the cornfields. Yet he would not admit to Ellen that, small and light though she was, pulling her up here was hot work. His pulses beat in his ears. It was some time before he realised that his mind had fitted a phrase of music to its beating.

"John! Stop it! You'll kill yourself."

"Stop what?"

"Pulling me up so fast."

"We're just up."

And now, indeed, they were. The road was running flat through the birch wood, and soon it would turn the corner, and there would be a seat and a view of the sea.

"Take off your hat and fan yourself, John."

He did as he was told. They were still capable of happiness together, these two—whenever the pressure of life relaxed itself, as it was doing now. Whenever they had time to remember they were man and wife, a gentle flame was lit once more between them.

"Take off your jacket." She put out her hand to help him.

"No. Leave it."

But now they were happy. As his breathing came back, John had begun to hum the phrase that was beating in his ears.

As they came out from among the birch-trees and turned the corner, Ellen's heart stopped.

There just in front, arm-in-arm, were Mr. and Mrs. Arthur Moorhouse!

It was a crowded moment. John. He had slammed the door in this woman's face. And Mrs. Moorhouse?

"Mrs. Netherton! And your husband! I had no idea you were in Brodick!"

So Mrs. Moorhouse had kept her head and was friendly. Her colour had risen. That was all.

"Arthur, I don't think you've met Mr. and Mrs. Netherton. You remember their daughter who played at Wil's wedding; who is with Lady Ruanthorpe now." Bel gave a hand to both of them.

With relief, Ellen saw her husband return Bel's handshake.

"Are you going this way? Can we walk back with you a

little?" Bel turned, pulled Ellen's arm gently, and left the men to follow.

John came behind with Arthur, gloomy and uncertain. His last meeting with Mrs. Moorhouse was vivid in his mind. Did her husband know?

But Arthur ambled along by his side easily, and, it would seem, at peace. He spoke of the fields. What was growing in them. When the hay would be ready to cut. He approved the condition of a herd of cows, that, finished with the evening milking, was fanning itself out into a green field from the door of a cowshed.

John made the right responses. They were, both of them, farmers' sons. They could, if they chose, speak farmers' language. He could understand Arthur's slow honesty. Could not dislike this merchant, who still could assume some of the country's ways.

"I know your boy, Mr. Moorhouse," he said, seeking on his side to be affable. "He was down in Partick the other night."

Arthur Moorhouse was quicker than he seemed. He was practised in the handling of men. He knew the story of the slammed door. But he guessed Bel's generosity was bearing this difficult man no grudge. "That would be my oldest boy," he said.

"A—a very nice boy," John said awkwardly.

Arthur was touched. But he knew better than show it.

"Aye, the boy's all right."

John Netherton and Arthur Moorhouse had met on the common ground of masculine goodwill.

But now Bel and Mrs. Netherton were turning round. They stood smiling until the men came up with them.

Bel's manner was genial. If John Netherton set down this geniality to a desire in Bel to prove that he was of so little

149

account that he was not worth quarrelling with, who shall say that he was wrong?

She was holding out her hand. "We were going the other way. We've kept you too long already. But I wanted to tell Mrs. Netherton how grateful we are that you allowed your daughter to go to Lady Ruanthorpe. Lady Ruanthorpe is delighted with her. And I wanted just to say again how sure I am that Miss Netherton will be happy." Bel paused, smiled and added, addressing John: "Mrs. Netherton has promised to bring you to see us."

John Netherton gave Mrs. Moorhouse his hand civilly, and the couples parted.

A welcome evening breeze had sprung up. Over yonder, on the evening calm of the sea, it was making dark patches where it struck the surface. Round about them the green corn was sprouting. Hens were cackling in a far-off farmyard. On the distant hillside a shepherd dog was barking.

Ellen walked beside her husband, stopping now and then to pick a gowan, a wild geranium, a scarlet poppy.

The Moorhouses had disappeared in the opposite direction.

"It's cooler," she said at length. She did not have to look at John to know his holiday mood was broken.

"Ellen, I'm not going."

"Going, John? Where?"

"To see Mrs. Moorhouse."

She knew better than to argue. "Don't bother about that, dear. I'll go, perhaps. I can make some excuse for you." She sensed that even this would not please him. But what was she to do?

"I don't know that ye should," he said uneasily.

She did not ask why. She merely put her arm through his and said: "It's nice and cool now, isn't it, John?"

"I wish these folks werena here. It has spoilt the holiday."

"Oh no, John! You don't need to see them again if you don't want to. They won't expect it. Mrs. Moorhouse only wanted to be kind."

But he said nothing more, and they walked on in silence.

V

It was Sunday evening, after ten o'clock, but not yet dark; for in Scotland in early July there is scarcely any darkness.

Mungo Moorhouse reminded his nephew Arthur that he had an early start for Glasgow in the morning, and that he had better think of bed. But Arthur was restless. He pleaded his need of a last breath of air, and came out into the stillness.

The high trees in the park beyond the lawn stood motionless in the half-light. A flock of sheep moved beneath them, step by step, cropping diligently, as cattle do at the end of a hot day. There were wisps of mist.

It had been a pleasant weekend. Charles and he had gone to see Lady Ruanthorpe more than once, which meant, of course, Elizabeth, too. On Saturday Jim and Winifred Ellerdale had come. Margaret had taken the occasion of Arthur's visit to invite them. In the afternoon Lady Ruanthorpe had come across to tea with her companion. Elizabeth had joined the other young people in games of croquet on the lawn. Then together they had, all of them, following Charles's prompting, discussed with Jim Ellerdale, who was thrust into the role of expert, the laying-down of a tennis-court.

Thus Arthur had seen much of Elizabeth. But now that he had said goodbye to her until next he should come to Duntrafford a black dispeace had fallen once more upon him. Now the Dower House drew him like a magnet. He followed a path that, here and there, led through the shrubbery, here and there came out on the open cliff above the gulf of the river, and ended finally at a viewpoint, close to the Dower House.

Distressed and thoughtful, Arthur sauntered slowly, his hands in his pockets, his eyes on the mossy path before him. Elizabeth. Everybody liked her. His mother was never done praising her. But he and she were both young. He was twenty-one, and she was less. Would a year be time enough before he declared himself? He would be more settled in his work then—more of a man. But by that time someone else might want to marry her. And if that should happen, and if Elizabeth did not even know that he, Arthur, loved her? Arthur felt a stab of dread. But what, then, was he to do? Moorhouse caution, virginal panic, and boyish inexperience joined themselves against his mounting passion. He felt unhappy and tormented.

The woods stood, damp and fragrant. Cushats murmured somewhere in the trees. Bird-notes sounded everywhere, and far away the crying of a lapwing came from a field beyond the river. A bat darted past him, fluttering black above the gully of the stream. Now another. Down there, almost on the surface of the water, caught for a moment in the waning light, Arthur glimpsed the blue of a kingfisher's wing. It was darker now. Here, where the shrubs came closer again, it was getting hard to see.

A step or two would bring him to the viewpoint, after which he must turn back, for it was late. Or perhaps he might cross the drive to the Dower House and stand for a moment unseen outside it.

Through this sombre stretch, then, where the branches met above him; the viewpoint; a look at the Dower House, then home by the open drive.

She was leaning on the wooden rail at the viewpoint, gazing down into the river. Now it was simple. The sight of her had wiped the trouble from his mind. He knew that he had come to seek her.

She turned. "I heard your footsteps," she said.

"How did you know they were mine?" His own voice was new to him.

She did not answer him, for the hoarseness of his tone had asked her heart a different, more important, question.

She had meant, if she found herself alone with him, to apologise for John Netherton's rudeness to his mother; to try to explain how life was not quite easy for her father; to make Arthur understand, so that he might go home and beg for John Netherton's forgiveness. But now her father and his behaviour were forgotten.

She found herself speaking low. "I just ran out for a breath of air. I shouldn't be here. I must go." But something made her turn to the rail once again and say: "Did you see the kingfisher? He flew across, just down there."

Arthur came beside her. He put out his hand to catch the rail, but it closed over the hand that already lay there. He seized it and swung her round.

Her eyes looked up at him.

"Elizabeth!"

"Arthur!"

They clung to each other, this young man and woman, their senses utterly astonished. What force was this that claimed them—they, who could know so little of each other?

But in a moment she slid a hand to his forehead and pressed him away.

They came apart, foolish and bewildered.

"I must go now, Arthur." Her voice shook.

"I'll write you, Elizabeth."

"Yes."

There was nothing to keep them from staying where they were. But, in their young fearfulness before this revelation, they walked to the drive in silence, and separated without another word.

Chapter Twelve

IT WAS A NEW ARTHUR who stepped from the afternoon steamer. His young man's heart was vividly awake.

This second Saturday afternoon of July was warm. The father and son made their way, with the rest of the weekend crowd, down the short length of Brodick pier, where, beyond the barrier, they could already see Bel and Isabel standing, waiting to greet them.

Arthur felt unreal. The sea lapping beneath them, among the barnacled supports and crossbeams; the wheeling gulls hanging above the steamer he had just quitted—luminous creatures of the air, bright as the light that clothed them. Unreal! The usual seaside noises. Friends meeting friends. The noise of the steamer's German band. The smell of seaweed. Pierhands wheeling luggage. He felt remote—rapt away from familiar things.

At the barrier his mother and sister stood waiting to greet them. His father paid the pier dues, and they passed through. His mother was familiar enough, and so was Isabel. But now, already as he greeted them, he was seeing them anew. His father bent to kiss his mother. For the first time Arthur saw him as her husband. He knew now something of what that meant. They, too, had once been assailed by enchantment, taken by surprise. And his sister Isabel, friendly and offhand. She was a young woman like Elizabeth, waiting until the spark should touch her.

"Did you have a nice journey, dear? Or was the boat too crowded?" His mother had taken his arm, and they went off, followed by his father and his sister.

"No. It was all right." Unreal. And yet it was easy for him to answer her, to make her the familiar replies.

She would have to be told, of course. But not yet. Not until he had seen Elizabeth again.

He had written Elizabeth at once—written early in the morning, indeed, before he had left for Glasgow. A deal of nonsense, as like as not, judged by any standards but the standards of very young love.

But they were words the girl had understood, and her reply was quite direct. Like himself, Elizabeth wrote, she had been swept away. But her love for Arthur meant everything. Why need she hide this from him? Yes, of course, they were young, and must be content to wait. But that was nothing, so long as they could see each other and write each other letters. Let him come soon to Duntrafford; but, please, say nothing meantime.

Arthur understood. She was still afraid, even as he was, of the flame that had flared between them. He would go to Brodick, as was expected of him, say nothing to anyone, and in the third weekend of the month reappear in Ayrshire.

"And how was everyone at Duntrafford, Arthur?"

"All right, I suppose." That sounded normal.

He walked along the shore road in silence now, arm-in-arm with Bel.

"Nice to see Brodick again."

"Yes."

"Is there much change?"

"Not much. Some building."

Everything was quite as usual. He was on the usual terms with his mother. Was it possible that Elizabeth had never happened? For the moment it almost seemed so.

Thus strange is the ebb and flow of feeling.

Old Mrs. Barrowfield sat knitting in a large wicker chair on the grass plot in front of the house. Before her was a little table spread with a tea-cloth of fine lace and bearing a large silver tray with silver tea-things, all of those glittering in the afternoon sunshine.

This grandeur was out of tune with Arran. But Bel had been determined. For once, she had given in to the family sentiment and come back to a month of simplicity. But standards were standards. They supported one's self-esteem. Even in Arran. It was less comfortable to relax certain conventions than to observe them. Hence the solid silver now in front of Bel's mother.

Mrs. Barrowfield, dressed in her best and whitest cap and shawl, sat, pleased and ready to pour tea for the Arthurs. She was much attached to her son-in-law, and adored her grandson. Besides, she preferred men about her. Her own sex, taking them as a whole, were, in her opinion, poor and purposeless creatures. She had said so many times since she had come to Brodick—much to the exasperation of Bel, who was driven at last to ask tartly who it was who was looking after her? Herself, Bel, a mere woman, or the Arthurs and Tom who were men? Mrs. Barrowfield evaded this question by managing to look hurt, and saying: "Ye know fine I wasna meaning you. Ye needna be so nippy." Which only added fuel to the fire.

Bel knew very well what had called forth these remarks. Mrs. Barrowfield had been disappointed that her elder grandson had not come to Brodick for their first weekend there.

"What's he needin' to go to Mungo's for? What way can he no' come here?"

This was sheer pettedness. Bel had no intention of pandering to it.

"Arthur's a man now, Mother. If he wants to go to Mungo's, why shouldn't he?"

"Maybe he wants to see that English lassie."

Bel intended her smile to be a smile of gentle indulgence towards an old woman's foolishness. But the foolish old woman knew her daughter. She saw that Bel was not displeased as she said: "Maybe he does."

But this did not suit Mrs. Barrowfield, whose delight it was to puncture Bel's smugness. "Or maybe that lassie from Partick, that ye sent to Lady Ruanthorpe."

That was better. Bel still had her indulgent smile, but now there was a glint of displeasure. "Perhaps he is, Mother. Who knows?"

"Ye wouldna like that."

"No."

"Well, what way did ye not make Arthur come to Brodick?"

"I can't *make* a son of twenty-one do anything, Mother."

"But maybe ye could try."

There was no rational reply to this. So Bel, to Mrs. Barrowfield's gratification, had turned away with a gesture of annoyance.

But now all was anticipation and pleasure. Both Arthurs would presently be here.

Surrounded by its scented hedge of yellow moss-roses and fuchsia, thick and deep, the little garden lay warm and sheltered. On a tartan rug beside her, her grandson Tom lay on his back motionless—a tousled, careless young male in knickerbockers and an open Norfolk jacket. An old linen hat belonging to his father covered his face. It was impossible to tell if Tom were asleep or merely basking.

The hedge about her was so high that Mrs. Barrowfield could see nothing beyond it. She must rely on sounds. She had heard the beat of the steamer paddles. Heard them stop, then, later, start up again. Now farmers' dogcarts were coming along the shore road, there, just on the other side of the hedge. And that was the clatter of the wagonette that climbed the String Road and crossed over with passengers bound for hamlets on the other side of the island. The family would be coming soon now.

Mrs. Barrowfield rolled up her knitting, put it on one side, touched her frilled cap and her curls to be sure they were in place for her menfolk, then, folding her hands, settled into complete stillness, gazing before her, smiling the patient, waiting smile of the very old. It was a smile that might have been outward expression of thoughts and memories, the reflection of things long since seen. Or a seeming smile, that was merely a gentle contraction of worn features, lying, for the moment, in repose.

White butterflies fluttered back and forth in the sunshine. Dragonflies hung in the air for a moment, then moved away again. She could not see their wings, vibrant transparency; only the little shining rods of green and blue. Bees worked unceasingly in the scented hedge, passing from one butter-coloured rose to another, dipping in and out industriously. Behind her, from the open window, she could hear the rattle of teacups as Sarah laid them ready to bring out.

Now she could hear the sound of familiar voices. She called to the sleeper at her feet. "Tom! Tom! Get up! There they are!"

Tom Moorhouse pushed back the linen hat from his sunflushed face, sat upright, rubbed his eyes, and pulled from between his teeth the blade of grass he had been sucking as he fell asleep. The latch of the garden gate clicked. Tom stretched himself and got up.

Mrs. Barrowfield was annoyed to see that, in addition to Bel and Isabel, there was yet another woman with them. For a moment she wondered who this odd little person in mauve linen and dangling chains could be. But as they crossed the grass to greet her, Bel called in explanation.

"Mother, this is Mrs. Netherton. You remember, we told you Elizabeth Netherton's parents were in Brodick."

As Mrs. Netherton shook hands with Mrs. Barrowfield, Bel called upon her mother to regret with her that it was only Mrs. Netherton who had come; Mr. Netherton having decided to climb Goat Fell on this hot afternoon. They had found Mrs. Netherton sitting on the rocks by the sea, and had, as Bel gaily put it, pounced upon her and brought her with them.

Mrs. Barrowfield saw no reason to support Bel's false regrets over John Netherton's absence by adding false regrets of her own.

Now Sarah had come with the teapot and things to eat. There was a running for chairs, a getting of rugs, the fetching of an additional cup, a disappearing to wash, a reappearing, a deciding where everyone was going to sit—whether on chair or rug—protests from all that they did not really mind what they did, in fact all the fuss of an improvised garden tea, when—as Sarah felt strongly, and said so in the kitchen— there would have been no fuss whatever had they drunk tea indoors.

"Arthur was at Duntrafford last weekend, Mrs. Netherton. Tell her that you saw Miss Netherton, Arthur," Bel was saying, as she settled back in her garden chair and began to pour out.

Mrs. Barrowfield watched her elder grandson with affection.

"Oh yes. I saw Miss Netherton several times." Arthur looked at the grass.

"I'm sure she must think it's a beautiful place," Bel prompted.

"She seems to think it's all right."

Bel laughed. "So like men! They won't tell you anything."

Mrs. Barrowfield drank her tea and listened.

Isabel and Tom asked news of Duntrafford.

The Ellerdales had come to play croquet, and they had discussed a tennis-court with Uncle Mungo.

"And did Miss Netherton play, too?" Bel asked.

"Yes."

Bel smiled at Mrs. Netherton as though to say: "You see. Your daughter is being treated like an honoured guest."

But there was a tension about her grandson, Mrs. Barrowfield felt. Something that was not quite the Arthur she knew. Was he worried by this talk of Miss Netherton? Had something happened to him in town? Or at Duntrafford? Had he fallen in love with that English girl? Or—no—not Miss Netherton?

And what of that woman? What did she think, as she sat there, submitting herself to Bel's rather condescending kindness?

Mrs. Barrowfield sat watching. Teacups tinkled. The garden hummed and breathed its perfumes. The talk flowed on round about her.

Ellen Netherton was grateful that mere chance had allowed her to pay a civil call upon the Moorhouses alone without her husband. Mrs. Moorhouse, it seemed, was seeking to be friendly, and for Elizabeth's sake it was right that she, Elizabeth's mother, should respond. She was too simple-minded to catch the note of patronage in Bel's voice—a note which was audible to Bel's family, and in particular to her son Arthur. For the first time in his life, perhaps, Arthur found himself unable quite to admire his mother's manner.

But presently the afternoon, having come to that late moment

161

where it would seem to stay poised before it passes over into early evening, had become sultry and still. Scent came, pungent from the rose-hedge. The bees seemed to become more industrious, as though they were eager to make it a bumper harvest before they flew home. Midges began to dance in the shade. Now and then there was a step upon the road outside, the sound of holiday laughter, the piping voice of a child coming home on bare, reluctant feet from summer sands.

Arthur lay back in his garden chair, ringed about by a world of his own.

IV

Mrs. Barrowfield watched her grandson. And more than once his face seemed lit by a look that had nothing to do with anything around him. It must be some girl.

The old woman was as much a snob as her daughter. It was she, indeed, who had made Bel what she was. If Mrs. Barrowfield made a cult of homeliness, it came, in part, from inverse snobbery; in part because she felt it was a rôle she could sustain; and in part because it suited her to play foil to the more genteel ways of her daughter and her daughter's children.

Yes, it would be a bad business if the boy were in the very act of attaching himself to some young woman who was nobody in the sight of herself and of the Moorhouses. The daughter of this church organist's wife, for instance. Something told Mrs. Barrowfield that this might be.

Having finished tea, Arthur's grandmother once more attacked her knitting, stabbing in the needle gloomily. She would talk to Bel, whenever Bel was free. But meantime she need not lose her head. She could continue to sit observing. And perhaps, after all, these disquieting signs would prove mere imagining, born of an old woman's anxiety and affection. Perhaps there would be no more of them.

But almost at once there *were* more of them. Next weekend would be the beginning of Glasgow's yearly fair. It would be, too, the beginning of the yearly holiday of both the Arthurs.

"Are you coming down on Thursday or Friday, Arthur?" Bel asked, alluding to this. "Arthur! Wake up! When are you coming here next week?"

The boy sat up blinking. "Next week? I'm going to Duntrafford until Monday or longer."

"Oh? Why?" There was disappointment in Bel's voice. And then, without waiting for Arthur to reply, Mrs. Barrowfield saw that she had rallied herself, thinking, no doubt, of the Ellerdales. "Well, dear, I suppose we can't stop you. It's very kind of your Aunt Margaret to want you again so soon."

So Bel was encouraging him? Was going to allow no difficulties to arise? She was now, indeed, on her son's side, parrying a surprised question from his father; turning the talk from Duntrafford.

Mrs. Barrowfield continued to knit. So there was something going on at Mungo's. But what? And with whom?

A light breeze blew into the garden. Tom and Isabel scrambled to their feet. Sarah came from the house, her starched streamers fluttering behind her, and set about taking away the tea-things.

Ellen Netherton stood up.

"Oh, Mrs. Netherton! It's early still!" Bel rose, too, smiling.

"I don't know when John will get down from Goat Fell, Mrs. Moorhouse. And he'll be hungry."

The others were on their feet bidding her goodbye. Bel went with her to the gate, then returned to help Sarah. The remainder of the family had scattered.

163

Now she was alone in the garden with her mother.

Mrs. Barrowfield continued knitting fiercely. "Where's Arthur?" she asked.

"Old or young?"

"Young."

"I don't know, Mother. I didn't notice."

"He went out after that woman."

"Oh, did he? Mrs. Netherton, do you mean?"

"Aye, Mrs. Netherton. Take a look out and see if he's walking down the road with her."

"Why?" But Bel went to the gate, opened it and looked. There were people about now. One or two couples taking the air. A party of children coming home from a picnic. A family of Arran tinkers pushing a cart along the dusty road; nut-brown all of them, with the dirty, cinnamon-coloured hair of their kind. And yes, there in the distance was Mrs. Netherton's slight figure going towards the village with Arthur, almost twice her height, pacing beside her.

Bel turned, came back and sat down. She took out her embroidery and searched for needle and thread. "Yes, Mother, he is," she said easily. "I don't know what he can have to say to her," she added, finding the things she sought.

Mrs. Barrowfield put down her knitting and looked at Bel as a stoat would look at a rabbit. It must be conceded that she found a sour pleasure in what she now had to say. "Bein' polite to his mother-in-law?"

"What, Mother?"

"Have ye no eyes and ears, Bel?"

"You think that Arthur and the Netherton girl—?"

"Just that."

"Nonsense!"

"Ye'll not stop it by sayin' nonsense."

Bel looked at her mother with rising annoyance. She knew

Mrs. Barrowfield liked to bait her, but this was serious. Baiting or no baiting, she must know what was in her mind. "Mother, what makes you think—?"

"Ye were surprised when he said he was going back to Mungo's next weekend, were ye not?"

Bel thought for a moment. "Not specially. He's been making new friends. That English family, for instance."

"Ye want him to like that English lassie, do ye not, now?"

"I can think of worse."

"Ah well, ye better think of it, then! It's not the English lassie's mother he's walking down the road with."

Bel bent over her work and began sewing nervously. "Arthur will have news of Miss Netherton," she argued. "After all, he was at Duntrafford last weekend, and he knows her mother will want to hear about her. Arthur is always very thoughtful to people of that kind."

"Aye, very thoughtful."

Apprehension made Bel lose her temper. This baiting was too much. She must hit back. Chancing to look up, she saw her husband in the doorway. "Arthur, do come and tell us how the men are getting on with Granny's telephone. Oh, I forgot! It was to be a surprise."

Arthur was in no doubt that his wife's words were deliberate. But neither then nor later could he understand why, after weeks of secrecy, she had asked him this, the most imprudent of questions, causing the old lady so much annoyance, and disturbing the peace of everyone's weekend.

V

But it was very well for Bel to apply a counter-irritant to her mother's cocksureness. Telephones or no telephones,

Mrs. Barrowfield had made her sharply aware of Arthur's danger.

Elizabeth Netherton. She had been a fool to make such a fuss of her. Why had she done it?

Bel was reasonably quick. But it was difficult for her to see her own motives. She could see the motives of others plainly enough. Mrs. Dermott, she saw, had used Elizabeth as a peg upon which to hang out her own importance. But she did not see that she herself had been doing just the same thing; that she had, indeed, allowed herself to be goaded by Mrs. Dermott into competition.

And now she must face the possibility of an attachment between this girl and Arthur!

Bel wanted the good things of this world for her children. And favourable marriage stood high among these.

Now this! Much disturbed, she got up, quite heedless that she was leaving her husband to take the weight of her mother's displeasure over the telephone, and, moving to the little garden gate, hung over it, seeking to compose her thoughts.

"Ye needna tell me, Arthur, that Bel's getting a telephone just because she's fashed about me and my health. Some of her grand friends'll have got one. And Bel has aye to be upsides."

To get away from the sound of wrangling, Bel opened the gate and went out into the road, walking along in the direction Arthur had taken.

The evening breeze coming in from the sea was stronger out here. It was blowing little eddies of straw and fine white dust along the road. From a field Bel caught the scent of new-cut hay baked by the afternoon sun, and, farther on, the warm farmyard odour from sleek, black Angus cows waiting by a gate to be taken home to the milking. But now she was hardly aware of these things.

Elizabeth Netherton. Bel tried to see the girl clearly. Stripping Elizabeth of the excellencies and charms in which it had amused herself to clothe her, what did she find? A young woman of reasonable good looks, who was straightforward and not a fool, who had no accomplishments except, perhaps, common sense. Bel wished she had taken Elizabeth more seriously, learnt more about her.

Yet why should she? The Nethertons were not in the same station as themselves. She could have no idea that Arthur— Oh no! It must not happen! Bel was shaken by the thought of it. Elizabeth might not be a Rosie. But her background! Her impossible father!

Bel moved slowly along, her brows wrinkled, her eyes on the ground, twisting a piece of straw in nervous fingers; her skirts neglected, trailing the dust.

"Hullo, Mother! Anything wrong?"

She looked up to find her son Arthur in front of her. His smile was affectionate and intimate. It helped her to take hold of herself. "Wrong? Why, Arthur? What could be wrong? It was hot in the garden, that's all."

Once more he slid his arm through her own as they turned to go back. This was reassuring and pleasant.

"I thought I should tell Mrs. Netherton about Duntrafford," Arthur said. "I thought she might like to know Miss Netherton was quite happy." His voice was casual.

Bel could deduce nothing from it. "It was nice of you to think of that, dear," she answered. "And is she?"

"She seems to be. They seem to like her."

"I'm glad."

"Did I tell you we're hoping to get Uncle Mungo to lay down a tennis-court?"

"We? Who are we?"

"Well, myself, I suppose," Arthur laughed. "And young

167

Charles, of course. He's mad about it. Jim and Winifred Ellerdale have played in England. They're going to teach us."

"And how was Winifred? Did she look nice?" No sooner was this said than Bel could have bitten her tongue out. It was so conventional—the question of every foolish mother who has a son of marriageable age.

"Winifred? Yes, all right. I like both the Ellerdales. They're coming again next weekend to Duntrafford."

"Your Aunt Margaret will be glad to have you there to help," Bel said, frightened now into caution.

"I suppose so. Look out, Mother!"

They stood aside as the herd of Angus cows was driven from the road, lowing, jostling each other, and stirring up the dust, as they were hurried along to the evening milking. Then they continued homeward, saying nothing more.

Bel felt reassured. Arthur was just as usual. She knew him through and through. She was so near to this boy, she told herself, that nothing could be hidden from her. Her mother had been talking nonsense.

Chapter Thirteen

MARGY BUTTER bounced in upon Sophia. "Here's a note from Alec, Mother. He was to meet me, but he says he can't. He says he's feeling wretched. He's been to the doctor again."

"Alec? Does he say what's wrong, dear?"

"The old thing. Done too much. Oh, he has no sense!"

"Margy! And what about the wedding?"

"Wedding, Mother?" The girl shrugged. "How can I tell? If Alec's ill, how—?"

"Yes, dear, but if—"

"Oh, I'm going to see him!" And Margy flung herself out of the room, leaving her mother dispirited and alone.

Sophia Butter did not often admit herself depressed. She was usually too busy fussing over people to notice what she felt. Besides, there was a certain apologetic bravery, a certain habit of cheerfulness about her that kept depression at bay. But now, for once, Sophia's mood was black.

It was the third week in July, the week of Glasgow Fair. For those who remained in Glasgow these were the dog days. Nothing happened. Shipyards and factories were closed. There was a Sunday traffic in the streets, a feeling of suspended animation.

Sophia crossed to the window of her stuffy, tasselled drawing-room in Rosebery Terrace, where Margy had found her, and looked out. She was in time to see her daughter bang out of the house. The girl gave her straw boater a tug to straighten it, dug her hands into white cotton gloves, clutched her skirts from the dust and strode off out of sight with the swinging steps of a man.

Sophia sighed. The drawing-room clock struck three. She looked up and down Rosebery Terrace. The sun was shining, but it merely served to give things, both inside and out, a look of shabbiness. The high railing on the other side of the street needed painting. The trees in the gulf of the Kelvin beyond it stood smoky and lustreless. The river below moved, shallow and stagnant. Even the fresh paint on the balustrade of the newly widened Kelvin Bridge looked blistered and dusty.

She turned back into the room. The sun, coming round now to the west, cast hot shafts of silver on the carpet. Sophia wondered if she ought to pull down the blind, but she had neglected to do so for so many years that the carpet was already faded. She decided not to bother. Perhaps William might agree to letting her have it dyed to make the room look nice for Margy's wedding. Or perhaps it was too worn to be worth while.

Margy's wedding. Depression changed to a quick pang of fear. If only Bel were at home, she would drop up to Grosvenor Terrace and talk to her. Bel could show impatience now and then, but in the end she always settled down to listen, and her help was always worth having.

Snatches of Highland singing, bleak and infinitely nostalgic, were coming from the kitchen, accompanied by the clatter of midday dinner dishes, as the heavy hands of the singer shuffled them about the kitchen sink. There was, too, a greasy smell of mutton chop leftovers that the singer had no right to be burning on the kitchen fire. Two bluebottle flies buzzed tormentingly about in the drawing-room, even as the thoughts of Alec Findowie and Margy were buzzing tormentingly in Sophia's brain.

No. She must pull herself together. She must either indulge

170

in a burst of weeping or a cup of tea. She was deciding that tea would, perhaps, be best and had begun to summon her courage to descend among the confusion of the kitchen, the Celtic singing, and the fumes of burning fat, when she heard the doorbell ring.

II

The singing stopped. And after such time as it takes for a pair of red hands to be wiped on a kitchen towel and a drugget apron to be untied and thrown down, there were steps in the hall, and presently Sophia heard her sister Mary's voice inquiring: "Is Mrs. Butter at home, Morag?"

Sophia was glad to see her. Mary, at least, was better than nobody. And the sight of the widow's bonnet with its draping of black crape rising towards her as she looked over the banisters gave Sophia courage to call: "Oh, Morag! Perhaps, if you're not too busy, you would bring Mrs. McNairn a cup of tea."

Mary presented Sophia with a plump, white cheek to be kissed. It was typical of her, even in such things as family salutations, to take the passive part.

The sisters had not in any way grown more close to each other since their children's marriage. They continued together in that familiarity, each with the other, that comes near to breeding contempt. Yet the family bond was there.

"What on earth is that girl of yours burning, Sophia?" Mary asked, preceding her sister into the drawing-room and pulling off her black gloves.

"Mutton bones," Sophia answered meekly. During their lives Mary had always kept a certain superiority over her.

"She should have put them in the ashpit," Mary said, taking

171

off her bonnet now, and smoothing down first her hair and then her black dress.

"Yes, she should," Sophia hastened to agree.

"Then why didn't you tell her, dear?" Mary folded one plump hand over another in her lap.

"Because it never entered my head she would try to burn them in the kitchen."

Mary smiled vaguely, looked out of the window for an instant, and said: "I always see to these things myself, dear."

As Sophia made no reply to this, Mary turned to look at her. She was surprised to see two large tears rolling down her sister's cheeks.

"Sophia, my dear," she said gently, "have I said—?"

"No, no!"

"What's wrong, then?"

"It's Margy and Alec Findowie."

"Alec Findowie? What about him? He hasn't broken off—?"

"No, no, Mary! Oh no, I hope not!"

"You *hope* not, Sophia?"

It was a relief for Sophia to give way. Mary was not very understanding, perhaps, but at least she was her sister. Sophia, therefore, allowed herself the luxury of a sob or two before she answered.

Had it been a stranger who sat weeping thus before her, Mary would have applied a tranquil, healing sympathy and, as one who had plumbed the depths herself, have pointed the way to resignation and peace. But such treatment would not, she felt, do for Sophia. Her sister knew her too well. She contented herself, therefore, by merely adding: "I do hope there's nothing going wrong with Margy's engagement, dear," and sat awaiting the arrival of tea.

Words began to tumble out of Sophia. "Oh no, Mary! But Alec Findowie is ill again."

172

"Seriously?"

"We don't know yet. Margy has just had a note. She's gone to see him. And the wedding was to be in September! And if it's put off, I don't know what I'll do; for Margy has been so awful ever since her engagement. Oh, I don't mean she has been specially rude or anything, Mary. But you know, dear, on edge. I'm sure I don't know why. Or perhaps I do. But it's an unnatural time for a girl, waiting to be married, isn't it, Mary? Especially when she's as crazy about a young man as Margy is about Alec. And I'm terrified she'll tire Alec out, being so much in love with him. You know what I mean, Mary. Men like that sort of thing, but not all the time, dear. At least, some don't. I've tried to tell her to hide her feelings a little, but— And then Alec's so attractive, isn't he, Mary?" Here Sophia stopped, wiped her eyes, felt better, and prepared to plunge again.

Mary sat considering. She had gone with Anne to hear the Reverend Alexander Findowie preach. The young man's magnetic good looks, his beautiful voice and a manliness coupled with a look of fragility—all these things had given Mary, an inveterate sermon-taster, a very pleasant Sunday morning. She had left the church in a state of uplift very little dimmed, really, by the thought that such a rare young man should be throwing himself away upon anyone so large and ordinary as her niece, Margy Butter.

"But why should you worry about him being so attractive, Sophia?"

"Well, dear, surely you must see. Oh, I don't mean anything unpleasant, Mary; but in church life a young minister meets so many silly women. And I've found out he's a little susceptible. Oh, I shouldn't be telling you, perhaps, dear; but I know you won't spread it. You see, I've found out that Alec was engaged before. I was having a cup of tea in Cranston's tearoom, and there was a lady at my table who was one of his congregation. I don't think she should have told me, but she said she felt I ought to know. She seemed to me a little presuming, dear, considering I had told her that Alec was going to marry— But I daresay she didn't mean— Anyway, he was engaged before. Everything but the ring. But the lady said it was the girl's fault. That she had given him no peace. I haven't told Margy. But I don't want people to say that she— And then after that there was something about Alec not being very discreet at a choir social. But the waitress came to count the scones and cakes the lady had eaten, so she didn't finish telling me about that. Of course, I didn't set much store— And it gave me a queer feeling of being disloyal. So I just let her go away. All the same I can't help—" Here Sophia stopped, looked at Mary, and added: "Of course, I would never dream of telling Bel or anybody but my own sister."

Mary knew this last statement to be quite untrue. But she saw that, for the moment at least, Sophia meant it. "It seems to me you were far too patient with the lady in Cranston's, Sophia," she said. "After all, how does a woman like that know when a fine young man like Mr. Findowie is only meaning to be kind?"

"But surely, Mary, it's something more than just being kind, getting engaged to somebody? Besides, he must have broken it off again."

Mary was thinking of the beauty of Alec Findowie's holiness, when she heard the rattle of tea-things. Thus the words, "Who are we that we should presume to look into the hearts of others and seek to judge them harshly?" were just as much directed at the singer of songs and burner of mutton bones as at Sophia. Then, as they could not, of course, continue thus in the presence of Sophia's maid, Mary hid her disappointment at the sight of a single plate of plain biscuits, smiled bravely

174

and said: "Well, Morag, this is nice," with an irritating friendliness, that seemed to convey to Morag that if she, Mary, were her mistress, life would be easier and more pleasant.

But as she poured out tea, Sophia returned to the subject. "Well, perhaps, dear, I'm worrying about nothing. I daresay I am. You know I'm so bad about understanding people. But I feel that if Alec's fit to be married at all, they ought not to put off the wedding. You see—well, seeing Margy's so restless— And if he *is* a little susceptible—well, after he's safely married there will always be Margy, won't there?"

Mary considered this. It was a pity, she could not help feeling, that any girl so ordinary as her niece should have the privilege of becoming the permanent mopper-up of the Reverend Alexander Findowie's exquisite sensibilities. Still, it would be a pity to allow a young man of such gifts to slip through the family fingers. "Yes, dear," she said. "I think you're quite right. The sooner he has a wife to look after him the better. If he has to go away again to rest his nerves, it might be a good thing for Margy to marry him at once—oh, very quietly, not to upset him, of course—and go away with him."

This suggestion did wonders for Sophia. She poured out another cup for Mary and offered her another biscuit. And it would be wonderful to have the house to herself with no Margy raging round it. "Yes," she said, a smile breaking, "I think that's a good idea, Mary dear. Very good." Then a thought struck her. "But if we tell nobody, what about presents? And, dear, they'll need them. And who's going to pay for the wedding?"

"Oh, the uncles will."

"Not that William won't do as much as he can for his own daughter, Mary." As Mary, however, took this coldly, Sophia hurried on: "But another expensive holiday! And with a wife this time! And Alec still only an assistant minister!"

Mary brushed this aside. "Margy and Alec could have their honeymoon at Duntrafford or Aucheneame, Sophia. Surely!"

Sophia sat back and sipped her tea more cheerfully. "I hope Margy comes back before you go, Mary," she said. "Then we'll know how things are." She had not liked her sister Mary so much for a long time.

III

The door opened, and Phœbe Hayburn came in.

Sophia was delighted to see her. The afternoon was cheering up.

"Phœbe dear! I didn't hear Morag letting you in."

Phœbe stood in the middle of Sophia's stuffy room, a radiant figure in a white summer dress. Taking off her gloves and hat, she pitched them on a chair. Thereafter she smoothed out incipient wrinkles over her svelte waist and stood regarding her half-sisters, arms akimbo. "Pooh! It's hot!" she said. Then, in reply to Sophia: "I let myself in. Your maid was standing at the door gossiping with a woman selling bootlaces and white heather. I walked past her."

"I would let that girl of yours go if I were you, Sophia," Mary said.

Sophia did not reply to this. Her maids had a way of letting themselves go, she found. She took refuge from Mary's criticism in addressing her younger sister. "Sit down, Phœbe dear. I'll call Morag to bring another cup of tea. I never dreamt you would be in town in Fair Week. Hasn't Henry closed his works?"

Phœbe flung herself into a chair, her legs sprawling in front of her, her handsome face flushed, and her strange eyes regarding her sisters as though she did not quite see them. "Yes, Henry has closed his works," she said. "But he's cleaning out the boilers or something. Anyway, he seems to be spending his time crawling about inside them."

"And—dear me!—are the fires still lit?" Sophia asked senselessly.

Phœbe did not reply to this. She merely allowed a shadow of contempt to flicker in her face. "Henry may be amusing himself, but it's not much fun for Robin and me. Tomorrow we're going to Duntrafford for a week."

"That should be nice, dear," Sophia said, rising to seek the promised teacup herself.

"It's you I wanted to see," Phœbe said, turning round in her semi-recumbent position to address Mary. "In fact, I called up at your house, then followed you here. It's about Rosie and the baby. I'm just on my way to see them now. I suppose you know that the child has been unwell again?"

Mary's dislike of her grandson's mother had reduced her interest in her grandson to somewhere below normal, but it would be out of character to let the family, least of all her half-sister Phœbe, know this. Besides, Phœbe's impetuous championship of Rosie and the child had raised the stock of the Jackie McNairns on the Moorhouse exchange. "Of course I know about it, dear," Mary said gently. "Are you forgetting he's my own wee grandson, my very own flesh and blood?"

Phœbe said nothing. For a moment she sat detached, examining the strange fact that Mary should bother to pose thus before herself. But presently she roused herself and said: "Jackie ought to take them out of town to the fresh air somewhere. He's on holiday this week, isn't he?"

"The poor boy has no money, Phœbe dear," Mary said with resignation. "And since the baby came he has had to pay for so much illness."

"David or Mungo could invite them," Phœbe said, following, rather, the train of her own thinking than in reply to Mary. "Both of them are in the country, and both of them are stiff rich." She sat up suddenly and looked at her sister. "Has it never struck you to ask them, Mary?"

It had not struck Mary. Besides, Phœbe was showing great gaucheness and a lack of understanding. Their brothers had their own dignity to think of, their own friends to invite. Rosie wouldn't even know how to behave before the servants at Aucheneame or Duntrafford. "Oh, my dear, I would never presume—!"

Phœbe slumped down in her chair again. This evasion of Mary's was not worth replying to. She lay staring at the ceiling. "David has turned into a frightful snob, of course," she said, addressing the plaster ornamentation round the gaselier.

Mary sighed. There was no discussing with Phœbe when she was in a mood such as this.

"But all that doesn't mean that Rosie and the baby are not suffering from the heat in town." Phœbe lay watching the two bluebottles crawling upside down over the scrolls of commercial rococo. Suddenly she sat up again. "I know what I'm going to do! I'll be at Duntrafford tomorrow. I'm going to ask Mungo to let Rosie and the baby go to the Laigh Farm. I'll tell him he's got to. There's plenty of room. There's only the grieve and his wife. She can look after Rosie. And if they have to stay on for a bit, Jackie can live with you."

Mary didn't like having her affairs arranged like this. Especially when it called for some exertion on her own part. And she did not like the idea of Rosie being shown in Ayrshire as her daughter-in-law. Besides, short, dutiful visits from Jackie were, she felt, now quite enough for her strength. But she must not appear to be placing hindrances. "It's very kind of you to worry about them, Phœbe," she said. "Perhaps you'll see what Mungo says and let me know. Wil and Polly were at Duntrafford over last weekend," she added, seeking to turn Phœbe's thoughts into suaver channels. "They hadn't paid a visit since they were married. Margaret wrote to Polly to say she wanted to get to know them better. You see—"

"Now, dear, there's a nice cup for you." Sophia, having returned, poured out some black, over-brewed tea and gave it to Phœbe. "Yes, Wil was here, and told us all about Duntrafford," she added, unwittingly stealing Mary's story from her. "Young Arthur was there, and there were all sorts of grand young people. It sounded just like a society novel."

"Was that English family there? The one that Bel is never done talking about?" Phœbe asked.

"Oh yes, dear. I think so."

"I know they were." Mary's tone came as near to sharpness as her principles would allow.

"I have an idea that Bel rather hopes that Arthur and the English girl—"

"She needn't trouble," Mary cut Sophia short.

"But why, Mary dear?"

"Well, Polly says the girl is in love with another young man. I forget his name, but he was there, too. And she says Arthur couldn't keep his eyes off that Netherton girl who has gone to Lady Ruanthorpe."

"But, Mary dear, how will Bel like that?" Sophia asked innocently.

"Not at all, Sophia."

Phœbe gulped down her tea and got up. She couldn't be bothered with her sisters' chatter. And probably there wasn't a word of truth in Polly's gossip, anyway. But if there was, what about it?

"I'm going to see Rosie now," she said. "Shall I give her your love, Mary?"

179

"Yes, dear. Of course. Please." Mary thought she could hear harmonics of mockery in Phœbe's tone, but she chose to ignore them.

IV

"Queer girl, Phœbe," Mary said. She leant over, took the lid off the teapot, and peered in.

"I don't think there's any tea left, dear," Sophia said, her tone needlessly apologetic. "I'll see if Morag has any hot water."

Mary allowed her sister to get up, cross the floor and open the door, before she called: "No, don't bother, Sophia. I've really had quite enough. Well, let me—" But Sophia was gone.

Mary sat back complacently. She had protested to Sophia that she did not want to trouble her, and yet at the same time she had made sure that hot water would now be brought. There was nothing else to do this afternoon, so she might as well go on drinking tea and waiting to see if anything more happened about Margy Butter and her handsome preacher. Margy might even bring him here. Then she, Mary, could really have a look at him, examining his attractions at close quarters. Her hopes were to be rewarded.

While Sophia was still gone from the room Mary heard the front door open, then the voice of Margy, followed by the tones of a man. A moment later the Reverend Alexander Findowie was being presented to his future Aunt Mary.

Mr. Findowie had looks that can only be described as sentimental. And he had a voice to match. It would be unfair, perhaps, to couple such looks with personality—a man may look like a bulldog and yet have a weak character; or like the Greek Adonis and yet have iron within him—but, looking at

180

Mr. Findowie, it was impossible, and for women especially, not to feel his charm. Whether his appeal was begotten of a stiff determination to love his fellow men, or whether it came from a mere shallow anxiety to please, it was impossible to tell.

And his future Aunt Mary had no wish to tell. She had heard him preach; on what, she could not now quite remember. But at all events it had been wonderful. "That young man will go far," she had said to Anne. "Your cousin Margy is a lucky girl. It will be a great privilege, a great responsibility for Margy having such a bright spirit in her keeping."

Anne had been somewhat unresponsive.

"Oh, Alec, dear! I'm glad you've come! Margy, go and get some more teacups and do some bread and jam. Sit down, Alec. This is your new Aunt Mary. I hear you've been out of sorts again. I hope it's nothing serious?" Sophia, whose very stupidity made her a more wholesome woman than her sister, accepted her prospective son-in-law quite straightforwardly. She had now quite forgotten Alec's looks. Which is not to say that, in her fussy, unfocused way, she did not like him—love him, indeed. But she loved him for what he had pledged himself to do: to take the over-eager Margy off her hands and make her happy. When she did think of the young man's attractions, indeed, it was with a stab of anxiety. There would always be some woman in his congregation with more sensibility than sense.

Margy came back with cups, bread, butter and a pot of jam. She preferred to make Alec's sandwiches here rather than in the kitchen among the fumes of burning refuse and the greasy steam from the sink. When she had a house of her own, things would be ordered otherwise.

"Here you are, Alec. Here's your tea, and here's some bread and jam for you. Now sit down and behave yourself."

He did as he was told, Mary saw. Margy, it appeared, had taken complete possession of him. And he seemed to be accepting this—to be enjoying, indeed, the girl's keen attentions.

"I hope you're feeling better," Mary said, her curiosity putting out a feeler.

"Of course he is, Aunt Mary. Look at him enjoying his tea."

Mary wondered that the young man looked up at Margy and smiled quite unresentfully. Surely he could answer for himself. The girl's intervention sounded almost like impertinence. But Margy had already learnt that it would be her duty to surround Alec Findowie with a cheerful, determined normality. That was what he needed. Her passion was instructing her bluntness. And it would be recompense enough for her to know that this gifted, highly-strung man was coming, more and more, to lean heavily upon her.

Mr. Findowie had not himself replied to Mary's question, as his mouth was full of bread and jam. But his smile, working even under these disadvantages, was so disarming that Mary at once decided to forgive Margy her pertness.

"Could I have some bread and jam, too, dear?" she said, addressing her niece gently. "A thin slice, and lots of jam, if it's not too much trouble."

Chapter Fourteen

YOUNG ISABEL MOORHOUSE sat in a window of the drawing-room in Grosvenor Terrace. Her fair head was bent industriously, as she laboured with needle and thread to repair the ravages that Arran had wrought upon her clothing.

Isabel was alone. The quiet of her mother's well-ordered house was about her. The gilded clock on the white marble mantelpiece ticked steadily. That was the only sound from within. The life of the kitchen was, very properly, shut away and suitably muted in the basement.

Now and then, to rest herself momentarily, Isabel would pause, straighten her slim body and look out at the evening through the looped lace curtains.

It was a watery, nondescript evening of early August, after a day of rain. The hanging clouds seemed to be in two minds whether they should knit themselves together into a black frown and descend once again, or part benignly to reveal a pale sunset.

The drive in front of the terrace was drying a little, as were the pavements of Great Western Road beyond. People had come out to take the evening air. There were one or two cabs, a hansom now and then, and, of course, the trams with their patient, plodding horses coming and going to the terminus at Kirklee. But, although it was eight o'clock or thereby, there were few private carriages. Wealthy Glasgow was out of town. The trees over there in the Botanic Gardens stood dark with the summer's green. The formal, close-planted flower-beds looked from here like brilliant, odd-shaped rugs flung down anyhow on the fresh expanses of the lawns.

Isabel's mood was negative. She was aware that industry stood between herself and boredom. Her parents had driven down to Monteith Row to visit her grandmother, to have the reassurance of seeing the old lady comfortably settled in her own quarters, and to instruct her reluctance in the uses of her newly-installed telephone. Young Arthur and Tom were gone for a walk.

They had, all of them, invited Isabel to come with them. But virtue had triumphed. Her things, she protested, were in tatters, and she must mend them some time, so why not on this dull evening?

Now, as she thought of it, Isabel smiled to herself at the battle which, even now, must be raging in her grandmother's sitting-room. "Don't be surprised if you hear your grandmother's voice," Bel had said to her, indicating, as she went, their own telephone newly fixed in the hall beside the grandfather clock. But Isabel had wondered.

Presently, as she worked, she became aware of some movement below, then, in a moment, of a muted footfall outside the door. The handle turned.

"Mr. James Ellerdale."

Isabel had just time to drop her workbox lid upon the more intimate parts of her mending and stand up. If her nineteen years were fluttered at this sudden appearance of a young man, if, in herself, she sought about for easiness and poise, there was nothing visible to Jim but a cool young figure silhouetted in the long window, the light making a nimbus of her fair hair.

"Hullo, Jim! How are you? Sarah, could we have tea?"

Sarah withdrew with a look of disapproval, wondering, quite unjustly, if that monkey of a girl had arranged this.

"Do sit down."

He did as he was bade, looking about as though he expected to find the others.

"Mother and Father have gone down to my grandmother's. The boys are out walking. I was busy, so I stayed at home."

Young Ellerdale half rose. "Then I'm disturbing you."

"No, please! I'm glad to have someone to talk to. Look, I'll go on working." Taking her workbox on her knee, Isabel opened it, and, using the lid as a screen, extracted some trifle of white silk and began stitching it. She was pleased with herself now. That Jim's eyes were upon her did not unduly disturb her. "We've been in Arran," she said in a moment. "I suppose you knew that?"

"Yes. I saw Arthur at Duntrafford more than once."

"He told me." She looked up and smiled. "I've been hearing about a tennis-court."

"Yes. There was talk about a tennis-court." For a moment he hesitated, as though something embarrassed him. Then he coloured, and a grin spread over his large, good-natured face. "I've got news for you. Winifred told me I was to come and tell you."

"News?"

"Winifred is going to be married."

"No!" Isabel laid her work on her lap and gave herself up to astonishment. "But who? Do we know him?"

Jim was amused. She looked like a little girl now, the embodiment of naive excitement. She made him feel very grown-up. "No, I don't think you do. Actually, he's a sort of cousin. We've always known him. He came to see us on his way to the Highlands. He's taken a shoot in Perthshire. And this is the result. It has been a quick business."

Isabel took up her sewing again, giving her visitor an odd little smile, which he found charming. "You must give me

185

time to think about this," she said. "You've taken my breath away, Jim."

Jim Ellerdale had expected to give his news to all the Arthur Moorhouse family. But it pleased him now to find himself here with Isabel. It pleased him, because he was a young man, alone in the presence of a fair slip of womanhood.

For a moment he sat watching the girl's busy fingers, thinking. Now things would be easier for him. Winifred was to marry a relative of substance some ten years her senior. The wedding would be soon. She would have an establishment and the background she was bred to. The burdens of family responsibility were lifting.

Isabel looked up, wondering at his silence. "What else, Jim? Tell me more about it."

"She wants you to be a bridesmaid," Jim said.

Isabel was expressing thanks and beginning to ask further questions when the door was opened and they could hear the noise of Sarah bringing tea. At the same moment the house was flooded with a loud ringing. Isabel jumped. "What's that noise? Oh, the telephone! It must be Mother at Granny's. I won't be a minute."

Outside the door she found Sarah. For a moment the bell stopped, allowing her to say: "Sarah, isn't it exciting? Miss Winifred Ellerdale is going to marry her cousin." At that moment the bell began again. It was so loud that Isabel must now shout: "That's Mother on the telephone. I'll give her the news."

"Aye, give yer Mother the news," Sarah said sourly.

Bel had gone to Monteith Row expecting to find her mother sullen. She had, indeed, begged her husband, Arthur, to accompany her to help with the old lady. For when Mrs. Barrowfield had returned from Arran her telephone was there, installed.

But Mrs. Barrowfield had been made prisoner by a downpour of rain that was as constant as it was dreary. Her day had been spent at the window, looking out over the sodden expanses of Glasgow Green, watching the water dripping from the trees, and telling herself that she was a lonely and forgotten old woman. Now, in her boredom, she would have welcomed a visit from Beelzebub himself.

She answered the doorbell herself. "Come away, my dears! It's verra kind of ye to come down and see yer old, dull mother," she said, receiving them with a meekness that could only arouse Bel's worst apprehensions.

The instrument stood fixed to a wall in the dark hallway, but both of them chose tactfully to ignore it; although for a moment, indeed, it occurred to Bel to say: "Oh, there's your nice telephone!" in the hope that this might break the ice. But somehow the words would not come, and they passed into Mrs. Barrowfield's old-fashioned sitting-room, while old Maggie, white-haired and more shaky than Mrs. Barrowfield herself, trotted in and out tremulously, bringing refreshment for Miss Bel and her husband.

"Maggie can't be very young now, Mother. And she doesn't look very strong," Bel said, making an opening. "Don't you ever think of getting someone younger? You know, for emergencies?"

"Emergencies? What emergencies, Bel?" Mrs. Barrowfield's voice was still provokingly meek.

Bel remained patient. "Well, dear, sudden illness—or—"

The only other word she could think of for the moment was "death", but she managed to finish by saying: "or—something."

"I know what ye mean, Bel. I know what ye mean," Mrs. Barrowfield replied plaintively. "But the Lord will call me hence when He wants me. Not a minute sooner; and not a minute later."

Bel was not disputing the exact timing of her mother's call. Still, it was only right she should have proper support when it did come. And it was evident that Maggie and the old cook might be too frail to give it—might, indeed, have received their own calls before then. "Oh, I don't know, Mother. But I just thought—if you had someone who was reliable and strong."

"These faithful lassies will never be turned out o' this house, Bel. Surely you know yer mother better than that! And forbye—" But old Maggie had come back.

Bel could only sit back and remember that Arthur had recently had much difficulty in persuading her mother to will a sufficient pension to her "faithful lassies" should they need it, so great had been her desire to leave every penny she possessed to her grandchildren.

Bel looked at Arthur now. His face was lit up in pious and sympathetic admiration for what his mother-in-law had just said. Had men no sense whatever? Couldn't he see that the old woman was merely at her parlour tricks?

Annoyance gave Bel courage. "Arthur has come down to show you how to work your telephone, Mother," she said. "I thought he would be able to show you better than I could. Men are always better at mechanical things, aren't they?"

Mrs. Barrowfield was pouring out tea. She continued to do so. She gave no sign of having heard, although her daughter had a strong suspicion she had done so. "Now there's a nice cup for you, Arthur," the old lady said. "And for you, Bel."

Bel looked again at Arthur. For the moment no help was coming from his direction. Suddenly she remembered her plan. She would ring up Grosvenor Terrace, bring Isabel to the telephone, then persuade the old lady to come and speak. Isabel could do anything with her Granny.

Mrs. Barrowfield was still bending over the tea-things. Bel got up. She whispered her intention low and hastily to Arthur, and left the room, closing the door behind her.

Arthur felt nervous. He could not help it. The old lady had been quite violent about the telephone in Arran. He drank down his tea in gulps.

Mrs. Barrowfield looked up. "Where's Bel?"

"She's just outside."

To his relief, this seemed to satisfy her.

Now he could hear the vigorous turning of a handle. Now his own number given. Now there was a period of waiting. Mrs. Barrowfield took his cup from him, refilled it and gave it back. Now he could hear Bel's voice, low and surprised. Now Bel had reopened the door, come into the room and closed it behind her. He turned, raising his eyebrows, questioning.

Bel's face was flushed, and there were shadows of displeasure that he could not read. She drank her tea in silence.

Mrs. Barrowfield did not appear to notice the change. Company had made her cheerful. She was gay now, with Arthur, living in her memories, telling him the old stories he had heard so many times before.

Instinctively he took the weight of her talking. Whatever had happened to Bel, she wanted to be left in peace. And he was not surprised when, in a little while, his wife stood up to go.

189

He rose, too. Screened by the sound of the old woman's remonstrances, he questioned Bel quickly. "But what about the telephone? What's wrong?"

"Nothing. But I can't stand a fight. Not tonight. Please, Arthur."

III

In the middle of the next morning Bel had a surprise visit from David Moorhouse. And in so far as a disappointed and worried woman could be glad to see anyone, Bel was glad to see David.

Bel and her husband's youngest brother were old allies. In the days before his marriage—days when the Moorhouses were simpler people—David had come close to Bel. They had given each other support on the sometimes stony paths that lead to achievement and success. There had been, indeed, a point in David's history when Bel had worried lest he should take a false step. But now, at forty-five, David, some thirteen years married, was safe, settled and bland; conditioned by his wife's adoration, his wife's wealth and the place in the world his wife had been able to give him.

He came now with a sheaf of Aucheneame roses, a hamper of summer vegetables, another of hothouse fruit and a message from Grace to Bel, expressing the hope that she was once more safe at home, that perhaps these few things would help to get her reopened house going again, and that Bel must drive down to Aucheneame very soon to see her.

Bel took the roses from him at the open door. "David! How nice of Grace to think of us!" She plunged her face in them. When once again she looked up, there was pleasure, affection and appeal in her smile. "David, how long is it since

I've had you to myself—even for a minute? We used to be friends, you know."

"Still are, I hope!" As he bent down to give her a brotherly kiss, he turned for her into the young, larkish David Moorhouse with all his hopes and fears before him.

David. Her own boy Arthur.

No, Arthur hadn't the wistful, pliable naughtiness of the young David. He was firmer, less predictable, inclined to smoulder. She must talk to David about Arthur.

"David, don't go at once. There's nobody in the world I want to see more—just this morning. I want to talk to you." Now Sarah appeared. "Sarah, look at all these beautiful things from Aucheneame. Take them in and bring up some cake and sherry. Tell MacDonald to come back for you," she said, nodding in the direction of the Aucheneame carriage.

"I really shouldn't. I've got a board meeting this afternoon. And I've got to look into some figures for it." And thus, having lightly underlined his importance, David called: "Come back for me in half an hour, MacDonald!" And shut Bel's front door.

Some moments later, family enquiries having been exchanged, Bel was pouring sherry for him as he stood before the empty fireplace in her parlour.

"I'm worried, David," she said at length, sitting down on a chair by the table and looking up at him. "It's about Arthur. My son Arthur."

David held up his glass of sherry to the light, tasted it, and put it down on the mantelpiece. Bel could not help noticing the curve of prosperity that had taken the place of the erstwhile elegant depression beneath David's lower waistcoat. "It's not his health, I hope, Bel?"

"No, not his health."

"Not a young woman, already?"

191

Bel took a gloomy sip of her own quarter glass of sherry before she answered: "Well, I don't know, David. That's just what I want to talk about. You know how his father is when it comes to discussing things like that. He's a little too—" Bel should have said "honest", but she said "matter-of-fact".

It was a great help to her to see that David was nodding wisely. David had not lost his understanding of the niceties. She could go on. "He didn't come much to Brodick last month," she continued. "He went down to Duntrafford for the first weekend, and spent nearly all his holiday there. I thought it was the Ellerdales."

David smiled, took a piece of cake from the table, broke off an end and put it into his mouth. "After Winifred Ellerdale, is he?"

Bel sighed. It was a great help that David was still so quick at this kind of thing. "She's engaged. I thought you might know. Jim Ellerdale came in for a moment last night. Isabel was here. He told her. It's to a cousin of her own."

"No, I hadn't heard." David looked down into Bel's face, wondering for an instant why she looked serious, but quickly he came to the right conclusion. "So you had hopes for Arthur in that quarter?" He laughed good-naturedly and shook his head. "The same old Bel!"

The cloud deepened in Bel's face. She was in no mood for teasing. "It's all very well, David. When your son's Arthur's age, you may have your troubles, too."

"Dear me! How old is Arthur? Twenty? Twenty-one? Surely there are as good fish—" David finished his wine and allowed Bel to refill his glass. "Had the boy any interest in Winifred?"

"No. That's just it. I thought he had. I thought all this going down to Duntrafford was because of her. Now I know it wasn't. He isn't worried in the least." Bel paused, then added: "And they're very nice people, David."

192

Nobody in the family could grasp all the implications of the word "nice" in Bel's mouth as David did. But still he was puzzled. "Well? If there are no bones broken, what does it matter?"

"But don't you see, David! With all this going to Duntrafford, there must be someone else?"

"Who *could* there be?"

"At Brodick Mother was certain it was Lady Ruanthorpe's companion, the girl Netherton."

"Netherton?"

"Oh, you won't remember." Bel explained, while David kept putting bits of cake into his mouth and swallowing his sherry.

"And now you see," Bel concluded, "why I wanted to talk to you. You can understand these things, David. You know that while neither of us are—well, snobs—we do see that there's such a thing as suitability. You do see, don't you, why the girl Netherton would never do?"

David, having finished, wiped his hands on a fine handkerchief, then plunged them into his pockets. No one knew better than he what was to be gained from a good marriage, and thus, conversely, what was to be lost by a bad one.

"No, Bel," he said, knitting his brows, and making a very good picture of troubled thoughtfulness. "It won't do."

Bel felt reassured. David saw her point.

But now—perversely, as was her way—a cobweb of doubt began to float across her mind, as she sat looking up at this handsome, complacent man, standing there delivering what, she sensed, might be a judgement that was, perhaps, too easy. Would David, the young David Moorhouse, back there in his twenties, have agreed with her so easily? For a moment she caught a glimpse of him. He would have made a tactful joke of her question and turned it aside, maybe, refusing to commit himself. Yet somehow in doing so he would have been the real David, a more honest, more sensitive David; declining to tamper with things so delicate as another boy's affections. Bel's inner eye followed the cobweb as it floated. If it had been his own son, would David have been so heavy-fingered?

"Have you proved that there's anything between Arthur and this girl?"

Bel let the gossamer float out of sight. She must, after all, be practical. "No, David. Nothing definite. How could there be? It's only that Mother is so certain. And Arthur has been— I don't know—different. Preoccupied. I left him to himself. I kept hoping. I refused to listen to Mother."

"How does your mother know?"

"She doesn't. We happened to see the Netherton girl's parents in Brodick, and she guessed from Arthur's behaviour. But, then, Arthur is friendly with everyone."

"What's Miss Netherton like?"

"She's very nice—for that kind of girl."

"I see."

Again Bel was assailed by the feeling that David had understood her too well. She felt a stab of doubt. For a moment she saw Elizabeth too clearly.

"If that's all, you can put a stop to it before it goes too far," he said.

"Yes, but how? I don't want to come into the open with Arthur."

"But you needn't. You can talk to her."

"What! Lecture the girl! But if there's nothing in it, I'll only look foolish; and if there is, it won't change anything, and make my own son hate me."

"I didn't say lecture Miss Netherton, Bel. But there are ways of warning her."

Bel sat considering for a moment. "Yes, I could do it somehow, I suppose."

"Certainly. Without being hard on anybody. You mustn't show you suspect anything, of course. After all, if you let it go on—"

"No! I can't do that."

David saw that her face was flushed, that her eyes were large with worry. He bent down, laughing, and kissed her, suddenly boyish. "Cheer up, old lady. Nobody's trying to murder you."

"I can't help feeling mean, David."

"You would feel more mean if this came to something when you could have stopped it."

"Yes."

"Well, then? And the sooner the better." David became jaunty. "I'll have another half-glass with you, and then I'll go away." He bent over the table and poured out for both of them. When he had done so, he stood beside her, laying a hand affectionately on her shoulder. "This is like old times, my dear. Here's to them. And very nice times they were."

Bel waved to his carriage as it drove off. Then she turned, went inside and closed the door. She must do as he suggested, of course, but she did not like it. She had been pleased to see David, she supposed; but she wished, now, that they could have talked of other things.

Chapter Fifteen

"AUNT BEL is coming to lunch." The tones of Charles Ruanthorpe-Moorhouse were charged with offhand importance.

"Oh, is she? I didn't know." Robin Hayburn had, on the whole, a very casual interest in his Aunt Bel, but as his cousin Charles was sounding important about her, Robin felt he had better sound important, too.

They had finished breakfast and were setting out from Duntrafford to walk to the Laigh Farm. Their cousin Jackie McNairn's wife Rosie, and her child, had arrived there a week ago. Phœbe Hayburn had made this arrangement. By way of occupying the boys' morning, Margaret had asked Charles to walk over with Robin, convey her regrets that she had not yet been able to come across, and to ask if there was anything she could do.

Such a commission suited Charles's importance admirably.

"Dandy, come here." He addressed himself to a half-grown Dandie Dinmont terrier his grandmother had given him on his last birthday. "Yes, old man. Walkies. It's walkies Dandie's going to have," he said, bending to pat the little animal, which was now wriggling on the carpet of the entrance hall in an ecstasy of expectation.

Charles was aping his mother, who, dignified and a little regal even with her nearest and most beloved, still possessed that full measure of British imbecility when it came to petting dogs. Yet Margaret's loud, self-confident tones could, some-how, give the most senseless gibberish a ring of importance.

They seemed to proclaim that this was the only possible way a house-dog could be talked to. Charles had caught the trick exactly.

Robin was embarrassed, a little, by this exhibition. His face was turned aside, as one might turn aside from a young mother who has, for the moment, lost her head over her baby.

At last the adorer of dogs straightened himself. His face was flushed with stooping, but certainly not with shame. "Stick?" he asked.

Robin hesitated, waiting for a cue. He allowed his eleven years to be guided in most things by Charles's thirteen. It was, after all, important to be right about these things.

"*I'm* taking one," Charles said decidedly. "It's a help for cross-country work."

Robin therefore chose a stick, too.

They set out. It was a bright August morning. There had been rain in the night, but now there was sunshine, clouds and a light breeze.

The two cousins were very good friends. They had, in fact, become inseparables. Charles, indeed, had insisted that Robin be allowed to remain at Duntrafford when Phœbe had gone home. This morning, however, Charles was in one of his august moods, and his talk tended to become formal.

"Is Aunt Bel coming alone?" Robin asked, striving to make conversation as they went. "Or is Isabel coming with her?"

"Alone, I think." Charles scotched the end of a nettle with his walking-stick.

"Why is she coming?"

"A visit, I expect. Hasn't seen Mother for quite a bit."

For a time they walked in silence, Robin wondering from his companion's rather offhand tone if, somehow, his question had offended. It came as a relief, therefore, when Charles presently broke silence.

"D'you see much of Aunt Bel's family in Glasgow?"

"Oh, here and there, you know." Robin was pleased with this. He felt Charles would like it.

Charles stopped, looked at a young pony grazing in the paddock, said: "Hullo, Lillie," then continued his walk, remarking: "That filly is improving." And as Robin made no reply: "D'you like her?"

"What, the pony?"

"No. Aunt Bel. Dandie, come here! Don't go biting Lillie Langtry's heels!"

Robin went carefully. "Yes, quite," he said uncertainly.

"A little bit pompous, wouldn't you say?"

"Well, perhaps."

"A bit too much gloves-and-feathers for me, if you see what I mean?" Charles said, decapitating a thistle.

Robin saw at once. He was anything but slow. But again he decided to go carefully. "Well—yes. Perhaps."

As Aunt Bel was proving no very fruitful topic of conversation, Charles took to slashing at everything within his reach—toadstools, dandelions, whin bushes, tufts of grass. At last, becoming too energetic, he hit Robin's leg. "Oh, I say! Look here! Did I hurt you? I didn't mean that."

"No. It's all right."

"Quite sure, Robin? I'm awfully sorry."

"No. It was nothing. Honest."

"Really? Quite sure?"

"Yes. Honest, Charles."

"Right you are, then." And Charles continued swinging his stick as dangerously as before.

Now, however, Robin saw to it that a safe distance was maintained between them. His shorter legs plodded manfully along through green lanes, by fields of yellowing corn, then by a sandy up-and-down path in the hazel-woods fringing the river. He was a well-built, bright-eyed child, small for his years. Had he not been dazzled by hero-worship, his darting perceptions might have seen his cousin funny.

"D'you know our cousin Rosie?" Charles asked presently.

"A bit. Mother's been taking an interest in Alastair."

"I thought she was married to Jack McNairn?"

"Alastair is the baby."

"I see." Charles reflected for a time. "I don't know anything about these cousins. What are they like?" he asked at length.

Privately, Robin thought the Jack McNairn family very tiresome. He had the natural recoil of any schoolboy from a young child that was strange to him, and he didn't like the child's mother. It had not escaped him that Rosie was uncharming and Jack McNairn was merely a grown-up cousin— a creature of no conceivable interest. But Robin felt it would be wrong to speak ill of Rosie, that his mother wouldn't like it, and that Charles might set him down as a gossip.

"What are they like?" Robin repeated Charles's words with a show of deliberation. "Oh, quite nice, I suppose. Alastair is delicate a bit."

"Then why don't they get him a nurse or something?" Charles asked. It was impossible for him to think of starting life without someone like the old Duntrafford nurse, Mrs. Crawford, who had nursed his dead Uncle Charlie, his mother, and finally himself.

"No money, I'm afraid." Robin's look proclaimed him the son of Henry Hayburn as he added: "If you ask me, Jack McNairn can hardly make salt to his kail."

"What's kail?" Charles asked, seriously interested.

"Cabbage. It's a Scotch word." Robin was pleased to find he had used an expression Charles did not know. "Not making salt to your kail means you can't earn enough money to live on," he said.

But now Charles merely looked aloof, hit the head of another thistle, and said: "I see. Always on the point of finding himself in Queer Street?"

Robin's quick wits could surmise what Queer Street meant, and he did not dare to ask, so he contented himself by saying: "I suppose so."

"Who *was* Rosie?" Charles asked presently.

"Was?"

"Yes. Before she married Jack. Who are her people?"

For a moment Robin wondered what to say. Didn't Charles know, then? Hadn't anybody told him Rosie's terrible secret? But Charles must know sooner or later. "Rosie was in a shop."

Charles stood still and looked at Robin. "A shopgirl?"

"So they say."

The elder boy walked on again in silence. Robin, wondering at his silence, began once more to fear he had offended.

At last Charles spoke: "Well, relatives are relatives. We must stand by them, whoever they are, mustn't we?"

II

Mrs. Arthur Moorhouse was coming to tea with Lady Ruanthorpe this afternoon. When Elizabeth Netherton heard this, she felt some alarm. She liked Mrs. Moorhouse, who had always been flatteringly kind to her. But now, at the end of this first week of August, it was a full month since Arthur and Elizabeth had promised to marry each other, and Elizabeth, her first emotions past, had begun to worry. How would Arthur's mother take it?

Since coming to Ayrshire she had learnt that the Moorhouses had had their beginnings here at the Laigh Farm as working tenant farmers; that ambition had driven all of them, except Mungo, to Glasgow, and that there these ambitions had been realised. They would, perhaps, look to realising them still further in their children. Was it likely, then, that they should want herself—an ordinary, musician's daughter—to become one of their number? Elizabeth's intelligence would not let her think so.

Yet Arthur loved her, and she loved Arthur. That, as her twenty years saw it, was all that mattered. But she wished now that their engagement were known to all the world. Not until it was would she feel safe.

Again, there was another, quite practical reason why she did not want to see Mrs. Moorhouse just this afternoon. Lady Ruanthorpe was old and fussy, and did not like to be left alone with a guest. But young Charles and his cousin Robin had come back from a visit to the Laigh Farm this morning, saying that Mrs. Jack McNairn was feeling very unwell, and that Mrs. Taggart, the wife of the grieve, was in distress about her. Margaret, finding it impossible to drive across herself, had begged Elizabeth to go immediately after tea. A dogcart would be sent to fetch her. All this had to be explained several times to a reluctant and objecting Lady Ruanthorpe.

Elizabeth expected Arthur's mother to arrive at the Dower House tea hour. She was surprised, therefore, to see her pass a window, elegantly shutting her parasol, half an hour before then. Elizabeth went to let her in.

III

Bel had no sort of idea how things stood between her son and this young woman. Deliberately at lunch today, seeking a sign, she had dropped the names of Arthur and Elizabeth Netherton side by side into the conversation.

And Margaret had responded, exclaiming at once: "Oh, Arthur and Elizabeth!" and laughed. But she had said no more, as, just then, the butler had reappeared in the dining-room.

"Arthur and Elizabeth, what?" Charles at once demanded.

But Margaret had merely smiled her vague, not-before-the-servants smile, and turned to tell Campbell that a basket of new-laid eggs, a pound of fresh butter and flowers must be made ready for Mrs. Arthur Moorhouse to take with her, back to Glasgow.

Margaret's quick exclamation and laugh had been anything but reassuring. It fixed Bel's determination to see Elizabeth alone, and—in the nicest way, of course—warn her to keep her distance from Arthur.

Lady Ruanthorpe, Bel learned, remained in her room until teatime. If she went across half an hour earlier, she would almost certainly find Elizabeth alone.

"You see, I feel a little responsible for Miss Netherton coming here, Margaret. It would only be kind to have a talk with her. And friendly, don't you think?"

Margaret saw no reason why Miss Netherton should be displeased with Bel's attentions. Hence the parasol elegantly shutting just outside the Dower House window sometime before four o'clock.

Bel's smile was nervously amiable—a little overgracious, indeed—as she greeted Elizabeth on the doorstep. "How are you, Miss Netherton? I came across early, just to ask you how you were getting on. They told me Lady Ruanthorpe would still be resting. I wanted to catch you by yourself." She gave the girl her hand, and followed her into the little Dower House drawing-room. "How pleasant it is here!" she said, sitting down and looking about her at the chairs covered with faded chintz, the family photographs in silver frames, the flowers. One of Sir Charles Ruanthorpe's house spaniels, a very old dog, was lying asleep in a splash of sunlight by the window. Outside the trees hung still and dark green in the afternoon sunshine. A pleasant room with a country distinction about it.

Elizabeth sat down, too. It was difficult to feel at ease, here in the presence of Arthur's mother. She wished with all her heart that the news was out—that the telling of it was over. It made her feel deceitful, somehow. And yet, was it not the most natural thing in the world for love to keep its secret for a time?

"It's very kind of you, Mrs. Moorhouse," she said lamely.

"The country seems to be agreeing with you. You look sunburnt," Bel smiled.

"I'm so much in the open air."

"Of course. If I meet Mrs. Netherton in Glasgow, I'll be able to tell her."

"I went home for a night last week. Just to see my parents."

"And how were they?"

"Very well, thank you."

"Did your parents tell you we had seen them in Brodick?"

"Yes, they did."

There was a pause. Each found herself smiling at the other in amiable vacancy. Each was doubtful of the other's next move.

"I do hope you like being here," Bel said a little desperately, adding: "You see, I feel it's my responsibility."

"Oh yes, Mrs. Moorhouse, I like it."

The hands of the clock on the mantelpiece told Bel that time was running on. Lady Ruanthorpe might appear at any moment. And she had not begun to turn the talk in the direction of Arthur. She cast about her for an opening. "I was afraid you might feel shut away from other young people." The remark, as she made it, sounded forced, but she had to begin somewhere.

203

Elizabeth allowed her eyes to twinkle. "Charles is a great friend of mine."

Bel's smile became bland. She gave the conversation a resolute twist. "No; I meant friends of your own age."

The girl's colour rose a little. "Oh, Mrs. Ruanthorpe-Moorhouse has been very kind. She invites me across very often when there are people."

"I'm glad. Yes. My son Arthur told me he had seen you." This was better. Bel felt she could go on from here. "Then you must know his friends, Jim and Winifred Ellerdale?"

"Yes."

"Nice, don't you think?"

"Very."

The clock ticked on. But Bel was coming nearer now. "Was Winifred Ellerdale's engagement a surprise to everybody here? Or did you expect it?"

"I don't know, Mrs. Moorhouse. Yes, I think we expected it. You see, she had brought her cousin a few days before, to introduce him. Everybody liked him."

"I'm glad." Bel stopped for a moment, gave a little laugh as though in excuse for the gossip she was about to allow herself, then said: "You know, Miss Netherton, we were almost afraid for my son Arthur to hear the news. We thought he was a little fond of Miss Ellerdale, you know."

Bel was surprised that Elizabeth did not respond to this manufactured gaiety. The girl's colour had deepened, that was all. But now she must finish. She was doing nothing that was cruel. She was merely issuing a sensible, hands-off warning.

"And in confidence, Miss Netherton, his father and I would not have been sorry if it *had* come to something. I can tell you this as a friend. Arthur is a good boy, and, naturally, both of us are anxious for him to make a good marriage." Bel hated this. It made her feel infinitely small to find herself talking

204

thus to this girl she scarcely knew. Still, Arthur was Arthur; the warning must be given, and now she had given it.

But as she turned to look at Elizabeth, she was surprised to see that the girl's face was crimson; that she—Bel—was being regarded by two smouldering eyes.

"What do you mean by a 'good' marriage, Mrs. Moorhouse?"

Why was Miss Netherton asking this? What did her expression mean? But Bel could only go on: "Well, good from every point of view. Goodness of heart. Goodness of looks. Goodness of manners. What else?"

"Good position in the world, Mrs. Moorhouse?"

"Of course. Wouldn't you want the same, if you were me?"

"Yes, I suppose so. If I were you."

A stab of apprehension ran through Bel. She wished she could feel calmer. Was the girl angry? Was she being impertinent? Or did—? But why had Elizabeth jumped up? Why was she standing now, her face turned away, looking from the window?

At a loss, Bel sat silent, watching Elizabeth's back and waiting. Suddenly the girl turned round. Bel could see now that there were tears in her eyes—whether of anger or distress, she could not tell.

But Elizabeth's next words decided that. "So you're warning me away from your son, Mrs. Moorhouse?"

"My dear girl! Why should I—? I never thought—" Bel stood up, too.

"You might have been a little less clumsy about it."

Bel gathered her pride about her. "Miss Netherton, I'm not used to being talked to like—"

"Oh, you are quite right!"

"Quite right, Miss Netherton?"

"Yes. I promised to marry your son Arthur four weeks ago."

"You—!"

"Yes."

Bel caught the mantelpiece and sought about to find words. "But why didn't he tell us?"

"I daresay, being your son, he was ashamed of falling in love with me." Impetuous anger had aimed these words at Bel. Yet almost before they were out of Elizabeth's mouth she knew they were unfair. But her father's obstinacy was hot within her. Her tears flowed freely, but they were not tears of weakness. She crossed from the window and faced Bel. "Don't worry, Mrs. Moorhouse. You can go back to Arthur and tell him he is as free as the air. I won't admit I am not good enough for him, but—"

"Miss Netherton, I didn't say that."

"Perhaps not, but you certainly thought it. Didn't you?"

"Well, I—"

"I knew it."

Bel was trembling. She, too, was angry. Elizabeth's outburst had surprised and shaken her. But might she not, after all, profit by the girl's hot-headedness? Might not this unpleasantness, and the unpleasantness that now must surely follow, yet result in disentangling Arthur? Might she not thus achieve what she had set out to do? It was difficult, for the moment, to act calmly. But she must try. And certainly do nothing to commit herself.

"I am sorry you feel like this, Miss Netherton," she said cautiously.

"So am I! I've nothing more to say, Mrs. Moorhouse. It's time I went to Lady Ruanthorpe."

Bel found herself standing alone, gazing at the door that Elizabeth had just shut behind her.

Elizabeth's state of mind took her safely through tea. Her anger at Bel Moorhouse stiffened her pride and forced her into a semblance of normality. Hot resentment bore her up, allowing her to do the things required of her: the arrangement of the tea-table; the right disposal of Lady Ruanthorpe by it. If somewhere, in the numbness of her senses, she was conscious of distress—a distress that must at last approach and over-whelm her—for the time, at least, she was surprised to find herself so calm. Calmer than Mrs. Moorhouse, indeed, who, flushed and scatterbrained, appeared to be allowing Lady Ruanthorpe to wrestle with the conversation.

And this mood persisted in Elizabeth when, tea being finished, she found herself, perched up beside a young groom in the Duntrafford dogcart, driving over to the Laigh Farm on her errand to Mrs. Jack McNairn. Outwardly things remained very much as usual. The afternoon sunshine was warm and mellow. The distances were lightly veiled by a summer haze. Berries were already turning red in the thorn hedges. She could perceive these things, find pleasure in them, almost, with the surface of her mind, though now she was aware that unhappiness and fear were moving nearer.

The young groom wondered at her animation. It was not usual for Miss Netherton to be so talkative, so restlessly excitable. The stables had, long since, declared in her favour; she was friendly and could see a joke; and she could control the more mischievous exuberances of Master Charlie. But now she was chattering recklessly. The boy beside her asked himself why.

In the Laigh Farm close the grieve's wife ran to meet her, helping her to descend. "I'm glad you've come, Miss Netherton. Did the Big House send ye? The lady's no' well!

To tell ye the truth, I was just goin' to send up to the fields to get one of the boys to go for the doctor."

Elizabeth was glad she could remain so collected. It kept her on the surface and gave occupation to her thoughts. "Have you any notion what's wrong, Mrs. Taggart?"

"I doubt it's fever. She'll eat nothing. She fed her bairn some time since, but she's worse since that. She's been lyin' greetin'. She's sure she's infectious. She thinks she's got something from tinkers that were in her railway carriage comin' here. She says they were that dirty, and that one o' their bairns was no' weel. She'll no' let me near her now."

"That's ridiculous! Where is she?"

The woman led the way into the farmhouse and up the scrubbed wooden staircase. She opened a door.

Elizabeth found herself standing by the bedside of a young woman. Rosie McNairn's eyes were closed, but she could see there had been tears. Her face was flushed unhealthily, and she moved her head restlessly on the pillow.

"Mrs. McNairn!" Elizabeth called, seeking to rouse her.

Rosie opened her eyes, seeming as though it took her a moment to focus them. "Who are you?" she asked.

"My name is Netherton. But never mind. I belong to Duntrafford. Mrs. Ruanthorpe-Moorhouse has sent me across to see how you are."

"I'm in for the fever or something. Will you send for the doctor? Oh, Jack should never have brought us here!" And Rosie, stripped now of all her usual pert confidence, began once more to cry.

Elizabeth became briskly cheerful. She was acting a part, in any case, this afternoon. It gave her little additional trouble to assume a mask of bright assurance—an assurance she certainly did not possess; for even her inexperience could see that the flush on Rosie's face was unnatural. "Oh, you'll be all right, Mrs. McNairn. Don't distress yourself. How do you feel?"

Rosie declared she felt hot and cold, that she had fits of violent shivering, was sick and had a racking head.

"You've caught a chill, I expect. I'll send the dogcart straight to fetch the doctor."

"Will you send a telegram to Jack?"

"Jack, Mrs. McNairn?"

"My husband."

"I don't think we should bother him unless we have to. We'll see what the doctor says."

"And what about him?" Rosie's eyes had been wandering—rather alarmingly, Elizabeth thought—but now they withdrew themselves from the dark beams of the ceiling and the crude pattern of the farmhouse wallpaper, and fixed themselves upon the old, wooden cradle of the Laigh Farm; the cradle that had, in its time, contained the three Moorhouse brothers and the three Moorhouse sisters; and now contained Alastair McNairn, the first of their grandchildren.

Elizabeth bent down to have a look at Rosie's baby. "He's all right. He's asleep," she said.

"But what if anything happens to me?" Rosie began to weep hysterically.

Elizabeth came back. "Look here, Mrs. McNairn, don't be silly. Pull yourself together. I'm going to straighten your bed and make you comfortable. And the doctor will be here immediately."

Even as she did so, it crossed Elizabeth's mind that if Mrs. McNairn were suffering from some contagion, this rearranging of her bed might be unsafe for herself. But her own distress had made her reckless. Did it matter now what she, Elizabeth, caught or did not catch?

"There," she said in a moment, "that's better. Now I'll tell

209

Mrs. Taggart I'm sending the doctor. He'll put you all right."

"Will you stay beside me?" Rosie implored.

"I can't do that. But I'll come again when I can." She bent quickly for a second time over the child, then left the room.

Elizabeth had spoken with Mrs. Taggart, and now, perched up once again in the dogcart, was driving quickly back the way she had come.

She had surprised her driver by the flow of her talk as they came. Now, returning, he marvelled at her silence.

Puzzled, he sought to break it. Was the young lady at the Laigh as ill as Mrs. Taggart thought?

Elizabeth feared she was. He must drive to the doctor and take him to the Laigh at once. To save time she, herself, would jump down as they passed the gatehouse, while he went on to the village.

But having said these things, Miss Netherton said no more. And the groom was left to wonder why she sat tearing at her handkerchief.

Rosie was a mere unhappy shadow in her mind now. Arthur's mother. Arthur. Anger had deserted Elizabeth, leaving her frightened and heartsick.

"There ye are, Miss. Will ye manage?" She had not realised that the dogcart was at a standstill before the Duntrafford gates.

"Oh, are we here already? I can get down, thank you. You will hurry, won't you?"

V

Elizabeth found herself continuing up the avenue on foot. The unhappiness that pursued her was now close behind, urging her to walk quickly.

What would Arthur say when his mother told him? How would he look? And what would his mother tell him? Would dislike distort her story? Would Mrs. Moorhouse go home and tell Arthur that she had proved beyond all doubt that she, Elizabeth, was a sharp-tongued adventuress—a nobody who had tried to catch him?

As though to get away from this thought, Elizabeth walked faster, arguing with herself in her excitement. No, really she wasn't. In all honesty, she wasn't. Arthur and she had met and loved each other quite simply, that was all.

In the distance there was the sound of carriage wheels. Quickly she drew her watch from her belt and looked at it. That must be Mrs. Moorhouse going to the railway station. Should she hide herself in the bushes until the carriage had passed? But why should she? Elizabeth controlled her steps, straightened herself, summoned her dignity and let the carriage come up the drive towards her. Now it was upon her. The head coachman, seeing her, touched his tall hat in greeting. She nodded in return. And was there a sign from a gloved hand inside? Elizabeth was not sure. But she bowed to the window stiffly and let the carriage pass.

But when it was out of sight she grasped her skirt and began to run. Unhappiness was upon her now; she could not escape it. Panting and sobbing, she hurried on, hardly knowing what she did.

It was only when she found herself in the Dower House standing in front of Lady Ruanthorpe and felt the old woman's eyes upon her that she came a little to her senses.

"My dear child! Whatever is wrong?"

"Nothing."

"Don't put me off like that! Has anything happened at the farm?"

"No, not exactly. I sent for the doctor, Lady Ruanthorpe."

211

"Well, what is there to be upset about? What is it? Come here, Miss Netherton. Sit down on my footstool and tell me. Come at once when I tell you! I may be old and ugly—"

"Oh no, Lady Ruanthorpe!"

"Don't contradict, Miss Netherton. I said ugly. And old! But I can still feel some things. And I've lived longer and felt more things than you have. What is it, my dear?" The old woman's voice softened as she laid, for a moment, a hand that was stiff and wrinkled upon the girl's hair.

This show of sympathy destroyed the last of Elizabeth's self-control. She sat bent on the stool at Lady Ruanthorpe's feet, weeping and telling her story.

The old woman sat upright, listening, and blinking shortsightedly before her. One hand rested on her ebony stick. The other sought, now and then, the dark head beside her. The sorrows of the young, she reflected, were, at most times, fleeting. Bereavement and irreparable grief usually came later. But young sorrow could be sore enough. And she was not so old, so drained of sensibility, that her heart could no longer understand it.

Now, as she sat listening, Lady Ruanthorpe's face darkened. Who were the Moorhouses, anyway? She and Sir Charles had made no objection when Margaret had wanted to marry their tenant, Mungo Moorhouse. Margaret had been thirty-eight, and wouldn't get anybody else anyway. And Mungo was all right. He knew better than give himself airs. But who did this Mrs. Bel Moorhouse think she was? An upstart town woman who seemed to imagine she was royalty! And this girl? Her father was a farmer's son, and her mother was a daughter of the manse. What was wrong with that? She was as good as any Moorhouse.

Lady Ruanthorpe moved Elizabeth aside and got up. "My dear Miss Netherton, you really mustn't take this to heart," she said. "I'm going to fetch you some wine." For a moment she remained standing over her.

"I must leave here!" Elizabeth cried. "I can't stay here any longer. Not after today."

The old woman stiffened. "You'll do nothing of the kind." She spoke angrily. "You'll stay here and stand your ground. Do you hear me? And you'll discuss this with nobody. At least you can keep your dignity, and leave the others to lose theirs. If that boy's worth his salt, he'll come to you, mother or no mother. And if he doesn't, he's not worth having." Lady Ruanthorpe began stumping from the room. At the door she turned. "Cheap, town snobbery was a thing that Sir Charles could never endure," she added, and her voice was sharp with contempt.

Chapter Sixteen

BEL arrived home utterly exhausted. She had gone to Duntrafford intending to drop a firm but gracious hint— a hint that would, as she had put it to herself, protect the young people from their own inexperience.

It wasn't only her son Arthur. For, after all, Elizabeth Netherton was a very nice child, too—according to her station, of course—and needed protection just as much as he did. Having got herself thus far along the road of self-deception, Bel had not stopped to question from whom, exactly, Elizabeth must be protected.

But now at their meeting everything had gone wrong. Bel was not even sure that she herself had got the best of it. The news of a secret engagement between Arthur and this girl had been a great shock. And really, Elizabeth's show of anger and pride had been very disturbing.

And, as a result, the girl had declared that Arthur might now consider himself free! Did Elizabeth mean this? Would she write and tell him? Or would she leave it to herself, Bel, to tell him? There was a bleak ray of light here. But Bel shrank back from the telling. For what would she say to her son? That she, his mother, had gone down to Duntrafford and broken off his engagement? The boy would never forgive her.

This thought began to dominate all the others. Her son Arthur would hate her. She had done this for his good. But it would be hard indeed to make his folly see this. And now, perhaps, she had set up a barrier between herself and him that would never again be broken down.

She was thankful, on the journey home, to have a railway carriage to herself. Here, at least, she need not heed appearances. She could relax, give way to self-pity, search her feelings and decide what next she must do.

Bel was not a hard woman. If the girl had shown anything but quick anger and icy pride, if she had wept and pleaded her love for Arthur, Bel's ambition might have given way to her, at times, highly inconvenient tenderness of heart.

But what was she to tell her son? Bel's thoughts went round and round. No. It was a problem she could not face tonight. She was too shaken, too exhausted.

This brought Bel to a decision. She would go home, report an ordinary visit to Duntrafford, and go at once to bed, pleading, very truthfully, that she was tired.

But as she lay in the darkness some hours later, thinking, she became aware of a hot resentment against life in general, and against her own family in particular. There was her husband Arthur, for instance, sleeping the noiseless sleep of a boy beside her. He had asked her if she had had a nice day in the country, and continued to read his evening paper, scarcely looking up. Tom and Isabel had merely looked in upon her, as she sat solitary over her late meal, to say: "Hullo, Mother! Back all right?" And young Arthur, who was the storm-centre of this whole unfortunate affair, had put his head round the dining-room door to ask: "Have they laid the foundation of the tennis-court yet?"

Bel had jumped nervously at the sight of him. But this son, whose thoughts she had always insisted she could read like a book, had merely exclaimed: "What's wrong, Mother? Did I give you a fright?" And thereafter continued asking about the Duntrafford tennis-court.

Bel had been appalled at his calm and practised deceitfulness. Keying herself up, she had replied: "I went across to see Lady Ruanthorpe this afternoon. I had tea with her and Elizabeth Netherton." But even before this news Arthur had been the very mirror of offhand unconcern.

Yes, the family took her too much for granted. They did not consider for a moment how she kept scheming and exhausting herself for them. It wasn't fair. Bel turned in bed and sighed. Lying wide-eyed in the small hours staring into the darkness, she almost found it in her heart to hate them.

Presently she wept a little and felt better. Oh, she didn't hate them. They were her own, and very dear to her.

Still, Arthur's behaviour tonight had stiffened her. She had no intention of giving way over this affair. Whether she brought the trouble to a head herself, or whether it developed of its own accord, for everybody's sake she must stand firm.

II

But it is difficult to stand firm in a vacuum. Bel found nothing to stand firm against.

Next morning she came down early, expecting to see a letter with an Ayrshire postmark addressed to her elder son—a letter which would, in all probability, occasion an explosion and give her something to stand firm about. But there was no such letter. Young Arthur appeared, said: "Good morning," got through his ham and eggs with his usual hurry and preoccupation, then went off to work, accompanied by his father.

After these had gone, Bel sat on, her elbows on the table, a cup of tea held in both hands. She sipped it reflectively, staring before her.

So Elizabeth Netherton had not yet written? There might

216

be a letter later in the day. She must watch for it. Or would Elizabeth herself come to Glasgow to see Arthur and her parents? And were her parents in on the young people's secret? And did they sympathise?

Bel refilled her cup and put her elbows back on the table. Of course they would sympathise! Why, indeed, shouldn't they? Their daughter had everything to gain from a union with her son. Most probably, indeed, Elizabeth's parents had encouraged it.

But here even Bel felt that her appalling Lowland Scots shrewdness was going too far. Elizabeth's mother was a foolish little woman, perhaps, but she was neither sly nor scheming. And as for John Netherton, he was morose and graceless. But somehow, it was impossible to imagine him occupying himself with any such plans for his daughter's advancement.

John Netherton. Now the thought of him troubled her. She had had one sharp rebuff from him already. Yes, an encounter with John Netherton would give her something to stand firm about. It was not, indeed, impossible that Elizabeth might appear here today, accompanied by a father come to demand an explanation. Bel took a large and hasty gulp of hot tea. It did little to dispel the sick emptiness that had invaded her stomach. Yet, cost what it must, and though he did come, she must stand firm.

"Good gracious, Mother! What are you looking so grim about?"

Isabel had come down, followed by Tom, both of them late for breakfast.

In her preoccupation, Bel was scarcely aware of their coming. She withdrew her eyes from whatever they had fixed their stare upon, allowed her face to soften and asked: "Grim, dear? Why should you think I was looking grim?"

"But you *were* looking grim, Mother," Tom said.

"I'm a little tired after yesterday, perhaps," Bel told her younger children gently.

"How was everybody at Duntrafford?" Isabel asked offhandedly, reaching for toast and butter.

"Very well, dear."

"Nothing new?"

"Nothing." And Bel hastened to cover this flagrant but necessary lie, both from herself and her children, by inquiring of Isabel: "Did you see Winifred Ellerdale yesterday?"

"Yes. And Mrs. Ellerdale. They were choosing clothes for Winifred."

Bel sighed at the thought of Winifred's wedding.

"We all had lunch together," Tom announced, much to Bel's surprise.

"You, too?" she asked.

"Yes. Jim telephoned. I happened to answer. He asked me to lunch in Ferguson and Forrester's, too. Said he didn't want to be the only man."

"Then it was quite a party!" Any regrets Bel might feel were covered now by her practised smile. "Nice Jim was able to be there."

"So Isabel thought anyway." Here Tom directed a large, tactless schoolboy wink in his mother's direction.

But for once Bel's curiosity was numb.

The clock struck ten. Outside the door Sarah was hovering sulkily, rattling a tray to remind them that it was late and that she wanted to clear away breakfast.

Bel got up. Yes, something must happen today. But what? She wished, whatever it was, that it would come.

218

She felt restless. Isabel and Tom had now gone out. Hanging round an empty house was intolerable. Bel determined to visit her mother. In this, at least, she could safely count on Mrs. Barrowfield's sympathy.

But she had better let her know she was coming, now that each had a telephone. She went to her own, turned the handle with energy, then gave her mother's number.

It took some time to receive any reply. The man at the exchange, indeed, asked Bel more than once if she were quite sure there would be someone at that number. But at last there were signs of life. Bel could recognise old Maggie's cracked voice, high-pitched and terrified, calling: "Yes, yes! Whit are ye ringing for?"

"It's me, Maggie—Miss Bel speaking."

"Miss Bel's no' here. She's oot at her hoose at Kelvinside."

"It's Miss Bel *speaking* to you. Keep calm, and don't shout so loud."

"I don't know whit ye're sayin'."

Bel dropped her voice, persuasive and firm. "It's Miss Bel. You must hear that."

"Oh, Miss Bel?"

"Yes. That's better." Maggie, Bel felt, had taken a step towards modernity. "Can you hear me now, Maggie?"

"Whit's that? Hear ye? Ay, I can hear ye."

"That's splendid, Maggie!"

"Whit? Oh ay? Ye just said 'Maggie'."

Now she had got some sense from her mother's old servant, why not try Mrs. Barrowfield herself? "That's right. Well, tell Mrs. Barrowfield I must speak to her. Say it's about Miss Netherton." The name Netherton would surely bring the old lady's curiosity to the telephone.

"Miss who?"

With infinite patience, Bel succeeded in teaching Maggie to repeat the name, finishing the struggle with a sigh and an encouraging: "That's it now, Maggie!"

"And whit am I to say aboot her?"

"Mention her name, and ask my mother to come to the telephone. That's all."

Bel stood in the hall waiting and listening for what seemed an eternity. The front doorbell rang. Sarah appeared to receive some letters from the postman. She left them on the hall table beside Bel. Bel fingered them impatiently. They were only bills. Again the doorbell rang. Sarah reappeared. This time it was a man offering to grind scissors. Sarah shook her head and shut the door. Still Bel stood waiting.

At last there were sounds of fumbling. Bel became alert. Had she accomplished the impossible? Was her mother going to speak? "Hullo, Mother. Are you there?" Her voice was warm with encouragement. But presently, after more fumbling, Maggie's voice said: "Ye're mother says she's no' speaking to no Miss Netherton."

"But I said she was to speak to me *about* Miss Netherton!"

"Whit's that?"

But Bel had given up. With a quick: "Oh, say I'm coming to see her", addressed more to her own impatience than to the telephone, she hung up and began ascending to her room. When she was half-way upstairs the telephone bell rang. She went down again and listened.

"Have ye finished speakin'?" she heard the exchange man's voice ask.

"Yes, thank you."

"Well, the other folks havena hung up right."

"Then you had better ring them, not me." Bel's voice was sharp with ill temper. But she heard herself, and was ashamed.

She was accustomed to see herself as the pleasant, cool centre of her own household, a creature of much gentle poise. That waspish voice had nothing to do with such a person. She was losing hold of herself. She must go out.

IV

As she stood waiting for a tram-car, Bel began to feel better. It was a clear mid-August day. The light breeze was refreshing. Things seemed more normal. She looked about her, taking note that Great Western Road seemed singularly empty. She felt herself regretting a little that this summer's arrangements should have forced herself and hers to be unfashionably at home during August. The tram-car, too, was strangely empty—empty, that was, of importance. One or two nondescript women going in to town, that was all.

As the horses halted opposite the Hillhead Steps, her niece, Polly Butter, came in and sat down beside her.

"Oh, good morning, Auntie Bel!"

Bel was not displeased to have her mind distracted by her good-natured, plump little relative. "Good morning, my dear," Bel said, a little formally perhaps, as was fitting, but still with affection. "How are you? And how is that husband of yours?"

Polly's round face blushed becomingly at the word "husband" and her smile broadened. "Oh, Wil's splendid. We're both splendid. And you're looking splendid, too, Auntie Bel."

Bel smiled indulgently. She was not feeling splendid. She was feeling worn, middle-aged and disillusioned. Still, she was touched by the morning splendour so rosily misting the eyes of this little beholder—a splendour that was so frail, so ephemeral. When Polly had sons of twenty-one— "Yes, dear," she said. "I'm very well."

221

But now Polly looked serious in so far as nineteen-year-old married rapture can look serious. "Have you heard about Jack's wife, Auntie Bel?"

"Yes. I was at Duntrafford yesterday. I hear she's staying at your Uncle Mungo's farm."

"Yes, but she's seriously ill."

"I didn't hear about that." Now Bel remembered Lady Ruanthorpe had said something at teatime. In her effort to master herself after her encounter with Elizabeth, Bel had paid little heed. "Oh yes, I did hear something. Lady Ruanthorpe's companion was being sent to find out how she was."

"Well, she has fever. Typhus. Jack got a telegram from Uncle Mungo first thing this morning. And Jack telephoned to us. You see, we had to get a telephone. Wil says all up-to-date young business men must have telephones. Jack was asking Wil to explain to his master why he wouldn't be working this morning. Isn't it terrible, Auntie Bel?" Polly looked now as though she rather enjoyed the importance of the telling.

"Yes indeed, Polly. Where did she catch fever?"

"We don't know yet. Uncle Mungo's telegram only said Rosie had typhus, and Jack had better come to Duntrafford at once."

Bel sat forward considering, her gloved hands folded over the crook of her parasol, swaying back and forth with the movement of the tram-car. Typhus at the Laigh Farm? Who had been there? Who was in danger of infection? Mungo, of course. He went to the farm every day. But he would be in the fields, not in the house. She remembered now that young Charles and young Robin had been at the Laigh yesterday. They had seen the child Alastair. But probably they had not touched him. She hoped they had not. For how could the poor little thing escape infection, since he was constantly in

222

his mother's arms? "Did the telegram mention the baby, my dear?" she asked.

"No, Auntie Bel. It would be terrible if Alastair—" Now Polly was solemn.

"It would be difficult for him to escape."

"Is typhus very infectious?"

"I've always heard it was."

Polly did not reply to this. She merely sat considering.

The brakes were screaming as the tram-car made its way down Renfield Street. The horses had dropped to a walk. Bel looked out on the dusty August street. In a few moments they would have reached the terminus.

Her own preoccupations would not let her be. Arthur. Elizabeth Netherton. The girl's angry face in the Dower House. Elizabeth's apparent composure as she gave them tea. Her cold goodbye as she left to go to the Laigh.

Polly wondered why her Aunt Bel's body had stiffened. She was sitting now, alert and upright. What had happened? Polly wondered if she had said something to offend.

Elizabeth Netherton had been to the Laigh, too, then. Had she seen Rosie? Had she risked infection? Bel remembered how, later, she had passed Elizabeth's expressionless, upturned face in the main avenue.

The tram-car had come to a standstill at St. Vincent Place. Everyone was getting out. Bel was glad to find her niece holding out a hand and apologising for leaving her thus abruptly. She must meet her mother and sister, she said. Bel's inattention did not catch where.

Left alone on the pavement, Bel stood considering. In some way, she felt, the news Polly had given her would alter everything. Yet how? What could it alter? If only she knew more!

If Elizabeth were infected? Suppose she were to die? Was it not, after all, because of herself, Bel, that the girl had gone to Duntrafford? What would John Netherton and his wife have to say? Would they lay Elizabeth's death at her door?

Should she walk across to her husband's office and ask if he had further news? No. Her son would be there, and she could not face him again this morning.

Bel sighed. She would walk down Buchanan Street and take another tram-car along Argyll Street to Monteith Row. The little bit of walk might help to clear this brain of hers writhing with conjecture. She was stepping from the kerb when someone caught her arm.

"Hullo!"

"David!"

"Is anything wrong, Bel? You were looking about as if you had lost something."

"Was I?" She looked up at him and smiled. "I'm tired, David."

"Tired? Did you go to Duntrafford?"

"Yesterday."

"And did you see the young woman?"

"Yes."

"That explains your tiredness." David laughed. "Well, you got it over, anyway. And I am sure you would do it beautifully."

Bel had been pleased to see David. She had wanted, indeed, just David's kind of sympathy. But his light-hearted picture of herself dropping charming but unmistakable warnings clashed with the picture of her real meeting with Elizabeth—a meeting with rough edges, angry words and hot resentment. "No, David. It was much more serious than that."

"What do you mean?"

"I am going down to Argyll Street. Walk down with me."

He took her arm and guided her safely across St. Vincent Place. It was getting near to midday, and the sun was shining hot above Buchanan Street. Bel could not continue to be displeased with David. This chance meeting with her old fellow-conspirator was wine and oil in her wounds.

They made a striking couple, this well-favoured brother and sister-in-law. Bel, fair and regal, walked with an air that somehow subtracted years rather than added to them. David's faultless frock-coat adorned a body that was gaining in importance what it was losing of youth. His hair still curled a little at the temples beneath the brim of his tall hat. But there, and on his cheeks, it was become darker, and now there were threads of white. But the advance into middle age was something of a triumphal march for both of them. People turned to look at their distinction, as they moved slowly down, arm-in-arm, talking earnestly beneath Bel's frilled parasol. These were folks of consequence.

Surely such a couple could not be troubled by the foolish independence of a young woman—a mere companion, a nobody?

Arrived at the foot of the street, Bel withdrew her arm and stood looking up at him. "So there I was, David. It was anything but pleasant. If I had known there was an engagement already I would never have—"

"She has given him up, hasn't she?"

"Yes. But she won't expect him to accept that."

David's eyes were following the traffic in Argyll Street. But Bel could see that their movement was mechanical. What was

225

he thinking, remembering? But now they blinked and came back to reality. "Still, you never know."

"She's not a wicked girl, or anything," Bel said quickly, with what seemed to David to be feminine irrelevance. "It's only just that she's—"

"I know." David knew.

Bel shrugged and held out her hand. "There's a car that will take me along."

He watched her as she closed her parasol, stepped up, and waved back a little ruefully.

VI

Bel turned, went inside and sat down. Alone once more, she remembered she was tired and that the day was hot. She regretted a little that she had taken this tram, the route of which lay in a working quarter of the city. It smelt stuffily of unwashed bodies.

In a far corner a dirty child was murmuring and complaining. Two women opposite with shawls over their heads were eyeing every detail of her clothes, their mouths gaping, stupid and curious. As she raised a white-gloved hand to stifle a yawn, their eyes followed it up to her face and back to her lap again.

But this second tram journey was, at least, short. Bel descended, thankful to be once more in the fresh air. The women's eyes followed her to the last. They turned to look at her, watching from the window, as the horses trotted out of sight. Now she was glad to find herself in her mother's sitting-room. The windows were open, and the trees before it rustled pleasantly in a light midday breeze.

Mrs. Barrowfield's reception was, as usual, fussy; but Bel

226

was ready for that. The old lady, she knew, would presently be done.

Yes, thanks, she would stay for a meal. Yes, she had come by tram. Yes, it had been exhausting. No, she did not quite know why she had not used the carriage, but at any rate here she was. Thus patiently did Bel cut her way through to the mother she had come to see.

It was only after their meal, when the mechanisms of life—mechanisms which go slowly with the very old—were over, and they found themselves settled together by the window, that Bel could begin her story.

Here, of all places, would she be certain to find the support she needed. (Was it not her mother who had given the first warning?) And on the whole she found it.

Mrs. Barrowfield listened with attention, exclaiming: "Did I not tell ye?" several times, in a manner that would have caused Bel sharp irritation had she been less eager for sympathy. And she appeared comfortingly shocked, too, by the news of the secret engagement.

"And was the lassie no' frightened to tell ye?"

"Frightened, Mother? She was very angry."

"Angry, Bel? At you?"

"Yes."

Mrs. Barrowfield said nothing.

Bel now remembered that there were few things that appealed to the old woman more than a show of spirit in the young. She was for ever complaining, indeed, that the young were backboneless. Elizabeth Netherton's having shown spirit would not count in her disfavour.

"But she said I was to tell Arthur he was quite free," Bel added hurriedly.

"And have ye told him?"

"No, Mother. I haven't had the chance."

227

"Ye'll have to tell him. And ye'll have to tell his father too," Mrs. Barrowfield said with foolish relish.

Bel's overwrought nerves gave way. The old woman was much surprised to see her daughter suddenly burst into tears.

Chapter Seventeen

O N THE SAME EVENING young Arthur Moorhouse, along with the others, was just finishing his meal, when Phœbe Hayburn burst into Grosvenor Terrace. She stood over them as they still sat at table.

"Phœbe, dear! Where have you come from?" Bel turned to look at her.

"Home. But I'm going to Duntrafford with a late train. Have you heard the news?"

"What? About Rosie McNairn?"

"Yes. Typhus. Jack McNairn went down this morning. He wasn't allowed to see Rosie. But he saw Alastair. He came back to Glasgow late this afternoon. Mungo had told him to get a fever nurse and bring her back at once. I've been helping to find one. We're all going down tonight."

"Why are *you* going, Aunt Phœbe?" Isabel asked.

"Because I'm worried to death. Robin was at the Laigh with Charles yesterday morning. I don't know if the boys were near infection." Anxiety made Phœbe flushed and sullen. "I must go down at once and find out."

Bel tried to reassure her. "I saw the boys at lunchtime, Phœbe. They didn't say they had gone into the farmhouse. I don't think they did. But it was they who brought back the news that Rosie McNairn was ill. Margaret sent Elizabeth Netherton over in the afternoon to see Rosie."

Arthur became alert. He looked at his mother, and wondered why she had gone red to the roots of her hair.

The talk was going on.

229

"Did Miss Netherton actually see Rosie?" Isabel inquired.

His Aunt Phœbe answered. "Yes. Jack says Elizabeth Netherton was in Rosie's room for some time."

"Then I hope Miss Netherton didna get the fever," Arthur Senior said.

The young man started.

"And what about the poor baby?" Isabel asked.

"Miss Netherton promised Jack she would go to the Laigh and look after him. She said she had risked infection, so she might as well go on risking it."

"Good lassie!" his father said.

Phœbe nodded. "Yes, she's good."

"Does that mean that Rosie and Alastair and Miss Netherton and the nurse will all be isolated together at the Laigh?" young Tom asked.

Again Phœbe nodded. She looked at the clock. "I must run for the train."

Young Arthur jumped to his feet. He must stop Elizabeth doing this! The McNairns could get all the help they needed. What right had she to expose herself to danger? She did not belong to the McNairns. She belonged to him. "I'm coming to Duntrafford with you, Aunt Phœbe!" he shouted after her as she went.

"You, Arthur? Why?" his mother asked.

"Because I must."

Bel had risen, too. She followed him as he went for his coat and hat. "Arthur! Why are you going?"

"Because, I tell you, I must."

"But, Arthur, you can't. I've got something to say to you. I must speak to you tonight. And what about your things?"

"Uncle Mungo will lend me things."

"Arthur, it's about Miss Netherton. I had a talk with her yesterday."

"What's wrong, Arthur?" His father was in the hall, too. Phœbe was opening the front door and signing to the cabman. "Father, please!"

But his mother still persisted. "Arthur! When I ask you!"

"Tomorrow, Mother, when I get back."

He broke from her, turned, bounded down the steps and jumped into Phœbe's cab.

II

The cabman banged the door, got up and drove off.

"Well, Arthur? Would you like to tell me what all this is about?" Phœbe's Highland eyes were upon him.

His reticence fought against the compulsion of them. But now it seemed he must answer. "Aunt Phœbe, I'm in love with Elizabeth Netherton."

"I thought it must be something like that."

He looked up, expecting, in his young man's foolishness, to find a look of amusement.

But Phœbe Hayburn had grown up with him. It was an old story that Arthur was her favourite nephew. Now he found only encouragement.

They did not speak again for a time. Explanation could wait.

The cabman, admonished by Phœbe, was urging his horse towards town and St. Enoch's Station. The cab shook and rattled as the nag's hastening, uneasy trot, developed, now and then, into a rocking-horse canter. Already the August dusk was falling. Lamp-lighters were at work.

Arthur moved in his seat uneasily. "You're the first person I've told," he said presently.

"Why?" She turned to look at him.

For the life of him he could not tell why. Or, at all events, he could not think of a reply that would truthfully give his feelings. Boyish shyness before a first passion are difficult things to make plain.

But she did not press him. "Are you frightened Elizabeth catches fever?" she asked.

"Yes. I must try to stop her from going to the Laigh."

Phœbe's courage liked people who took risks. "I'm not sure that you should. They'll need all the help they can get up there," she said.

"It's all very well for you to say that. What if—?"

She turned again to look at him. The words were spoken hotly. And he was looking out of the window now, twisting the leather window-strap with restless, unhappy fingers. Phœbe was moved. But an elaborate show of sympathy was not in her make-up. "It'll be all right, Arthur," was all she said. Then, as the cab was climbing the ramp leading to St. Enoch's Station, she added: "There's Jack with the nurse, waiting. We'll tell them your mother and father have sent you down tonight, so that you can bring them back news in the morning."

III

It was easy for Arthur to drop off at the Dower House. The Laigh Farm gig had picked up Jack McNairn and the nurse at the village railway station, leaving himself and Phœbe to go to Duntrafford.

The velvet darkness was about them as they lay back in the carriage. But Phœbe, once more in the country of her childhood, could always tell where they were from dips and turns of the road, from the echoes of the horse's hooves in the trees above them, from the flash of a cottage light.

232

Now they were in the drive.

Arthur sat up. "Tell me when we get to the Dower House," he said.

"But it's nearly eleven."

"I must try to see Elizabeth tonight!"

"Lady Ruanthorpe goes to bed early."

"It doesn't matter. I must try."

"All right. We'll see a light if there's anybody still about."

And there was a light. Arthur called to the coachman, and got down.

The front door of the Dower House was bolted for the night, but the blinds had not been lowered in the lamplit drawing-room. He went to a window and looked in. Lady Ruanthorpe sat by the fire, scanning a newspaper with the help of a magnifying-glass. Sir Charles's old spaniels lay on the rug in front of her. Arthur looked for Elizabeth. She was not to be seen.

For a moment the old woman continued reading, unaware of any movement outside. But the dogs began to bristle, then to bark, causing her to cast dazed glances about her.

Arthur went to the front door and knocked.

In answer, there was a still greater barking of the dogs; then, in a surprisingly short time, the drawing of a bolt. A servant must have heard. Or better, perhaps, Elizabeth herself.

But when the door was opened it was Lady Ruanthorpe—quite fearless, it would seem, of the night or of a latecomer.

"Who is it?" She looked into the darkness blankly.

Arthur was embarrassed. In his excitement it had not occurred to him he would have to explain his late appearance to this imperious old woman. "It's Arthur, Lady Ruanthorpe," he said lamely, holding out his hand.

She stood leaning on her ebony stick, gathering her wits. The spaniels had come out from behind their mistress, and were showing their teeth. "Who did you say you were?" she said, seeking to identify Arthur's features in the beam of light escaping from the door.

"Arthur. Arthur Moorhouse, Lady Ruanthorpe."

"I can't hear a word for those beasts!" she said crossly. "You had better come in." She prodded the dogs with her stick, then stumped before him into the drawing-room. Once there, she turned round to examine him with that cold, somewhat glassy stare that goes, sometimes, with old age and lifelong habits of authority. "I see who you are now," she said. "You're the Moorhouse young man from Glasgow."

Lady Ruanthorpe's reception had done nothing so far to remove his embarrassment. To Arthur, Lady Ruanthorpe had never been more than a rather tart, formal old lady. But he could not stand here in the lamplight without giving some account of himself. "Yes. I've just come down from Glasgow with Aunt Phœbe. She drove straight to the House. I dropped off here."

"Why?" The old eyes, pale, tired and commanding, were still upon him. Yet, if his confusion had allowed him to look straight into them, Arthur might now have detected a glint of wickedness.

But, for her own reasons, she had turned from him without waiting for an answer, and was poking a lump of coal in the dying fire with her stick. "There. That's better!" She settled herself once more into her chair, leaned forward on the stick, and looked into the flames she had just stirred up, as though she had forgotten her question.

Still the young man stood waiting.

Presently she looked up. "You must be tired," she said. "If you go into the dining-room, you will find a decanter on the sideboard and a box of biscuits. Take one of the candles from the hall table if it's too dark."

234

He did as he was told.

Lady Ruanthorpe had turned again to the fire. The wrinkles it illumined had formed themselves into a smile. She was remembering her words to Elizabeth: "If that boy's worth his salt, he'll come to you!"

So the boy had come. In spite of his silly, upstart mother. Sir Charles had always said the Moorhouses had a core to them. Even in the days when he and she had known them only as hard-working farmer lads. Now it was showing itself in the next generation. She was glad. For, after all, her own grandson was half a Moorhouse.

She was pleased with this large, fair young man, who was back in the room, sitting awkward and silent, and helping himself to wine and biscuits. But she was determined to give him no help. Though now she knew very well whom he was seeking.

"So you came down with Phœbe Hayburn?" Lady Ruanthorpe said by way of breaking silence.

"Yes. And Jack McNairn and a nurse." He sat alert, looking about the room and at the door, as though he expected someone to come in.

"Oh, I'm glad they've got a nurse."

Again there was a strained pause.

"Wine all right?"

"Yes, thank you, Lady Ruanthorpe." Then, after a moment: "Is there any news from the Laigh tonight?"

"Well, I don't know what you've heard. The whole farm is quarantined, of course. Your uncle has given orders to throw away the cows' milk even, as, of course, nobody will want it. Although, actually, very few people have been in contact with your cousin's wife and child."

"Has the child caught fever, Lady Ruanthorpe?"

"No, not yet. We can't tell for a bit, of course."

And now, at last, the question she was waiting for: "Who's looking after the child, Lady Ruanthorpe?"

No, she would make his impatience say it. "They say typhus may take some days to develop, even in a very young child."

"Is Elizabeth Netherton looking after the baby?"

"Yes." She raised her eyes to look at him.

"Is she there now? Oh!—I'm sorry." The thin stem of his wineglass had snapped in his fingers.

"Never mind. There wasn't much left to spill. I see there's another glass on the tray."

As he jumped up in confusion, the old woman continued talking: "Yes, Miss Netherton went across this afternoon. That's why I'm alone tonight. You see, she had been in contact already, so she felt that she—"

"Lady Ruanthorpe, why did you let her go?"

"Why should I stop her? She couldn't very well stay here and risk spreading infection. Could she?"

He was standing over her now, looking flushed and feckless. She waited for him to speak, to make his confession to her, but words seemed impossible.

"Why do you mind so much about this, Arthur?"

He put a hand on the mantelpiece, and for a moment his lip trembled. But at last the words came: "Because we have promised to marry each other, Lady Ruanthorpe."

IV

To his surprise, she turned from his confusion with no show of wonder. She leant forward, and once more she stirred the fire with her stick. "Of course. I was forgetting," she said.

He could not believe that she had understood him. "Forgetting?"

236

"Yes. Elizabeth Netherton told me two days ago." Then, after an instant in which her inward eye saw a fashionably dressed woman with much distaste, she added: "Yes. You see, Miss Netherton had been discussing it with your mother."

"Mother!"

"Why not? Didn't your mother tell you?"

"No."

"How odd! I thought she had given your mother a message for you."

The old spaniels at Lady Ruanthorpe's feet raised their heads, sniffed and wagged their stumps of tails as though they saw a third person in the room. Was it the wraith of their gruff old master, Sir Charles, come to tell his wife to stop this frivolous, sentimental frisking with the young people's love affairs?

But she and he had always made a point of disobeying each other whenever they felt like it, and though she might feel the presence, it could not stop her now.

"Message, Lady Ruanthorpe? What kind of message?"

"I understand Miss Netherton told your mother you might consider yourself quite free from any engagement to her."

Arthur sat down again. He looked at her with eyes that were full of misery and doubt. "Why, Lady Ruanthorpe? And why didn't Mother tell me?"

"Perhaps your mother didn't think it important."

"Important!"

The spaniels had gone to sleep again. The wraith, it seemed, had withdrawn himself in disgust.

"Then you had better go back to your mother and ask her all about it."

"I must see Elizabeth first!"

"You can't. She's in quarantine." Was Lady Ruanthorpe actually looking a little smug? Was she pleased in some way with how things were going?

237

He sought to touch her sympathies. "Lady Ruanthorpe, Elizabeth's life may be in danger."

Deliberately, she added fuel to the flames of his distress. "Yes. Miss Netherton is a brave girl."

Again the fire was burning low. The old dogs snuffed and snorted in their sleep. The marble clock on the mantelpiece ticked away the seconds.

Arthur sat silent, his handsome features glum with unhappiness, seeking a key to things he could not understand.

His mother. She had moulded him so much after her own desires that it was difficult for him to see her actions as anything but right.

But what had she said to Elizabeth—the Elizabeth that she herself had drawn into the circle, extolling her excellences? What had happened between them? What had she done, that Elizabeth should want to be free? And why hadn't he been told? He remembered now that she had sought to stop him from coming here tonight. Didn't she want him to see Elizabeth, then?

A dog, hearing one of the servants outside, raised his fat body, got up and slowly went to the door. Arthur came back to his surroundings to find Lady Ruanthorpe's eyes still upon him.

"If I write a letter to Elizabeth, Lady Ruanthorpe, will you see she gets it in the morning?"

The door opened. A maidservant had come to attend the old woman to bed.

"I let Mr. Arthur Moorhouse in myself," Lady Ruanthorpe said, answering the woman's surprise. "Is there anyone still about who can take word over to the House that he's staying here tonight?"

"Yes, Ma'am."

"All right. Tell them to get a room ready for him here. I'm

just coming." Lady Ruanthorpe got up and stood leaning on her stick. "I thought you wouldn't want to be bothered going over and answering questions. You'd better see your room, then come down again and write your letter. And be sure you put out the lamps properly. I don't want the house set on fire." She held out her hand. "Good night, Arthur."

"Good night, Lady Ruanthorpe, and thanks very much." He searched her face, bewildered. But now, though there was still a smile, there was no longer any hint of mockery. It was merely the wrinkled smile of a tired old woman, seeking to be kind.

Lady Ruanthorpe turned and hobbled from the room.

V

It was eleven o'clock in the morning.

Bel turned from her own, somewhat pale reflection in her dressing-table mirror, to see who had opened and shut her bedroom door so quickly. "Arthur!"

Her son was throwing down his hat and coat on her bed.

"Arthur, where have you come from? Why aren't you at work?" But already she was apprehensive.

"Mother, what did you say to Elizabeth Netherton?" His voice was boyish and hoarse, and there was anger in it.

"What did I say?" She was giving herself time.

He had thrown himself into a chair by the window, and now, both of them, son and mother, sat confronting each other.

She tried to fall back on her everyday authority. "Arthur, what has upset you? Why are you sitting there, looking at me as if I was a criminal? Come and kiss me, and say good morning."

He rose, kissed her and sat down again, his expression

exactly as before. He had, she felt, merely cleared formality out of the way.

"I want to know what you said to Elizabeth Netherton, Mother."

So he wasn't to be softened. He was determined to hold her to it. But still she struggled. "Arthur, are you all right? You're behaving so queerly."

"I'm all right, Mother. I want you to tell me what happened."

"Happened? Where?"

"You know very well where."

"Arthur, I don't know you, angry like this! Tell me what has happened."

"That's what *I* want to know, Mother! You went to the Dower House and saw Elizabeth Netherton the day before yesterday."

"Yes. Well?"

"And Elizabeth gave you a message you haven't given me yet."

"Message?"

"Yes. That I could consider myself free of her. I'm asking what you said to make her say that?"

"Arthur, I won't be bullied like this." She turned away from him, trembling. She, too, had spent a night of little sleep. But she made a very good show of self-control by taking time to straighten her comb, her brushes and her crystal bottles before her on the dressing-table. So the girl had been seeing Arthur; had been playing on his sympathy? "Perhaps you will remember that I wanted you to stay at home last night? I've had no chance to speak to you. I wanted to see you quietly and alone, to tell you just what Miss Netherton did say." If this was dishonest, Bel was, at least, as dishonest with herself as she was with her son.

"And what difference does that make now?"

"What did Miss Netherton say to you?"

"I didn't see Elizabeth, Mother."

"Didn't see—? Then where have you been?"

"At the Dower House."

"Then whom did you see, Arthur?"

"Lady Ruanthorpe."

A chill struck at Bel's vitals. "Lady Ruanthorpe!" She paused in bewilderment. But again she must have time to consider the implications of this. To gain it, she asked another question. "But where was Elizabeth Netherton?"

"At the Laigh Farm, risking her life."

"Risking—!"

"She's shut herself in with Rosie McNairn. She's trying to save the baby." Arthur spoke bitterly. If he had hurled the words: "And that's more than you would ever do—you with your plotting and your scheming," after his reply, he could not have conveyed his anger and contempt more clearly.

No. This was a strange young man. A changeling Arthur, who had stolen the form of the beloved son who had always thought her every action perfect. She turned again to look at this new creature. Her eyes were great with fear, but they could find nothing but accusation in the eyes that met them.

"Elizabeth may easily catch typhus and die," Arthur said. He had meant to speak coldly, but he ended the sentence in distress.

"Oh, Arthur!" But she was grateful, at least, that he could be softened, that his voice had lost its ice.

"It's true, Mother."

Quite suddenly—and perhaps a little by intention—Bel broke down. Anything, anything, she told herself, rather than this. She leaned her elbows on her dressing-table and hid her face in her hands. But Arthur, to her surprise, did not come to comfort her.

He got up, thrust his hands into his pockets and began striding about the room. The force of his anger against her had made him callous. He was determined not to be softened. She had explained nothing yet, justified herself in no way. A little astonished at himself, he turned now and then to watch her convulsive shoulders, merely waiting.

After a time Bel turned a tear-stained face to him and held out a hand. She did not know it, but with this gesture she was beginning to renounce her sovereignty over that part of her son's manhood that could never belong to her. "Arthur, we can't go on like this! What am I to do?"

"Do, Mother?"

"No, dear. Bring your chair and sit beside me, and give me your hand. You're far too—" She did not know exactly what she wanted to say. Too cold, too hard, too inaccessible, perhaps. But instead she broke down once more and wept; resenting that the clay of her son's emotion was no longer soft in her hand; resenting that even her genuine distress was failing now to move him. She had begun to yield ground, but, as yet, it was hard for her to see that she had lost the battle.

Arthur had not come to her. He was still pacing the room. "It won't be very nice for you, having a dead girl on your conscience."

She dried her eyes, turned and looked at him. "On my conscience, Arthur?"

Seeing now, in part, perhaps, the tangle of her motives, Arthur spoke with decision, seeking to cut his way through. "Mother, listen to this. I love Elizabeth Netherton. You may not like it, though I don't know why you shouldn't, but there it is. If Elizabeth catches fever and dies, I don't know how you'll feel about it; but I'll never want to look you in the face again, now that I know you tried to come between us."

"I tried—?" But she could not cheat herself or Arthur any more. She turned away from him. She could see that her last ramparts were down. Arthur had set the issue squarely before her. She must make her peace with Elizabeth Netherton whatever happened, whether she liked it or not.

She strove to pull herself together, and stood up. "All right, Arthur. I'll go and see Elizabeth Netherton's parents today. She may have written and told them. And after I've seen them I'll write a letter to Elizabeth."

"What will you say to her?" Arthur, it seemed, was determined to let her off nothing, determined to underline his victory.

She stood, one hand seeking support from her dressing-table, the other wiping her eyes. "I don't know, Arthur. You must let me think. When I went to see Miss Netherton at Duntrafford I had no idea that things had gone so far between you." She took her handkerchief from her eyes and looked at him. She saw that still he was doubtful of her—that even now he was not fully reassured. "Oh, Arthur! Can't you ever forgive me? Can't you ever believe that I'll do everything I can to put this right?"

She made a lost, uncertain gesture towards him, and once again her tears came. But they had lost their bitterness; for now Bel was held close in the arms of this son of hers, who had, overnight, broken from her and was changed into a grown man.

At last she disengaged herself, turned to the mirror, examined her face in it, reached for her flask of eau-de-Cologne and her brushes, and began to repair the ravages of battle. Because she had lost was no reason why her retreat should be disorderly. "You had better hurry down to business, dear," she said over her shoulder in a voice that tried to be normal. "Your father will be wondering what has happened to you."

Chapter Eighteen

I N THE MIDDLE of this same August morning Arthur Moorhouse, Senior, was standing at the door of Arthur Moorhouse and Company in the Candleriggs. He had just concluded a deal with a business friend of many years' standing, a farmer from the Newton Mearns district to the south of Glasgow. There had been, as was the case with most of Arthur's negotiations, little haggling. For each trusted the other. The farmer offered Mr. Moorhouse only of his best. And the merchant, knowing his man, had been ready to take what was offered.

Arthur led his friend from the counting-house, where they had closed their deal over a glass of whisky. Custom demanded this; although Arthur, who was nothing if not moderate in all things, saw to it that his own drink was not large. At the warehouse door he bade the farmer goodbye, at the same time running a caressing hand over the thin, elegant muzzle of his collie. The dog, which was used to following his master everywhere, even to town, had been sitting waiting on the pavement outside, his nervous eyes darting hither and thither, his high-strung body trembling before the sights and noises of this busy street of warehouses.

The sun, high, and not far off midday, was striking down the narrow street. Now the farmer, followed by the handsome, bewildered beast, was disappearing round the corner. Arthur raised his hand in a final, distant salute.

It was hot this morning—too hot to have to pass the day in this street where so much of Glasgow's food was bought and sold: a street of straw, packing-papers and dust, of clattering hooves and oaths, of sweating warehousemen and hurrying merchants. One or two of these last greeted the head of Arthur Moorhouse and Company with respect as they passed him, wondering, perhaps, where Mr. Moorhouse had got that natural air of distinction, which, somehow, set him apart from themselves.

Arthur stood looking about him, tempted by the sunlight to remain outside for a moment longer.

Where had that boy of his got to? Why had he run off to Duntrafford with Phœbe last night? When was he going to reappear?

And what about Bel? She had been so restless, so on edge. But he had asked no questions. And, as a family man of some twenty-two years standing, Arthur was not too worried. He guessed that, in the end, Bel would tell him everything. She wouldn't be able to help it. Arthur smiled to himself. And no doubt, as heretofore, he would pour oil on such waters as were troubled, receive his wife's contrition, and thereafter Bel would return to her smiling usual.

But what about that boy? It wasn't like him to neglect his work like this. He would have to give a very real reason for his truancy, or for discipline's sake something must be said. Arthur cast a final glance up and down the Candleriggs, as though in hope that his elder son might, even now, chance to be pushing his way up the crowded pavement, then he turned to go inside.

"Mr. Moorhouse."

Arthur turned back. "Yes?" For a moment he could not remember where he had met this man before—where he had seen this worn tweed suit, this wide-brimmed hat and this thin, red beard. But the newcomer did not keep him guessing.

245

"I'm John Netherton, Mr. Moorhouse. Mebbe ye'll mind me?"

"Yes, yes, Mr. Netherton. In Arran. I was trying to place ye." Arthur extended his hand with homely kindliness.

"I would like to have a word with ye, Mr. Moorhouse."

"With me, Mr. Netherton? Well, come away in, then, and ye can speak to me in my office, where it's quiet."

The cheese merchant led the way past his well-ordered shelves to his own private office at the back. It was a plain little place with a window, where Arthur could talk in private, yet keep an eye on what was going on. He set a chair for John Netherton, then swung round in his own desk chair, regarding him with eyes of friendly inquiry.

As Elizabeth's father took off his hat, wiped his pale face and stroked his damp hair, he looked more like a faded messiah than ever. "It's about my girl, Mr. Moorhouse."

Yes. Arthur remembered all about him now. A stiff, difficult sort of man, a man that needed handling. A musician, wasn't he? And wasn't his daughter now going to the Laigh to help with Rosie McNairn or something? But why had Netherton come here? "Your girl, Mr. Netherton?" Arthur's voice was purposeful. His instinct knew better than to sound the note of patronage.

It was difficult to tell if John Netherton was angry as he took an envelope from his pocket. "Her mother got this, this morning. My girl has gone to some farm—my wife thinks it belongs to yer brother—and she's shut herself in there with a young woman and her bairn. She says the young woman has the typhus fever. My girl has taken the bairn to look after."

"That's my nephew, Jack McNairn's wife and bairn," Arthur said, avoiding comment.

John Netherton did not speak again at once. For a time he

remained sullenly staring before him. "The typhus fever is very dangerous," he said at length.

"Aye, yer daughter's a good girl." Still Arthur was feeling his way.

Anger suddenly cracked the crust of the other man's reserve. "It's all very fine to sit there and say she's good, Mr. Moorhouse. She's no business to be in that farmhouse, risking her life. What right had your folks to send her to any such place? I never wanted her to go to Ayrshire. I made it clear enough to yer wife at the time. But they petted and pleased her, and got her to go—'just to be a daughter in the house'—" John spoke these last words with bitterness. "But the devil of a daughter of your own would you send to nurse typhus fever!"

Arthur had not bothered himself over the family politics that had gone to the sending of Elizabeth to Lady Ruanthorpe. But he knew that Bel, along with Mrs. Robert Dermott, had been deep in them. Had this man, then, come here in his distress to accuse Bel and to try to hold himself, Arthur, responsible?

He hesitated. This was a serious business. Arthur wished he knew more of the real facts now. John Netherton's eyes were watching him steadily, reproachful and angry. But what could he say? Bel, he knew, had sent the girl to Duntrafford. She was a great planner, Bel! But certainly she had meant no harm.

Arthur stood up, striking an attitude of deliberation to give himself time. He knitted his brows, looked down at the scrubbed floorboards, thrust one hand deep in a trouser pocket, while he felt his chin and smoothed his cropped side-whiskers with the other. Yes, this was difficult.

"I don't know very well what to say to ye, Mr. Netherton," he said, still looking down. "Ye see, I don't know all the circumstances. I quite see, of course, that with your girl in danger—"

The door of the little office was thrown open. Both men looked up to find young Arthur holding the handle. His father, feeling himself in a tight place, had seldom been better pleased by an interruption.

"Come in, son, come in!" he called with sudden geniality. "Did ye go to Duntrafford last night?"

"Yes; I—"

"Well, here's Mr. Netherton come to ask about his daughter. You're just the one to tell us. Did ye hear about Miss Netherton?"

Young Arthur came in and shut the door. He merely said: "Yes, I heard," and sat down in the chair his father had just risen from, saying nothing more.

Tired of riddles, his father addressed him sharply. "Well? And what about her, Arthur?"

But the young man had turned to John Netherton. "I've just had it out with Mother, Mr. Netherton," he said. "She's going down to Partick to see you and Mrs. Netherton this afternoon."

"See us? What about?"

"About Elizabeth. Mother's very sorry."

"Yer Mother may well be sorry. My girl's no' a fever nurse."

Young Arthur was uncertain how to take this. Was Elizabeth's father angry only because she had been exposed to infection? Or had Elizabeth written telling of his mother's visit to the Dower House, and what she had said? His eyes passed from one to the other. When he spoke his voice was strained, but determined. "Anyway, Mother knows now that Elizabeth and I want to be married. And, that typhus or no typhus, nothing is going to change that."

The older men looked at each other in amazement.

It was Arthur Senior who found his voice first. "Well, Mr. Netherton? What are we to say to that?"

John Netherton put his hands on his knees and shook his head.

"Did ye know?" Arthur Moorhouse asked him.

"No. Did you?"

"No. What have ye to say to it, Mr. Netherton?"

John Netherton got up. "I can't tell ye," he said, in some bewilderment. "I'll need to see my wife first."

"And it seems ye're going to get a visit from *mine*."

Suddenly John Netherton swung round on the young man. "Did yer mother try to come between you and my girl?" he asked suspiciously.

So Elizabeth's parents didn't know. And how much better it would be if they never did. After a mere instant to collect himself, young Arthur answered. "Of course Mother is not trying to come between us, Mr. Netherton. Would she be coming to see you and Elizabeth's mother if she were?"

And, standing by, watching, Arthur Moorhouse applauded his son. Good boy! He would make a quick-witted merchant out of him. "I'll see ye to the door," he said, taking John by the arm. "No, you stop here, son. I want a word with Mr. Netherton." As he led John to the street his mind was working. So Bel had been up to something? Just what, was not yet plain to him, but at least he could protect her.

Out in the sunshine, he gave Elizabeth's father his hand. "I want to ask a favour of ye, Mr. Netherton," he said. "Just between ourselves, my wife's a managing kind o' body. But she's all right. She's not hard. If she comes to see you today, I would like to ask ye to keep mind o' that. I havena thought about the young folk yet; but if it happens that they're serious about wanting one another, then yer girl needna be frightened

249

for my boy's mother. And we'll see about this fever nursing. I'll send word to Duntrafford right away."

John Netherton returned Arthur Moorhouse's handshake, then turned and went. He had said nothing in reply, but Arthur had taken reassurance from his expression.

Back in the little office, he examined his watch, then looked at his son. "I think, mebbe, if yer mother's going down to see these folks today, I had better go home and go down with her." He snapped his watch shut. "We'll go and get our lunch. And you can tell me what's been going on."

III

John Netherton stood on his own landing, feeling for his latchkey in the pocket of his trousers. Before putting it in the lock, however, he once more took off his hat and mopped his brow. It had been hot work toiling upstairs. As he pushed the door open, his wife's high voice greeted him.

"Is that John?"

"Aye."

She left the cooking of his midday meal and came to him in the little sitting-room. "Well, did you see Mr. Moorhouse?"

John Netherton sat down, still mopping his brow. "Aye," he repeated.

She knew she must give him time. "John, you look warm. Take off your jacket for a minute." She came to him, smoothed his hair with timid, affectionate fingers, and helped him out of his jacket. "And what about Elizabeth? What did Mr. Moorhouse say?"

"Well, she's doing what she wrote she was doing."

"Oh!" Elizabeth's mother gave a foolish little cry of fear. "But, John, didn't you ask about her? Didn't you tell Mr.

250

Moorhouse that we didn't like her having to nurse fever? That she must be taken away at once?" She felt so impotent, and John, for all his obstinacy, could be so ineffective, too.

He did not speak, and it was impossible for her anxiety to tell what he was thinking. "Oh, John, tell me!"

"Mrs. Moorhouse is coming here today. Ye can ask her."

"Mrs. Moorhouse? But why is she coming here, dear? It's very kind. But didn't Mr. Moorhouse tell you all about it at the office?"

John Netherton stroked his beard, then, grasping his right wrist in his left hand—a habit he had learned from his accident—turned in his chair and looked up at his wife. "It'll surprise ye to hear, Ellen, that the young man Moorhouse wants to get married to Elizabeth."

Ellen Netherton turned away, merely smoothing down the loose smock she was wearing with agitated, fluttering fingers. Her husband waited. "Young Mr. Moorhouse, dear?" she said at length. "But how do you know? Who told you?"

"Young Moorhouse told me."

"Young Mr. Moorhouse! And what do his parents think about it, John?"

"He told his father at the same time as he told me."

"At the office this morning? And what did Mr. Moorhouse say?"

John Netherton merely shrugged.

Ellen Netherton looked about her like a flustered pigeon— quite at a loss. If only Elizabeth were here! Elizabeth would tell her what to feel about this. "That must be why Mrs. Moorhouse is coming here, John," she said foolishly.

"I wouldna be surprised."

"I must get your dinner, John." It was a relief to scurry back into her kitchen. There, at least, her hands would be busy.

251

"Arthur!" Bel turned. She stood in one of the long windows of her drawing-room. Her husband had come upon her there. She had been gazing out, restless and disturbed at the thought of the visit she had undertaken to pay this afternoon.

His appearance in Grosvenor Terrace in the early afternoon of a working day was something very unusual. She was uncertain whether to be pleased or apprehensive. "Arthur, what are you doing—home at this time of day?"

He crossed the room and stood beside her. "I've just had my lunch with the boy," he said.

She looked at him quickly, noted his expression and took heart. "Well, dear?" she asked.

"He talked to me about the Netherton lassie."

"Yes." Bel's colour rose. She moved away from her husband and crossed to the empty fireplace.

Arthur had sat down in a chair by the window, and now appeared to be intent upon the passing traffic in Great Western Road. "He wants to get married to her," he said.

"Yes. He told me this morning."

"I don't suppose ye were too well pleased, Bel?" As there was no immediate reply, he turned round to look at his wife. "Well?"

In Bel's eyes there were tears hanging. She shook her head. Suddenly she burst out: "Oh, Arthur, why should I like it? She's a nice girl. But you know what the Nethertons are!"

He shook his head slowly, indulgently. "Bel! Bel! John Netherton was a farmer's son, just like me."

She turned from him, leaning against the mantelpiece. "Oh, I know, Arthur. But after all these years. It's no use pretending you and he are the same now."

He did not answer this. He merely sat looking from the window, considering.

Bel would have given the world to know what he was thinking. How much of this morning's stormy talk with her son had been told him?

"The boy's very determined," Arthur said at last. "We'll not stop him."

"No."

"Well, take my advice, Bel, and don't try any more."

In self-justification, she burst out: "I wasn't going to. Didn't he tell you? I'm going down to see the girl's parents this afternoon. I promised him I would."

"Aye. That's all right, then, my dear. I'm glad ye are. The boy said ye were." His voice was kind, but firm, as he added: "And if anything comes of this, the better friends we are with the lassie's father and mother, the better for everybody, Bel."

"This visit won't be very easy for me, Arthur."

His eyes took a long time to follow some vehicle as it passed outside the window. They were still turned from her when he did say: "It'll mebbe be easier than ye think."

"I don't see why, Arthur."

"I'm coming with ye."

"My dear!" She went to him and stood, laying a caressing hand upon his shoulder, uncertain and emotional.

Arthur put up a hand to grasp Bel's, then took once more to window-gazing. "John Netherton came to the office this morning," he said.

"John Netherton?"

"Aye. His girl being in danger of fever was all that concerned him, as far as I could see."

"But I saw Miss Netherton three days ago. I said something to her. I've never had time to tell you, Arthur."

"Well, she canna have had time to tell her father and mother either. He didna seem to know."

"But, listen, Arthur—"

Arthur raised his voice. "The boy's away back down this afternoon. I sent him. I gave him a message to the lassie."

"A message? From yourself?"

"I wrote her a line, for I thought he wouldna mebbe could see her. I said that you and me were to see her folk today. That we wanted to be friends. And that she would be silly if she did anything to change that. No matter who had said what."

Bel's grasp tightened on Arthur's shoulder. She felt grateful, ashamed, and at the same time consumed with curiosity. How much, then, did he know? But now she dare not ask him— dare not make confession, even. And she felt that she would never dare.

There was the sound of hooves outside. Arthur looked out and rose to his feet. "There's McCrimmon," he said. "Get on your things, and we'll away down to Partick."

Chapter Nineteen

LATE AFTERNOON of the same day.

The August sunshine that had been beating down on the Candleriggs this morning was beating with an afternoon fierceness on the ripening grain, the reddening berries, the yellow stubble of the hayfields. It beat on the backs of Mungo's sleek Ayrshires, as they came, jostling each other from the water-meadow by the river, their mouths still dripping from the grasses they had found there. It beat on the slate roofs and whitewashed walls of the Laigh Farm. It struck down through the south window of the "room", as the formal, little-used farm parlour was called; on the tongue fern in the brown china flowerpot; on the little bamboo table; on the plush sofa and on the Turkey carpet.

Particles of silver dust floated towards the iron fireplace and the tasselled mantelshelf, adorned with crude photographs and cupid ornaments, bought a quarter of a century ago from a wandering bagman by Sophia or Mary Moorhouse—relics of the days before they had quitted the Laigh and gone to be with their then bachelor brother Arthur in Glasgow.

A low, lazy fire burned in the fireplace—a fire that could be roused when, later, the temperature dropped. For this was the room assigned to the baby Alastair McNairn and Elizabeth Netherton. It was here that Elizabeth must remain tending her charge and watching for the symptoms of fever in the child and in herself; a prisoner, but for the solitary airings she must give him, and for communication without contact at door and window.

The "room" lay across the width of the farmhouse. There was thus, in addition, a north window on the shaded side. This now stood open. From time to time a cool breath came gratefully to her as she sat by it listless, in an armchair. In a corner of the room Rosie's child lay asleep in his cradle.

A bumble-bee buzzed in the south window, striking little padded blows against the glass as it sought to fly through and out into the sunshine. Now and then there was a distant footfall within the house, the creaking of a floorboard. Everything seemed close and muted. For the hundredth time today, Elizabeth found herself wondering how the fight was going. Whether the mother of the sleeping child would live or die.

A breeze, rather more fresh, came to her through the open window—a sign that the afternoon was passing, that the sun was losing strength.

Elizabeth sat forward in her chair. She glanced at the baby who had come so strangely into her inexpert care, tried to remember her instructions, wondered if there was anything that she should now be doing for him, then decided there was not.

She stood up, turned to the open window and took an envelope from her belt. It contained the letter Arthur had written to her at midnight in the Dower House. She did not open it. She held it in her hand, pondering. The envelope merely bore the words "Miss Netherton". It had been brought here by a servant.

Elizabeth leant her head against a window-shutter. Numbness, along with fatigue, had descended upon her feelings. Two days ago her bitter meeting with Arthur's mother. The excitement and danger of typhus. The anger and vexation that had driven her to a stubborn decision to come here, shut herself up and risk infection. Had emotion been overstretched, that she could stand, now, feeling so little?

She had dropped tears on the letter this morning. Arthur

was so hotly anxious that nothing his mother had said should come between them. He wrote that her talk of freeing him was a thing he could not hear of. His earlier letters had been conventional, self-conscious, a little. But distress and shame tumbled out of this one without ceremony. Presently, when she could feel again, the thought of Arthur would be sweet to her. But then the bitterness against his mother would come back, too. Yes, she must be thankful for the present vacuum in her senses.

A stronger breeze ballooned the stiff lace curtains. It brought with it the distant cackle of hens and the lowing of the cows as they ambled, heavy with milk, into the farm close. She could hear, too, the farm collies barking.

These things, coming from the other—the working—side of the farm, merely increased her sense of isolation—a sense for which she was grateful. This stuffy, decorated farmer's best room had become her fortress, her retreat. Here she must make herself useful, heedless of her feelings, heedless of the risks she took, free of all responsibility except to her charge. She sighed. So be it. In this mood of dull, smouldering unhappiness she could not be in a better place.

II

There was the sound of a step by the window; then her name: "Elizabeth!"

She looked up to see young Arthur Moorhouse. So strange was everything, so numbly felt, that for a moment she wondered if her own thinking had projected his image for her, there, just outside.

But he was speaking, urgent and excited: "Elizabeth!"

"Arthur." She wondered at the lack of surprise in her own voice.

"Are you all right? You look worn out."

"I'm all right, Arthur. What are you doing here?"

"What do you think? How could I stay away?"

She had no reply for that.

"Did you get my last night's letter?"

"Yes." Instinct somehow had prompted her to hide it from him.

"So, you see, I know all about you and Mother."

Again she did not speak.

"But it's going to be all right, Elizabeth."

"Is it?" Her voice was flat.

"Yes. I brought you a letter from Father."

"Your father?"

"He said I was to come here and give it to you."

Why had Arthur's father sent him? What did that mean? She took the letter from him, broke it open and read:

"DEAR MISS NETHERTON,

My son has just been telling me how things are between you. He should have told me long ago. It would have saved a lot of bother. He spoke about a meeting between yourself and my wife. It was the kind of meeting that never should have taken place. Let me ask you most earnestly to forget it, and above all not to tell your parents. For I have every reason to believe that Arthur's mother is now truly sorry for what she said to you. As a proof of that, we are going today to see your own mother and father. Please be assured that whatever happens, you will now meet with nothing but our goodwill; and, if the tie becomes closer, our sympathy and real affection.

Yours very sincerely,

ARTHUR MOORHOUSE."

She folded the letter, made to give it to him through the open window, then remembered. "No. It may be infected."

"Don't be silly." He took it from her and read it.

She stood watching him: his fair hair falling forward, the curve of his cheek as he read, his conventional, town clothes dusty from the journey.

She caught an echo of Bel Moorhouse in the flushed, bending face of Bel's son, and her heart, forgetting its numbness, rose in rebellion.

As Elizabeth stood now by the window she felt herself in a trap. Not the trap of quarantine. Not the confinement in the stuffy farm room. Not the danger of infection. She was trapped between her own hot pride and her love for that young man there, outside the window. Which way was she to turn? What must she do? She could only keep her pride by the outraging of her heart. And if she yielded him her heart, her pride must be humbled.

Arthur raised his head. He looked pleased. "Well, Elizabeth?" He saw her face was flushed.

"Your father is very kind," she said in a voice that gave him no clue to her feelings.

"Not kind, Elizabeth. He only wants to put things right between you and Mother."

"Couldn't your mother put things right herself?"

"She will, Elizabeth."

She did not reply to this, and they stood silent, both of them at the window for a time.

There were faraway sounds of cartwheels, of the cows as they were being chained up in the byre. The farmyard cock had begun his afternoon crowing. But here, in the shadow at the front of the Laigh, they were quiet. Nothing came near them.

He raised his eyes to hers. He could not read her thoughts, but he saw she was unhappy. Unhappy like himself. He had no idea what to say to her, what tangle of stubborn, woman's unhappiness he must cut to reach her.

He let his instinct guide him. "Elizabeth, I love you."

She flinched, bent her head, but said nothing.

"Do you love me?" And as again she said nothing, he persisted: "Elizabeth—Elizabeth! I must know!"

She nodded, and a tear fell on the windowsill.

"Oh, Elizabeth!—But that's all right, then."

"No." She looked up at him, her eyes full. "Arthur, I'm sorry. Please go away now. When all this is over I'll—I'll talk to you."

"What will you say to me?"

"I don't know."

"But you're leaving here almost at once, Elizabeth. It's to be arranged."

"I don't care what they've arranged. I'm staying here."

"But you can't. It's dangerous."

"I'm keeping my promise to that child's mother. Oh, don't think I'm good! I want to stay here. I want to let things straighten themselves out. For me. For everybody."

"But the danger? You could—"

"I'm staying here. Now go away, please, Arthur. I'll be all right."

He saw that she meant it.

"Very well." He made a gesture of helplessness. "Can I come back and see you?"

"Leave me until this is over. Don't insist."

"All right. I'll write to you. Goodbye, Elizabeth."

"Goodbye, Arthur."

He turned and passed out of sight.

Elizabeth stood at the window until she could hear his footsteps no longer. Then she turned and bent over Alastair McNairn.

The child's eyes were wide open. They were looking up at her, impersonal and candid.

Chapter Twenty

JUST BEFORE LUNCH Mrs. Robert Dermott had telephoned.

"I've just been reading this morning's *Herald*, Bel. I see your family were at Ayr yesterday, at the Ellerdale wedding. Are you free, my dear? Come across this afternoon, will you? I must hear all about it."

And Bel had been too weary, too preoccupied, to invent an immediate excuse for not going. These telephones, she was beginning to find, had their drawbacks, as well as their conveniences.

Now, on her way to Mrs. Dermott's house in Hamilton Drive, she halted at the end of Grosvenor Terrace for a moment before crossing over. The early September afternoon was mellow. Great Western Road was full of animation. Carriages were out again. People were home. The autumn was coming into full swing. Bel picked up her skirts and crossed.

Through the main gates of the Botanic Gardens she could now see the throng of starched and streamered nursemaids, the shining perambulators, the frilled or sailor-suited children. And, in addition, here and there, a hunting couple of soldiers from the barracks across the river, with their moustaches waxed, their pillbox hats, their red monkey-jackets, their braided trousers and their canes; out, no doubt, to make havoc among the nursemaids.

Bel would fain have sat on one of the seats up there by the great hothouse, watching this pleasant afternoon rabble and admiring the green lawns set with flower-beds of begonias, dahlias and asters. It would have been so much less of an effort than meeting Mrs. Dermott's energetic questions. But she must continue on, past the new Queen Margaret College.

Was this college education of her own sex a good thing, Bel wondered? Would that group of young women over there on the steps in trenchers and swinging scarlet gowns be of greater use to their husbands when they got them? She could hear from their voices that they were the daughters of gentlemen. But weren't they behaving too noisily? Too conspicuously? Wasn't their laughter too unselfconscious?

Bel pondered these things, as she went down Hamilton Drive. She felt less sure of herself these days, less certain of her standards.

II

"My dear Bel! How nice of you to come!" Mrs. Dermott rose from a group made up of her own daughter Grace, together with Mary and Sophia.

Bel had expected to find the old woman alone, and on the whole she would have preferred it. But she must do her best.

"Isn't it great fun having you all here, Mrs. Moorhouse?" Mrs. Dermott asked genially.

"Yes. Where have you all come from?" Bel exclaimed foolishly, hoping she was giving a plausible imitation of sisterly interest.

Sophia was bursting with news. "Bel dear, do you know what's happening? Margy and Alec are being married some time this month. And do you know where the wedding's going to be? At Aucheneame. A garden wedding. Well, the ceremony in the house, but the rest in the garden. Just very quietly, because of Alec's nerves. Only ourselves." (Ourselves, Bel

reflected, could be quite numerous enough to be tiresome.)
"And, of course, Alec's mother. She's a widow in Kilmarnock."

Mrs. Dermott, the organiser, turned to her calendar.

"Let me see. What's today's date? September the second.
You've got time to have cards printed, Sophia."

"Oh, it's all to be very informal, Mrs. Dermott."

"Still, Sophia, things should never be left vague. It's horrid
to have hitches. I always remember—" Here Mrs. Dermott
gathered her own meek daughter, Grace Dermott-Moorhouse,
along with Sophia Butter into the tent of her own commanding
talk, leaving Bel to turn to Mary McNairn, who, so far, had
been giving her attention to Mrs. Dermott's cake.

Bel asked the question expected of her. "And how is poor
Rosie, Mary?"

Mary wiped her fingers on her handkerchief, reached for
another piece, and said: "Holding her own, dear."

"I'm glad, Mary."

"Oh, the crisis is still to come, Bel. You can never be sure."

"Still, Mary, if she has held her ground so far—"

"They say that doesn't mean anything."

Bel's eyes wandered to the slab of cake. Today she could
find little sympathy for Mary. "This is news about Margy
and Mr. Findowie!" she exclaimed with dry brightness.

But Mary had no intention of giving up. "And to think of
my poor wee baby grandson, Bel!" she said plaintively.

"Do I hear you talking about your grandson, Mary?" Mrs.
Dermott had suddenly turned round. "He hasn't taken fever,
has he?"

"No. But—"

"No, of course he hasn't!" The old woman's forcefulness
blew Mary aside. "And do you know why he hasn't, Bel? It's
that wonderful girl I got for Lady Ruanthorpe. Grace got a
letter from Margaret Moorhouse this morning. You remember,

263

Bel, a nice girl called Elizabeth Netherfield, that Mary had to play at her daughter's wedding?"

Bel thought she could remember.

"Well, there Miss Netherfield has been. Shut up in that dreadful, fever-stricken farmhouse, looking after the child, just out of the goodness of her heart. I was certain she was a girl with character."

Mrs. Dermott having struck the note, the room burst into a chorus of praise for Elizabeth Netherton. She was good. She was brave. They remembered what a pretty girl she was; how well she had played at Wil and Polly's wedding.

Bel succeeded in throwing a smile and a nod now and then, as she listened to the magpie chatter of these women.

Elizabeth. Arthur.

Her husband had gone with her to the Nethertons' a week ago. Elizabeth's mother had been birdlike, talkative and anxious. Her father had sat solemn and amazingly civil. There had been no thunder on his brow.

When they had spoken of Elizabeth and Arthur, John Netherton had, indeed, pronounced a considered decision. "It's like this, Mr. and Mrs. Moorhouse. If the young folk want to get married, then Elizabeth's mother and I will do nothing to stop them. But for one thing"—and here he had turned to Bel, speaking, surprisingly, in a voice of gentle reason—"unless it should be that we feel we're bein' asked to let the lassie go where she's not wanted."

"Ye'll never feel that," Bel heard her husband say, and she had, as was expected of her, hastened to echo this.

"No, no. I would never think of giving a wedding lunch, Grace dear. Yes. A nice tea. That would be lovely. Margy and Alec would be delighted with a nice tea. The ceremony at two; and then— What do *you* think, Bel dear? Grace is being far too good, isn't she?"

Bel, without quite marking where the talk had got to, found herself assenting that Grace was far too good.

"And when do you expect the crisis, Mary?" Grace's mother was asking.

"In four or five days. You can't imagine what this waiting and uncertainty—"

But Mrs. Dermott had risen and was coming towards Bel.

"Now, my dear, I'm going to sit beside you to hear all about the Ayr wedding. You see, young James Ellerdale has become a great friend of mine. He comes here to dinner sometimes. Such nice manners he has. English. (Grace is sending both her children to school in England.) And David says that in spite of that, Mr. Ellerdale has quite a good business head."

Bel was glad to listen to Jim Ellerdale's excellences. It was less of an effort than having to describe his sister's wedding. She would excuse herself soon and escape.

Thus, a little later, and much to her relief, she found herself free and alone in the Botanic Gardens, walking slowly in the direction of home. The chatter of these women about Elizabeth Netherton had set her nerves on edge.

Yes, she had promised to gather herself together and go to see this girl. Whether she would ever like Elizabeth, she did not know. It would be her duty, she supposed, to try.

She walked along, her eyes on the ground, heedless that the crowd had thinned, that the sunshine had begun to slant, oblique and golden.

She had liked Elizabeth at first, genuinely. That was, of course, when there had been no thought of her marriage with Arthur. What was it, then, that had changed her? With complete honesty, now, Bel put the question to herself. But the light she had turned inwards was too revealing.

Her step quickened, she pushed through the little wicket-gate into Great Western Road and crossed over to Grosvenor Terrace.

III

And Elizabeth's stock kept rising. Letters from Mungo to her husband; from Margaret to herself. News from all quarters. Elizabeth Netherton had become a heroine in the Moorhouse family. Her spirit. Her bravery. Her sense of devotion.

In a few days it was known that Rosie McNairn had passed the crisis of her illness; that she was alive, and would now recover; that neither Elizabeth nor the child had taken fever, and that the danger was passing.

In these dragging days of September the tension between mother and son did not slacken. Arthur was strained and restless. Bel felt his eyes were upon her, waiting.

It was becoming more than she could bear. She must see Elizabeth at once, whenever she came home. What she would find to say to her must be left to the time of their meeting.

And, as chance fell, it was Bel who first learned that Elizabeth was in Glasgow. Two days before Margy Butter's wedding, young Charles Ruanthorpe-Moorhouse appeared at Grosvenor Terrace with his cousin, Robin Hayburn.

"My people are coming up the day after tomorrow," Charles explained, as he sat with Robin drinking Bel's lemonade. "They've sent me on ahead. I'm staying with Robin."

"Did you come by yourself, Charles?" Bel asked, wondering a little that the much-cherished heir to Duntrafford should be allowed to make the journey to Glasgow unattended.

"Well, as a matter of fact, Aunt Bel, no. You see, Granny's Miss Netherton was coming, so we came together."

Bel had been waiting for this. Yet she heard it with a

266

sense of shock. "Miss Netherton! Was she able to leave—?"

"Oh, my dear aunt, yes! Didn't you know? Cousin Rosie is getting on like a house on fire."

So that was that. The thing had come, and she must face it.

On that same day, therefore, Bel was in Partick, ringing the Nethertons' doorbell. Ellen Netherton answered her ringing.

Bel greeted her. "I hear your daughter has come home?"

The little woman burst into a chatter of pleasure and relief.

"Please, Mrs. Netherton. It's very important for me to see Elizabeth by herself."

For a moment Bel stood alone in the Nethertons' sitting-room; then Elizabeth came, closed the door behind her, and leant against it.

So often, at the turning-points, it is triviality that lingers. When she came to look back, Bel was to remember that the wallpaper near the door was rubbed and dingy, that the carpet at Elizabeth's feet was worn, that a sheet of music had fluttered from John Netherton's piano and was lying on the floor.

In the last weeks this girl's image had seldom been out of her mind. She had thought of her with the dislike that is born of shame. Now, as she looked at the real Elizabeth, Bel knew she had been hating a shadow. Elizabeth was merely a young woman like any other, standing there embarrassed and waiting.

"You wanted to see me?" she was saying.

"Yes, I—" There was one thing about Bel Moorhouse—a thing that surprised her anew each time it happened. When she had decided to capitulate, her generosity, her humanity took charge and forced her to capitulate fully and handsomely. It had been thus with her in smaller capitulations. Now in this larger one she was to find it happen, too.

There were tears in her eyes as she went to Elizabeth,

stretching out her hand. "I've come to apologise for what I said to you at Duntrafford, my dear."

Elizabeth gave Bel her hand in return. But she did not answer.

"Won't you forgive me, Elizabeth?"

Still Elizabeth did not speak.

"Please, Elizabeth."

Elizabeth turned to her almost wearily. "Why are you trying to apologise now, Mrs. Moorhouse? Why have you changed your mind?"

Bel drew back. Was her welcome uprush of warm feeling to be repulsed? Didn't the girl see it was genuine? Couldn't she trust her? Dismayed and baffled, Bel sat down by the sitting-room table.

Presently she looked up. She saw Elizabeth still leaning against the door, exhausted and unhappy. Their eyes met. In Elizabeth's she could see nothing but a smouldering distaste. It gave Bel a measure of the wound she had inflicted, a measure of the girl's dislike. What had she said at Duntrafford that had cut this child so deeply?

Bel was shocked and bitterly sorry. She was seized by a womanly impulse to run to Elizabeth, to take her in her arms and thus ask forgiveness. But what if Elizabeth should draw away? What if, once again, she should not respond?

"I'm going to be honest, Elizabeth," Bel said at length. "You see, at Duntrafford I thought I was only giving a hint—a hint that would hurt no one."

"You still don't think I'm—"

"Please! I had no idea then that my son loved you. Or that you loved my son. Now I know. Oh, Elizabeth, he's been so unhappy!" And as Elizabeth made no reply: "My dear, you promised to marry him. Do you want to break his heart?"

Bel was at the end of her forces. Her voice trembled. She

could think of nothing now but to have this girl's forgiveness. And there the girl stood, weeping resentfully, and looking as though her only wish were to get away from her. "What can I *do*, Elizabeth? What can I say to you?"

Elizabeth crossed to the window, turning her back on Bel. She stood looking out, seeing nothing. Could she really believe in this woman's sudden change of heart? And must she forgive her just because she was Arthur's mother? Forgive her, or risk losing him? Why must her pride be forced to this hard choice?

"Elizabeth, can't you say it will be all right?"

The girl turned. "Will you ever think I'm good enough for your son?"

Bel waited before she answered. It would be very easy to say yes, to give quick reassurances. But she could guess now that these things would count for little with Elizabeth; that they might leave her merely scornful. But she must try. "I love my son, Elizabeth. And so do you. I had hoped that for his sake you could forgive me. Oh, what else can I say to you?" And as Elizabeth said nothing: "Am I to go back to him and tell him I've tried to say I'm sorry, but that you won't listen to me? Oh, I daresay Arthur will come to you whatever happens. But will he be happy? Can he go on liking a woman who has cut him off from his own?"

Elizabeth had flung herself into an old armchair by the window. Now her weeping was convulsed and bitter, while love and pride fought out their war within her.

Distressed and powerless, Bel could only sit waiting for the storm to pass. But at length, when it had spent itself, she rose and stood looking down upon her. "Elizabeth, I'm going now. What am I to tell Arthur? That you've forgiven his mother? And that you want to see him?"

Bel had to bend over Elizabeth to catch the low, shaken reply. "Yes, say that. Say that I want to see him."

269

Bel pushed back Elizabeth's hair and kissed her brow. Then she tiptoed across the room and let herself out of the Nethertons' flat.

Outside on the landing she halted. She could give way now to her own quivering feelings. But her task was done.

For her son's sake she had fought a strange battle—the last battle she had ever looked to fight.

In the winning of it lay her own defeat.

IV

Amid shouts of affection and farewell, David banged the shining, monogrammed door of the Aucheneame carriage upon the Reverend Alexander Findowie and upon the young woman who, until some two hours since, had been Miss Butter of Rosebery Terrace, Glasgow. The cockaded coachman shook his reins, the sleek horses took up their prancing, and the newly-married pair were borne off into a life that could not fail to combine rapture with usefulness and high-thinking.

The carriage disappeared. Cambric handkerchiefs, having blown sentimental noses, were now being rearranged in the front pockets of frock-coats. Fine lace ones, having done more duty less adequately, were going back into reticules, and the Moorhouse clan, standing there on the front lawn, began to draw breath and look about it.

It had been a house wedding. The young preacher, accustomed to conducting more elaborate ceremonies in church, had been grateful for the simplicity of his own.

"Grace, dear," Sophia was exclaiming tearfully, "William was just saying this morning that we could never finish thanking you enough for what you've done for Alec and Margy. Didn't you, William?"

William said nothing.

Grace smiled—a little mistily, perhaps. William Butter, she knew, would certainly never finish thanking her, because he would never begin. He was standing now, between his wife and the bridegroom's mother—the lady whom Sophia had described as "a widow in Kilmarnock"—fat, hairy and static, wearing, though no one had any idea how it had got there, a tea-rose in his buttonhole.

But Mrs. Findowie, a faded woman with some of her handsome son's intensity, hastened to take her cue from Sophia. She praised Grace's kindness to the Reverend Alec with such incontinent and embarrassing eagerness that Grace, having said everything she could think of in self-depreciation, was driven at length to escape her, muttering something about seeing to additional food and drink before her guests went home.

And, indeed, Grace had been kind. In the middle of August, on a hint dropped by Sophia to Mrs. Dermott, whose enthusiasm forthwith magnified the hint to a command, Grace had invited Margy's prospective husband to Aucheneame, seeking to restore him with the calm of her well-ordered house and her sunny garden. Luxury and peace had done their work. Then Grace, knowing something of her niece's anxieties, had gone on to arranging this wedding-day.

The wedding guests began to break up into groups wandering about the front garden. It was a warm autumn day. In a cornfield just beyond the lawn the harvesters were busy. The sun shone, yet seemed to cast no shadow; for a thin mist hanging in the still air diffused its light, golden and impartial, everywhere, rendering objects a little unreal, sounds a little muted. And, like the mist, a soft nostalgia hung everywhere. A sense of the passing year.

The guests seemed to feel this. Their voices were subdued, as they moved in twos and threes, talking. Of the bridal couple

271

who had just left them. Of Rosie McNairn's recovery. And, strangest of all, of the engagement, just announced today, between young Arthur Moorhouse and this girl Netherton. Eyes kept turning to Elizabeth as she stood with Arthur, Isabel and Tom, making a ring about Mrs. Robert Dermott. A most surprising happening. Not that they had anything against her, of course. They had heard, indeed, that she had been wonderful at the Laigh. But would Bel really like it?

Only Bel could answer that.

She stood now looking about her with her elegant, "Queen-of-the-Family" smile, as her daughter Isabel called it—a smile that might be masking anything.

Bel's host took her by the arm. "Well, my dear?"

"Well, David?"

They, too, began walking about on the lawn in front of the large, graceless house, that old Robert Dermott had built for himself some thirty years since.

Scraps of talk came to them. Sophia, with William and the bridegroom's mother still tagging behind her, was explaining to her brother Mungo's impatience just what a terrible rush this wedding had been for poor Margy; but how Mrs. Findowie had found a splendid dressmaker in Kilmarnock, who, though Sophia had been obliged to have her staying in the house for several days, which had made housekeeping more difficult, had been a perfect brick and worked like a Trojan.

Mary was reading a letter to Arthur and Margaret Ruanthorpe-Moorhouse. Bel, interpreting her husband's look of self-control, guessed it was a eulogy of his mother from young George McNairn in America.

In the distance, Henry Hayburn and young Wil Butter were gesticulating at each other as though they might come to blows. Bel and David decided they must be having a business talk.

Phœbe Hayburn was holding the hand of little Meg Dermott-

Moorhouse as she walked in rapture up and down the top of the wall that divided the lawn from the harvest-field.

The three boy cousins—Robert, Robin and Charles—ran past and out of sight, shouting something about plums in the kitchen-garden.

Jack McNairn stood with his twin sisters, answering questions about his wife and child. He looked shabby and tired in this prosperous company.

The group round Mrs. Dermott were obliging her robust good-nature with a burst of laughter. Now Elizabeth and young Arthur were going off by themselves.

"Don't go too far, children," Bel called.

David had time to see Bel's eye meet Elizabeth's, and the smile that passed between them. What had happened, he wondered? Obviously the young people had won.

Bel and David now stood by the wall at the foot of the lawn. He turned and leaned his folded arms on the top of it, waiting for her to speak. She had turned with him, but she said nothing. Thus they stood for a time, looking at the harvest-field, the half-grown trees of the drive, and down into the gossamer distance, where the masts and funnels of a great steamer moved slowly up the river on a high tide.

At last he spoke. "So Arthur has had his own way about Miss Netherton?" he ventured.

Bel continued to look ahead of her, as though the movements of those masts and funnels were all that mattered to her. It was a moment before she answered: "Yes, David. He did."

"Are you pleased, Bel?"

"I like Elizabeth very much."

David could not tell from Bel's voice if her answer was conventional. And he felt resentment. After all, she had sought his advice about this girl.

He would have questioned her further, but a manservant had appeared to say that the guests might now come inside.

Bel turned to go back with him. In the middle of the lawn they met Elizabeth and Arthur.

Mixing together the right proportions of elegance and affection in her smile, she drew the girl's arm through her own. And thus, linked together, before the family, Bel and her future daughter-in-law led the way from the garden, up the stone steps of the main entrance, and into Aucheneame.

Her husband, Arthur, having done at last with Mary and her letter, turned to look after them. As he watched Bel now, he saw that the ranks had closed; that Bel, whatever her private feelings, had thrown her loyalty resolutely and openly on the side of this girl their son had chosen.

She had, of course, told him of the visit to Partick. How, when she had seen the girl, she had been ready to open her arms, to make free and full amends for any injury done her.

He could believe it. Bel was like that; with her quick, warm changes of heart. But it hadn't been so easy. It had taken all Bel's forces to break down the girl's hot reluctance and smarting pride.

Well, as his fairness saw it, he couldn't say that the lassie had been in the wrong, either. And, after all, her behaviour had shown that she loved his boy dearly, whatever she felt about Bel.

Deep in thought, Arthur put his hands behind him and, forgetting the others, moved slowly across the grass.

He remembered now, as he went, John Netherton's morning visit to the Candleriggs, and his own words as they said goodbye. "My wife's a managing kind o' body. But she's all right. If it happens that the young folk are serious about wanting one another, then yer girl needna be frightened o' my boy's mother."

Surely if the lassie had as much sense as everybody said she had, she would very soon come to see that for herself. When she did, it wouldn't be Bel's fault if a real affection didn't grow up between them.

Arthur felt a hand on his arm. Turning, he found his elder son beside him.

"What are you thinking about, Father?"

"You."

But as there was a look of teasing in the older man's face, and as circumstances had made young Arthur more than usually shy today, he did not hazard a further question.

Thus together, without saying more, the two Arthur Moorhouses, father and son, passed with the others up into the house.

KING'S ROYAL

John Quigley

An epic story of bitter rivalry, illicit passion and soaring ambition, set in Glasgow at the height of the Victorian era, *King's Royal* follows the changing fortunes of the King family—Fergus, the patriarch of a whisky empire, who gained his wealth from a string of sleazy drinking houses; Gwen, the beautiful daughter betrayed by a faithless husband; and Robert, the son whose forbidden love fires a ruthless lust for power—which threatens to destroy everything the family have worked for.

'Rich and fascinating'
THE SCOTSMAN

*'A first class novel . . .
compelling and altogether believable'*
SCOTTISH FIELD

*'A wide-ranging saga . . . filled with
fascinating whisky expertise and vivid writing'*
DAILY RECORD

---

*Available from
all good bookshops,
or direct from
B&W Publishing.*